DATE			

Kipling's Fantasy

John Brunner
PRESENTS

Kipling's Fantasy

STORIES BY
RUDYARD KIPLING

A Tom Doherty Associates Book
New York

JOHN BRUNNER PRESENTS KIPLING'S FANTASY

This book is printed on acid-free paper.

A Tor Book
Published by Tom Doherty Associates, Inc.
175 Fifth Avenue
New York, N.Y. 10010

Library of Congress Cataloging-in-Publication Data

Kipling, Rudyard, 1865–1936.
[Short stories. Selections]
Kipling's fantasy / Rudyard Kipling; presented by John Brunner.
p. cm.
"A Tom Doherty Associates book."
"Tor books"—
ISBN 0-312-85354-8
1. Fantastic fiction, English. I. Brunner, John.
II. Title.
PR4852.B73 1992b
823'.8—dc20 92-24915
CIP

First Edition: November 1992

Printed in the United States of America

0 9 8 7 6 5 4 3 2 1

Contents

For much of the information on Kipling's career I am indebted to Charles Carrington's excellent study *Rudyard Kipling: His Life and Work* (Pelican Books, London, 1970), and the twenty contributors to *Rudyard Kipling: The Man, His Work and His World* edited by John Gross (Weidenfeld & Nicolson, London, 1972). The opinions are of course my own.

—JKHB

Kipling's Major Publications

1886	*Departmental Ditties*
1888	*Plain Tales from the Hills*
1889	*From Sea to Sea*
1890	*The Light That Failed*
	Soldiers Three
	Wee Willie Winkie
1891	*Life's Handicap*
1892	*The Naulahka* (with Wolcott Balestier)
	Barrack-Room Ballads
1893	*Many Inventions*
1894	*The Jungle Book*
1895	*The Second Jungle Book*
1896	*The Seven Seas*
1897	*Captains Courageous*
1898	*The Day's Work*
1899	*Stalky & Co.*
1901	*Kim*
1902	*Just So Stories*
1903	*The Five Nations*
1904	*Traffics and Discoveries*
1906	*Puck of Pook's Hill*
1909	*Actions and Reactions*
1910	*Rewards and Fairies*
1913	*Letters of Travel*
	Songs from Books
1917	*A Diversity of Creatures*
1919	*The Years Between*

1923	*Land and Sea Tales*
	The Irish Guards in the Great War
1926	*Debits and Credits*
1927	*Brazilian Sketches*
1928	*A Book of Words*
1930	*Thy Servant a Dog*
1932	*Limits and Renewals*
1937	*Something of Myself* (posthumous)
1937–9	"The Sussex Edition": complete edition of RK's acknowledged works
1940	"The Definitive Edition of Rudyard Kipling's Verse"

About Rudyard Kipling

In a book by David Frost entitled *I Could Have Kicked Myself,* a compilation of decisions that their makers lived to regret, it is asserted that in 1869 the editor of the *San Francisco Examiner* sacked Rudyard Kipling from his job as a cub reporter, saying, "I'm sorry, Mr. Kipling, but you just don't know how to use the English language."

Which was, I suppose, scarcely surprising, since at the time RK was rather less than five years old.

But he was a prodigy, even if not quite on Mr. Frost's scale. His first collection of verse, *Schoolboy Lyrics,* was published when he was sixteen, albeit without his permission. On learning what his mother had done with his juvenile effusions, reportedly he "sulked for three days." And one might almost say that that epitomized the pattern of his life. During his lifetime approximately 15,000,000 copies of his works were sold in English alone. So popular were they in French translation that on one visit to France he was described as being treated "like a national hero." He was the first British author to receive the Nobel Prize for Literature. He would never admit to writing poetry, only "verses," yet T. S. Eliot was among his staunchest champions. He was twice offered, twice refused, a knighthood. He was made a Companion of Honour, but that was much to his annoyance. He declined the Order of Merit, arguably the most coveted distinction in Britain, and forbade his name to be put forward for the post of Poet Laureate. Universities and learned societies awarded him medals and honorary degrees—those he did accept—and toward the end of his life he became a close friend of King George V.

Yet he was never able truly to enjoy his astonishing achievement, for the passage of his days was marred by suffering, both physical and mental, and by such tragedies as, perhaps, the ancient Greeks would have attributed to Nemesis. Here, in outline, is his story.

Born in 1865 in Bombay, where his father was the principal of a recently founded school of art, he was sent to Britain for his education and spent most of his childhood separated from his parents, although his sister Alice (known as "Trix") went with him. The woman to whose care they were confided maltreated the boy to such a degree that when, during an unexpected visit, his mother came to kiss him good night, he automatically flung up his arm to ward off the blow he had been conditioned to expect. In later life Trix became deranged and, their parents being dead, RK had to accept responsibility for her care; perhaps it was at this time that the seeds of that burden were sown.

However, he spent a month each year with his mother's sister, who was married to the prominent artist Sir Edward Burne-Jones, and later described their home as "a paradise which I verily believe saved me." This and other links with the artistic and literary life of London were in young adulthood to stand him in equally good stead.

He was far happier at the school where he passed his early teens, which he later adapted as the setting for his "Stalky" stories; in particular, the headmaster gave him the run of his study and encouraged his omnivorous reading. By now it was obvious he was both intelligent and gifted. But university fees were beyond his parents' means, so just before his seventeenth birthday in 1882 he returned to India, where they had obtained him a job on a newspaper.

The next few years marked him for life. Although, after being lionized in London in 1889–90, he paid only one more visit to India, his apprenticeship there as a journalist and commentator on the social and political scene provided the first significant outlet for his talents and shaped his preference for the range of styles and choice of subjects that were to earn him his almost incredible popularity. To the end of his days he retained his admiration, dating from his late teens, for the tough hard-headed individualist; for "the man who's good at what he has to do," be his calling villager or Viceroy; for the skillful engineer, the cunning strategist, the silver-tongued confidence man. . . . And, perhaps above all else, for India's fantastic, colorful, endlessly varied store of tales and myths and legends, with which his childhood had so richly stocked his mind.

Such was the success of his early stories that he could afford to travel to England via Japan, the U.S.A., and Canada—quite a voyage for a twenty-four-year-old. He was made much of in London, but despite his many acquaintances felt desperately lonely until he fell in with a young American named Wolcott Balestier. They became close friends and even collaborated on a novel, *The Naulahka.*

Tragedy, though, was waiting in the wings; while RK was making another long voyage, to South Africa, Australia, and New Zealand, Wolcott was struck down in Germany by typhoid fever and died at thirty.

Conceivably *in memoriam* (no one will ever be sure), RK proposed to and married Wolcott's sister, Carrie Balestier, and they settled on her family's estate in Vermont. The next few years ensured that America became the second great influence on his work, after India. In addition they saw the birth of children, the publication of *Many Inventions* and the two *Jungle Books* . . . and an almost farcical but most unpleasant feud with his brother-in-law, which in the end drove him and Carrie back to England.

It was on a return trip to the U.S.A., to visit the Balestier family, that tragedy again invaded their lives. In a bitter New York winter RK fell ill with inflammation of the lungs. Often delirious, he fought for his life for nearly seven weeks. Meantime, his baby son developed bronchitis and both his daughters succumbed to whooping cough . . . from which the elder died.

Despite his background in journalism (or maybe because of it) he always hated publicity. Perhaps, though, it was on some level a consolation that by now he was so famous and indeed so beloved a writer that when, at the same time, Pope Leo XIII also fell ill, the *Pall Mall Gazette* issued posters with the headline KIPLING AND POPE—in *that* order.

Then, for a while, the Kiplings' life grew calmer and more bearable. Having rented houses in various parts of Southern England, in 1902 they found the home ("Bateman's," near Burwash in Sussex) where they were to settle for the rest of their lives—the place where evolved the third and ultimately greatest of the influences on his writing. After India, after America, it was the turn of the mother country: England.

For whose future RK was becoming increasingly concerned. Having served as a war correspondent during the Boer Wars, he foresaw the likelihood of a major European conflict at a time when most "experts" regarded it as out of the question. In the event he was proved only too right—and fate dealt him yet another blow in consequence. Serving with the Irish Guards in 1915, his only son John Kipling was reported missing, and though the family clung to hope as long as possible they were forced in the end to admit that he must be dead.

During and after the war, although he would never accept the seat in Parliament that was his for the asking, RK played a distinguished part in politics and public affairs, notably on behalf of the War Graves Commission. (It was he who proposed that in Westminster

Abbey a tomb be erected to The Unknown Soldier.) However . . .

Though he continued to write—*A Diversity of Creatures, Land and Sea Tales,* and the story collection many people regard as his finest, *Debits and Credits*—a permanent shadow had fallen over his life. He lightened it with travel; having been a keen motorist since the pioneering days, he often enjoyed tours in France, a country he had come to love almost as much as his own, and he even visited parts of the world that he had missed in his youth: Brazil, and the West Indies. But he, who had always appreciated good food and had even written a story whose hero was hopeless at everything except cooking ("His Gift," in *Land and Sea Tales*), was chronically ill with abdominal pains, so even the pleasures of the table were denied him. When a French doctor finally diagnosed that for fifteen years he had endured untreated gastric ulcers, he was too weak for the operation that might have given him relief. He died in January 1936.

He was a baffling, paradoxical man: fiercely patriotic, yet among the keenest and most unrelenting critics of his country; an advocate of Empire, who made no secret of his lifelong affection and respect for those whom others casually dismissed as "wogs" or worse; a man of letters whose greatest admiration was reserved for men of action; a confidant of at least one president and one king, whose reputation was founded on his tales and songs concerning peasants, barbarians, and that next-to-barbarian, the common soldier; a dreamer who, despite being endlessly fascinated by practical details—of government, of steam engines, of medicine and electricity and radio—did not hesitate to apply his talent to far-out tales of the fantastic, to horror stories, even to what in his day people had scarcely begun to refer to as science fiction . . . a truth, I trust, amply demonstrated in this and its companion volume.

He has been dead for more than half a century. But what other writer of his generation could, in the 1980s, have inspired an American editor to invite contributions for an anthology of SF stories modeled on or influenced by that person's work?*

In the manner of Robert Louis Stevenson, whom he corresponded with but never met, Kipling wrote his own epitaph. Perhaps we should not attempt to resolve the contradictions of his nature, but be content to obey the injunction with which it concludes:

Seek not to question other than
The books I leave behind.

—JKHB
South Petherton
1988

*The editor was David Drake. The collection, entitled *Heads to the Storm,* is published by Baen Books, and I'm delighted that it includes my story "Mowgli." RK influenced my work more than anybody, more even than did Wells—who, surprisingly, a decade later, echoed and approved RK's opinion of crowds as expressed in "As Easy as A.B.C." (See Book Three, Chapter Two of *Men Like Gods.*)

By Word of Mouth

FROM *PLAIN TALES FROM THE HILLS* (1888)

Let's begin with a ghost story in the classic tradition—indeed, in the tradition of the Appointment in Samara. It was written when, in his early twenties, RK was working for the *Civil and Military Gazette* in Lahore, although by the time it was collected in book form he was a special reporter on a much more distinguished paper, *The Pioneer*, in Allahabad. He had already made a considerable mark, being improbably well informed on every subject. According to Charles Carrington, he was said to know "more about the low life of Lahore than the police," while informants constantly brought him news of "the unruly, almost unknown world of Central Asia beyond the Khyber Pass." Moreover he astonished the cavalry subalterns with his knowledge of horses and steeple-chasing.

But, as well as making his mark, he was being marked. Death was a frequent visitor in the India of those days; over and over he mentions epidemics—smallpox, or as here typhoid and cholera—and casualties of war, murder, even suicide. It is against this background that one must picture him puzzling about the meaning, the point, of the lives that were so often cruelly curtailed. And one must also remember that Indian folklore is full of ghosts and revenants; there is one especially unpleasant kind, the spirit of a woman dead in childbirth. Manifestations of the supernatural, and indeed the gods themselves, were very real to the Hindus around him.

Whether he himself believed in ghosts doesn't matter. Out of this one he wove a neat and powerful tale.

A "march" is a day's journey at walking pace, its length dependent on the country to be traversed. "Bearer" was the common term for a native servant. A dâk-bungalow provided accommodation for travelers on a less than luxurious scale: in effect, an inn without an inn's conveniences. (*Dâk*, from Hindi, means the post [U.S. mail] by extension from its original sense of a relay of runners. There are hotels and inns in Britain still called The Post House.) Simla was the hill-town, cool because of its altitude, to which the Viceroy's court, and other Britons who could, retired from the plains during the hottest time of year.

Sahib = a term of respect for persons of rank, in RK's time especially Europeans. *Memsahib* = madam, the lady. *Salaams* = greetings.

By Word of Mouth

Not though you die to-night, O Sweet, and wail,
   A specter at my door,
Shall mortal Fear make Love immortal fail—
   I shall but love you more,
Who, from Death's house returning, give me still
One moment's comfort in my matchless ill.

Shadow Houses

This tale may be explained by those who know how souls are made, and where the bounds of the Possible are put down. I have lived long enough in this India to know that it is better to know nothing, and can only write the story as it happened.

Dumoise was our Civil Surgeon at Meridki, and we called him "Dormouse," because he was a round little, sleepy little man. He was a good Doctor and never quarreled with anyone, not even with our Deputy Commissioner who had the manners of a bargee and the tact of a horse. He married a girl as round and as sleepy-looking as himself. She was a Miss Hillardyce, daughter of "Squash" Hillardyce of the Berars, who married his Chief's daughter by mistake. But that is another story.

A honeymoon in India is seldom more than a week long; but there is nothing to hinder a couple from extending it over two or three years. India is a delightful country for married folk who are wrapped up in one another. They can live absolutely alone and without interruption—just as the Dormice did. Those two little people retired from the world after their marriage, and were very happy. They were forced, of course, to give occasional dinners, but they made no friends thereby, and the Station went its own way and forgot them; only saying, occasionally, that Dormouse was the best of good fellows though dull. A Civil Surgeon who never quarrels is a rarity, appreciated as such.

Few people can afford to play Robinson Crusoe anywhere—least of all in India, where we are few in the land and very much dependent on each other's kind offices. Dumoise was wrong in shutting himself from the world for a year, and he discovered his mistake when an epidemic of typhoid broke out in the Station in the heart of the cold weather, and his wife went down. He was a shy little man, and five days were wasted before he realized that Mrs. Dumoise was burning with something worse than simple fever, and three days more passed before he ventured to call on Mrs. Shute, the Engineer's wife, and timidly speak about his trouble. Nearly every household in India knows that Doctors are very helpless in typhoid. The battle must be fought out between Death and the Nurses minute by minute and degree by degree. Mrs. Shute almost boxed Dumoise's ears for what she called his "criminal delay," and went off at once to look after the poor girl. We had seven cases of typhoid in the Station that winter and, as the average of death is about one in every five cases, we felt certain that we should have to lose somebody. But all did their best. The women sat up nursing the women, and the men turned to and tended the bachelors who were down, and we wrestled with those typhoid cases for fifty-six days, and brought them through the Valley of the Shadow in triumph. But, just when we thought all was over, and were going to give a dance to celebrate the victory, little Mrs. Dumoise got a relapse and died in a week, and the Station went to the funeral. Dumoise broke down utterly at the brink of the grave, and had to be taken away.

After the death Dumoise crept into his own house and refused to be comforted. He did his duties perfectly, but we all felt that he should go on leave, and the other men of his own Service told him so. Dumoise was very thankful for the suggestion—he was thankful for anything in those days—and went to Chini on a walking-tour. Chini is some twenty marches from Simla, in the heart of the Hills, and the scenery is good if you are in trouble. You pass through big, still deodar forests, and under big, still cliffs, and over big, still grass-downs swelling like a woman's breasts; and the wind across the grass, and the rain among the deodars say—"Hush—hush—hush." So little Dumoise was packed off to Chini, to wear down his grief with a full-plate camera and a rifle. He took also a useless bearer, because the man had been his wife's favorite servant. He was idle and a thief, but Dumoise trusted everything to him.

On his way back from Chini, Dumoise turned aside to Bagi, through the Forest Reserve which is on the spur of Mount Huttoo. Some men who have traveled more than a little say that the march from Kotegarh to Bagi is one of the finest in creation. It runs through dark wet forest, and ends suddenly in bleak, nipped hillside and black rocks. Bagi dâk-bungalow is open to all the winds and is bitterly cold. Few people go to Bagi. Perhaps that was the reason why Dumoise went there. He halted at seven in the evening, and his bearer went down the hillside to the village to engage coolies for the next day's march. The sun had set, and the night-winds were beginning to croon among the rocks. Dumoise leaned on the railing of the verandah, waiting for his bearer to return. The man came back almost immediately after he had disappeared, and at such a rate that Dumoise fancied he must have crossed a bear. He was running as hard as he could up the face of the hill.

But there was no bear to account for his terror. He raced to the verandah and fell down, the blood spurting from his nose and his face iron-grey. Then he gurgled—"I have seen the *Memsahib!* I have seen the *Memsahib!*"

"Where?" said Dumoise.

"Down there, walking on the road to the village. She was in a blue dress, and she lifted the veil of her bonnet and said—'Ram Dass, give my *salaams* to the *Sahib,* and tell him that I shall meet him next month at Nuddea.' Then I ran away, because I was afraid."

What Dumoise said or did I do not know. Ram Dass declares that he said nothing, but walked up and down the verandah all the cold night, waiting for the *Memsahib* to come up the hill, and stretching out his arms into the dark like a madman. But no *Memsahib* came, and, next day, he went on to Simla cross-questioning the bearer every hour.

Ram Dass could only say that he had met Mrs. Dumoise, and that she had lifted up her veil and given him the message which he had faithfully repeated to Dumoise. To this statement Ram Dass adhered. He did not know where Nuddea was, had no friends at Nuddea, and would most certainly never go to Nuddea, even though his pay were doubled.

Nuddea is in Bengal, and has nothing whatever to do with a Doctor serving in the Punjab. It must be more than twelve hundred miles south of Meridki.

Dumoise went through Simla without halting, and returned to Meridki, there to take over charge from the man who had been officiating for him during his tour. There were some Dispensary accounts to be explained, and some recent orders of the Surgeon-General to be noted, and, altogether, the taking-over was a full day's work. In the evening Dumoise told his *locum tenens,* who was an old friend of his bachelor days, what had happened at Bagi; and the man said that Ram Dass might as well have chosen Tuticorin while he was about it.

At that moment a telegraph-peon came in with a telegram from Simla, ordering Dumoise not to take over charge at Meridki, but to go at once to Nuddea on special duty. There was a nasty outbreak of cholera at Nuddea, and the Bengal Government being short-handed, as usual, had borrowed a Surgeon from the Punjab.

Dumoise threw the telegram across the table and said—"Well?"

The other Doctor said nothing. It was all that he could say.

Then he remembered that Dumoise had passed through Simla on his way from Bagi; and thus might, possibly, have heard first news of the impending transfer.

He tried to put the question and the implied suspicion into words, but Dumoise stopped him with—"If I had desired *that,* I should never have come back from Chini. I was shooting there. I wish to live, for I have things to do . . . but I shall not be sorry."

The other man bowed his head, and helped, in the twilight, to pack up Dumoise's just opened trunks. Ram Dass entered with the lamps.

"Where is the *Sahib* going?" he asked.

"To Nuddea," said Dumoise softly.

Ram Dass clawed Dumoise's knees and boots and begged him not to go. Ram Dass wept and howled till he was turned out of the room. Then he wrapped up all his belongings and came back to ask for a character. He was not going to Nuddea to see his *Sahib* die and, perhaps, to die himself.

So Dumoise gave the man his wages and went down to Nuddea alone, the other Doctor bidding him good-bye as one under sentence of death.

Eleven days later he had joined his *Memsahib;* and the Bengal Government had to borrow a fresh Doctor to cope with that epidemic at Nuddea. The first importation lay dead in Chooadanga Dâk-Bungalow.

The Finances of the Gods

FROM *LIFE'S HANDICAP* (1891)

Throughout his working life Kipling enjoyed fabricating what might more aptly be termed fables than actual stories. Often, whether it was true in point of fact or not, he attributed them to sources other than himself. Many of the items in *Life's Handicap* that were originally published in Indian newspapers but collected in book form after his success in London and the appearance there of his first novel, *The Light That Failed*, are of this kind. In an introduction he describes his meeting with the old holy man Gobind, at the *chubara* (Hindu monastery) of Dunni Bhagat, "full of brick cells, gaily painted with the figures of Gods and kings and elephants, where worn-out priests could sit and meditate on the latter end of things. . . . Clumps of mangoes sprouted from between the bricks; great pipal trees overhung the well-windlass that whined all day; and hosts of parrots tore through the trees. Crows and squirrels were tame in that place, for they knew that never a priest would touch them."

Such is the setting for this wholly charming morality tale.

Cow-dung was, and is, used as fuel in wood-poor India. Rupees (from Urdu *rupiya*) are the unit of Indian currency. The cowries (Hindi *kauri*) in the holy man's begging-bowl are shells "used in certain primitive societies as money and magical objects" *(Chambers Twentieth Century Dictionary)*. One *lakh* = 100,000.

The Finances of the Gods

The evening meal was ended in Dhunni Bhagat's chubara, and the old priests were smoking or counting their beads. A little naked child pattered in, with its mouth wide open, a handful of marigold flowers in one hand, and a lump of conserved tobacco in the other. It tried to kneel and make obeisance to Gobind, but it was so fat that it fell forward on its shaven head, and rolled on its side, kicking and gasping, while the marigolds tumbled one way and the tobacco the other. Gobind laughed, set it up again, and blessed the marigold flowers as he received the tobacco.

"From my father," said the child. "He has the fever, and cannot come. Wilt thou pray for him, father?"

"Surely, littlest; but the smoke is on the ground, and the night-chill is in the air, and it is not good to go abroad naked in the autumn."

"I have no clothes," said the child, "and all today I have been carrying cow-dung cakes to the bazaar. It was very hot, and I am very tired." It shivered a little, for the twilight was cool.

Gobind lifted an arm under his vast tattered quilt of many colors, and made an inviting little nest by his side. The child crept in, and Gobind filled his brass-studded leather waterpipe with the new tobacco. When I came to the chubara the shaven head with the tuft atop, and the beady black eyes looked out of the folds of the quilt as a squirrel looks out from his nest, and Gobind was smiling while the child played with his beard.

I would have said something friendly, but remembered in time that if the child fell ill afterwards I should be credited with the Evil Eye, and that is a horrible possession.

"Sit thou still, Thumbling," I said, as it made to get up and run away. "Where is thy slate, and why has the teacher let such an evil character loose on the streets when there are no police to protect us weaklings? In which ward dost thou try to break thy neck with flying kites from the house-tops?"

"Nay, *Sahib*, nay," said the child, burrowing its face into Gobind's beard, and twisting uneasily. "There was a holiday today among the schools, and I do not always fly kites. I play ker-li-kit like the rest."

Cricket is the national game among the schoolboys of the Punjab, from the naked hedge-school children, who use an old kerosene-tin for wicket, to the B.A.s of the University, who compete for the Championship belt.

"Thou play kerlikit! Thou art half the height of the bat!" I said.

The child nodded resolutely. "Yea, I *do* play. *Perlay-ball. Ow-at! Ran, ran, ran!* I know it all."

"But thou must not forget with all this to pray to the Gods according to custom," said Gobind, who did not altogether approve of cricket and Western innovations.

"I do not forget," said the child in a hushed voice.

"Also to give reverence to thy teacher, and"—Gobind's voice softened—"to abstain from pulling holy men by the beard, little badling. Eh, eh, eh?"

The child's face was altogether hidden in the great white beard, and it began to whimper till Gobind soothed it as children are soothed all the world over, with the promise of a story.

"I did not think to frighten thee, senseless little one. Look up! Am I angry? *Aré, aré, aré!* Shall I weep too, and of our tears make a great pond and drown us both, and then thy father will never get well, lacking thee to pull his beard? Peace, peace, and I will tell thee of the Gods. Thou hast heard many tales?"

"Very many, father."

"Now, this is a new one which thou hast not heard. Long and long ago when the Gods walked with men as they do to-day, but that we have not faith to see, Shiv, the greatest of Gods, and Parbati his wife, were walking in the garden of a temple."

"Which temple? That in the Nandgaon ward?" said the child.

"Nay, very far away. Maybe at Trimbak or Hurdwar, whither thou must make pilgrimage when thou art a man. Now, there was sitting in the garden under the jujube trees, a mendicant that had worshiped Shiv for forty years, and he lived on the offerings of the pious, and meditated holiness night and day."

"Oh father, was it thou?" said the child, looking up with large eyes.

"Nay, I have said it was long ago, and, moreover, this mendicant was married."

"Did they put him on a horse with flowers on his head, and forbid him to go to sleep all night long? Thus they did to me when they made my wedding," said the child, who had been married a few months before.

"And what didst thou do?" said I.

"I wept, and they called me evil names, and then I smote *her*, and we wept together."

"Thus did not the mendicant," said Gobind, "for he was a holy man, and very poor. Parbati perceived him sitting naked by the temple steps where all went up and down, and she said to Shiv, 'What shall men think of the Gods when the Gods thus scorn their worshippers? For forty years yonder man has prayed to us, and yet there be only a few grains of rice and some broken cowries before him after all. Men's hearts will be hardened by this thing.' And Shiv said, 'It shall be looked to,' and so he called to the temple which was the temple of his son, Ganesh of the elephant head, saying, 'Son, there is a mendicant without who is very poor. What wilt thou do for him?' Then that great elephant-headed One awoke in the dark and answered, 'In three days, if it be thy will, he shall have one *lakh* of rupees.' Then Shiv and Parbati went away.

"But there was a money-lender in the garden hidden among the marigolds"—the child looked at the ball of crumpled blossoms in its hands—"ay, among the yellow marigolds, and he heard the Gods talking. He was a covetous man, and of a black heart, and he desired that lakh of rupees for himself. So he went to the mendicant and said, 'Oh brother, how much do the pious give thee daily?' The mendicant said, 'I cannot tell. Sometimes a little rice, sometimes a little pulse, and a few cowries and, it has been, pickled mangoes, and dried fish.' "

"That is good," said the child, smacking its lips.

"Then said the money-lender, 'Because I have long watched thee, and learned to love thee and thy patience, I will give thee now five rupees for all thy earnings of the three days to come. There is only a bond to sign on the matter.' But the mendicant said, 'Thou art mad. In two months I do not receive the worth of five rupees,' and he told the thing to his wife that evening. She, being a woman, said, 'When did money-lender ever make a bad bargain? The wolf runs through the corn for the sake of the fat deer. Our fate is in the hands of the Gods. Pledge it not even for three days.'

"So the mendicant returned to the money-lender, and would not sell. Then that wicked man sat all day before him offering more and more for those three days' earnings. First, ten, fifty, and a hundred rupees; and then, for he did not know when the Gods would pour down their gifts, rupees by the thousand, till he had offered half a *lakh* of rupees. Upon this sum the mendicant's wife shifted her counsel, and the mendicant signed the bond, and the money was paid in silver; great white bullocks bringing it by the cartload. But saving only all that money, the mendicant received nothing from the Gods at all, and the heart of the money-lender was uneasy on account of expectation. Therefore at noon of the third day the money-lender went into the temple to spy upon the councils of the Gods, and to learn in what manner that gift might arrive. Even as he was making his prayers, a crack between the stones of the floor gaped, and, closing, caught him by the heel. Then he heard the Gods walking in the temple in the darkness of the columns, and Shiv called to his son Ganesh, saying 'Son, what hast thou done in regard to the *lakh* of rupees for the mendicant?' And Ganesh woke, for the money-lender heard the dry rustle of his trunk uncoiling, and he answered, 'Father, one-half of the money has been paid, and the debtor for the other half I hold here fast by the heel.' "

The child bubbled with laughter. "And the money-lender paid the mendicant?" it said.

"Surely, for he whom the Gods hold by the heel must pay to the uttermost. The money was paid at evening, all silver, in great carts, and thus Ganesh did his work."

"Nathu! *Ohē* Nathu!"

A woman was calling in the dusk by the door of the courtyard.

The child began to wriggle. "That is my mother," it said.

"Go then, littlest," answered Gobind; "but stay a moment."

He ripped a generous yard from his patchwork-quilt, put it over the child's shoulders, and the child ran away.

"The Finest Story in the World"

FROM *MANY INVENTIONS* (1893)

When Kipling wrote this he was living alone in London, invited now and then to Society dances and receptions on the strength of his literary achievements, but acutely aware that, as he himself said, "Unless it happened that I was the fashion of the moment, you'd let me die of want on your doorstep."

He was consumed with homesickness. On Christmas Day, 1890, he wrote at midnight to his family in India: "there are five million people in London this night and, saving those who starve, I don't think there is one more heartsick or thoroughly wretched than that rising young author known to you as—Ruddy."

Among his few close friends was his cousin Ambrose Poynter, nicknamed Ambo, whom Charles Carrington diagnosed as suffering "the common misfortune of a successful man's son; he had inherited his father's nervous temperament without his father's talent." It is possible that the character of Charlie Mears, who didn't recognise the treasure under his hand, owes something to Ambo, for he also had unattainable literary aspirations.

What is certain is that at the end of last century there was widespread speculation about the content, function, and nature of dreams, even before Freud and his colleagues of the Viennese school of psychology elaborated their theories of the unconscious. RK often wondered whether they might reveal hidden memories, or even recollections of previous lives. See, for example, "In the Same Boat," in the companion collection of his science fiction.

And what is definite, for this story proves it, is that within months of his arrival in Britain he knew nearly as much about London as he had known about Lahore and Allahabad, and could fix it just as accurately on the page.

The choice of epigraph, incidentally, is by way of a thank-you to its author, who published RK's "Barrack-Room Ballads" in his literary journal, the *Scots Observer.*

Longfellow's black wharves are from "My Lost Youth"; the equinoctial storm-wind, from "Seaweed." *Treasure Island* is of course by R. L. Stevenson. Skraelings, so says Farley Mowat in *Westviking,* were most likely Dorset Eskimos. *Tit-Bits* was a popular but scarcely intellectual weekly paper.

As to the Hindi words which the narrator uses to Grish Chunder, Mr. H. V. S. Manral of the Indian High Commission kindly informs me that *tulsi* "is a holy plant held in great reverence by the Hindu ladies of India and is generally planted in the courtyard." *Purohit* = family priest. *Khuttri* is "a Hindu belonging to the warrior class of the old times." *Desi* = national, of the country, native.

"The Finest Story in the World"

Or ever the knightly years were gone
With the old world to the grave,
I was a king in Babylon
And you were a Christian slave.
W. E. HENLEY

His name was Charlie Mears; he was the only son of his mother who was a widow, and he lived in the north of London, coming into the City every day to work in a bank. He was twenty years old and was full of aspirations. I met him in a public billiard-saloon where the marker called him by his first name, and he called the marker "Bullseye." Charlie explained, a little nervously, that he had only come to the place to look on, and since looking on at games of skill is not a cheap amusement for the young, I suggested that Charlie should go back to his mother.

That was our first step towards better acquaintance. He would call on me sometimes in the evenings instead of running about London with his fellow-clerks; and before long, speaking of himself as a young man must, he told me of his aspirations, which were all literary. He desired to make himself an undying name chiefly through verse, though he was not above sending stories of love and death to the penny-in-the-slot journals. It was my fate to sit still while Charlie read me poems of many hundred lines, and bulky fragments of plays that would surely shake the world. My reward was his unreserved confidence, and the self-revelations and troubles of a young man are almost as holy as those of a maiden. Charlie had never fallen in love, but was anxious to do so on the first opportunity; he believed in all things good and all things honorable, but at the same time, was curiously careful to let me see that he knew his way about the world as befitted a bank-clerk on twenty-five shillings a week. He rhymed "dove" with "love" and "moon" with "June," and devoutly believed that they had never so been rhymed before. The long lame gaps in his plays he filled up with hasty words of apology and description, and swept on, seeing all that he intended to do so clearly that he esteemed it already done, and turned to me for applause.

I fancy that his mother did not encourage his aspirations; and I know that his writing-table at home was the edge of his wash-stand. This he told me almost at the outset of our acquaintance—when he was ravaging my bookshelves, and a little before I was implored to speak the truth as to his chances of "writing something really great, you know." Maybe I encouraged him too much, for, one night, he called on me, his eyes flaming with excitement, and said breathlessly:

"Do you mind—can you let me stay here and write all this evening? I won't interrupt you, I won't really. There's no place for me to write in at my mother's."

"What's the trouble?" I said, knowing well what that trouble was.

"I've a notion in my head that would make the most splendid story that was ever written. Do let me write it out here. It's *such* a notion!"

There was no resisting the appeal. I set him a table; he hardly thanked me, but plunged into his work at once. For half an hour the pen scratched without stopping. Then Charlie sighed and tugged his hair. The scratching grew slower, there were more erasures, and at last ceased. The finest story in the world would not come forth.

"It looks such awful rot now," he said mournfully. "And yet it seemed so good when I was thinking about it. What's wrong?"

I could not dishearten him by saying the truth. So I answered: "Perhaps you don't feel in the mood for writing."

"Yes I do—except when I look at this stuff. Ugh!"

"Read me what you've done," I said.

He read, and it was wondrous bad, and he paused at all the specially turgid sentences, expecting a little approval; for he was proud of those sentences, as I knew he would be.

"It needs compression," I suggested cautiously.

"I hate cutting my things down. I don't think you could alter a word here without spoiling the sense. It reads better aloud than when I was writing it."

"Charlie, you're suffering from an alarming disease afflicting a numerous class. Put the thing by, and tackle it again in a week."

"I want to do it at once. What do you think of it?"

"How can I judge from a half-written tale? Tell me the story as it lies in your head."

Charlie told, and in the telling there was everything that his ignorance had so carefully prevented from escaping into the written word. I looked at him, wondering whether it were possible that he did not know the originality, the power of the notion that had come in his way? It was distinctly a Notion among notions. Men had been puffed up with pride by ideas not a tithe as excellent and practicable. But Charlie babbled on serenely, interrupting the current of pure fancy with samples of horrible sentences that he purposed to use. I heard him out to the end. It would be folly to allow his thought to remain in his own inept hands, when I could do so much with it. Not all that could be done indeed; but, oh so much!

"What do you think?" he said at last. "I fancy I shall call it 'The Story of a Ship.' "

"I think the idea's pretty good; but you won't be able to handle it for ever so long. Now I—"

"Would it be of any use to you? Would you care to take it? I should be proud," said Charlie promptly.

There are few things sweeter in this world than the guileless, hot-headed, intemperate, open admiration of a junior. Even a woman in her blindest devotion does not fall into the gait of the man she adores, tilt her bonnet to the angle at which he wears his hat, or interlard her speech with his pet oaths. And Charlie did all these things. Still it was necessary to salve my conscience before I possessed myself of Charlie's thoughts.

"Let's make a bargain. I'll give you a fiver for the notion," I said.

Charlie became a bank-clerk at once.

"Oh, that's impossible. Between two pals, you know, if I may call you so, and speaking as a man of the world, I couldn't. Take the notion if it's any use to you. I've heaps more."

He had—none knew this better than I—but they were the notions of other men.

"Look at it as a matter of business—between men of the world," I returned. "Five pounds will buy you any number of poetry-books. Business is business, and you may be sure I shouldn't give that price unless—"

"Oh, if you put it *that* way," said Charlie, visibly moved by the thought of the books. The bargain was clinched with an agreement that he should at unstated intervals come to me with all the notions that he possessed, should have a table of his own to write at, and unquestioned right to inflict upon me all his poems and fragments of poems. Then I said, "Now tell me how you came by this idea."

"It came by itself." Charlie's eyes opened a little.

"Yes, but you told me a great deal about the hero that you must have read before somewhere."

"I haven't any time for reading, except when you let me sit here, and on Sundays I'm on my bicycle or down the river all day. There's nothing wrong about the hero, is there?"

"Tell me again and I shall understand clearly. You say that your hero went pirating. How did he live?"

"He was on the lower deck of this ship-thing that I was telling you about."

"What sort of ship?"

"It was the kind rowed with oars, and the sea spurts through the oar-holes, and the men row sitting up to their knees in water. Then there's a bench running down between the two lines of oars, and an overseer with a whip walks up and down the bench to make the men work."

"How do you know that?"

"It's in the tale. There's a rope running overhead, looped to the upper-deck, for the overseer to catch hold of when the ship rolls. When the overseer misses the rope once and falls among the rowers, remember the hero laughs at him and gets licked for it. He's chained to his oar of course—the hero."

"How is he chained?"

"With an iron band round his waist fixed to the bench he sits on, and a sort of handcuff on his left wrist chaining him to the oar. He's on the lower deck where the worst men are sent, and the only light comes from the hatchways and through the oar-holes. Can't you imagine the sunlight just squeezing through between the handle and the hole and wobbling about as the ship moves?"

"I can, but I can't imagine your imagining it."

"How could it be any other way? Now you listen to me. The long oars on the upper deck are managed by four men to each bench, the lower ones by three, and the lowest of all by two. Remember it's quite dark on the lowest deck and all the men there go mad. When a man dies at his oar on that deck he isn't thrown overboard, but cut up in his chains and stuffed through the oar-hole in little pieces."

"Why?" I demanded amazed, not so much at the information as the tone of command in which it was flung out.

"To save trouble and to frighten the others. It needs two overseers to drag a man's body up to the top deck; and if the men at the lower deck oars were left alone, of course they'd stop rowing and try to pull up the benches by all standing up together in their chains."

"You've a most provident imagination. Where have you been reading about galleys and galley-slaves?"

"Nowhere that I remember. I row a little when I get the chance. But, perhaps, if you say so, I may have read something."

He went away shortly afterwards to deal with booksellers, and I wondered how a bank-clerk aged twenty could put into my hands with a profligate abundance of detail, all given with absolute assurance, the story of extravagant and bloodthirsty adventure, riot, piracy, and death in unnamed seas. He had led his hero a desperate dance through revolt against the overseers, to command of a ship of his own, and at last to the establishment of a kingdom on an island "somewhere in the sea, you know" and, delighted with my paltry five pounds, had gone out to buy the notions of other men, that these might teach him how to write. I had the consolation of knowing that this notion was mine by right of purchase, and I thought that I could make something of it.

When next he came to me he was drunk—royally drunk on many poets for the first time revealed to him. His pupils were dilated, his words tumbled over each other, and he wrapped himself in quotations—as a beggar would enfold himself in the purple of emperors. Most of all was he drunk with Longfellow.

"Isn't it splendid? Isn't it superb?" he cried, after hasty greetings. "Listen to this—

" 'Wouldst thou,'—so the helmsman answered,
'Know the secret of the sea?
Only those who brave its dangers
Comprehend its mystery.'

"By gum!

> " 'Only those who brave its dangers
> Comprehend its mystery,' "

he repeated twenty times, walking up and down the room and forgetting me. "But *I* can understand it too," he said to himself. "I don't know how to thank you for that fiver. And this; listen—

> " 'I remember the black wharves and the slips
> And the sea-tides tossing free;
> And the Spanish sailors with bearded lips,
> And the beauty and mystery of the ships,
> And the magic of the sea.'

"I haven't braved any dangers, but I feel as if I knew all about it."

"You certainly seem to have a grip of the sea. Have you ever seen it?"

"When I was a little chap I went to Brighton once; we used to live in Coventry, though, before we came to London. I never saw it,

> " 'When descends on the Atlantic
> The gigantic
> Storm-wind of the Equinox.' "

He shook me by the shoulder to make me understand the passion that was shaking himself.

"When that storm comes," he continued, "I think that all the oars in the ship that I was talking about get broken, and the rowers have their chests smashed in by the oar-heads bucking. By the way, have you done anything with that notion of mine yet?"

"No. I was waiting to hear more of it from you. Tell me how in the world you're so certain about the fittings of the ship. You know nothing of ships."

"I don't know. It's as real as anything to me until I try to write it down. I was thinking about it only last night in bed, after you had lent me *Treasure Island;* and I made up a whole lot of new things to go into the story."

"What sort of things?"

"About the food the men ate; rotten figs and black beans and wine in a skin bag, passed from bench to bench."

"Was the ship built so long ago as *that*?"

"As what? I don't know whether it was long ago or not. It's only a notion, but sometimes it seems just as real as if it was true. Do I bother you with talking about it?"

"Not in the least. Did you make up anything else?"

"Yes, but it's nonsense." Charlie flushed a little.

"Never mind; let's hear about it."

"Well, I was thinking over the story, and after awhile I got out of bed and wrote down on a piece of paper the sort of stuff the men might be supposed to scratch on their oars with the edges of their handcuffs. It seemed to make the thing more life-like. It *is* so real to me, y'know."

"Have you the paper on you?"

"Ye—es, but what's the use of showing it? It's only a lot of scratches. All the same, we might have 'em reproduced in the book on the front page."

"I'll attend to those details. Show me what your men wrote."

He pulled out of his pocket a sheet of notepaper, with a single line of scratches upon it, and I put this carefully away.

"What is it supposed to mean in English?" I said.

"Oh, I don't know. I mean it to mean 'I'm beastly tired.' It's great nonsense," he repeated, "but all those men in the ship seem as real as real people to me. Do do something to the notion soon; I should like to see it written and printed."

"But all you've told me would make a long book."

"Make it then. You've only to sit down and write it out."

"Give me a little time. Have you any more notions?"

"Not just now. I'm reading all the books I've bought. They're splendid."

When he had left I looked at the sheet of notepaper with the inscription upon it. Then I took my head tenderly between both hands, to make certain that it was not coming off or turning round. Then . . . but there seemed to be no interval between quitting my rooms and finding myself arguing with a policeman outside a door marked *Private* in a corridor of the British Museum. All I demanded, as politely as possible, was "the Greek antiquity man." The policeman knew nothing except the rules of the Museum, and it became necessary to forage through all the houses and offices inside the gates. An elderly gentleman called away from his lunch put an end to my search by holding the notepaper between finger and thumb and sniffing at it scornfully.

"What does this mean? H'mm," said he. "So far as I can ascertain it is an attempt to write extremely corrupt Greek on the part"—here he glared at me with intention—"of an extremely illiterate—ah—person." He read slowly from the paper, *"Pollock, Erckmann, Tauchnitz, Henniker"*—four names familiar to me.

"Can you tell me what the corruption is supposed to mean—the gist of the thing?" I asked.

"I have been—many times—overcome with weariness in this particular employment. That is the meaning." He returned me the paper, and I fled without a word of thanks, explanation, or apology.

I might have been excused for forgetting much. To me of all men had been given the chance to write the most marvelous tale in the world, nothing less than the story of a Greek galley-slave, as told by himself. Small wonder that his dreaming had seemed real to Charlie. The Fates that are so careful to shut the doors of each successive life behind us had, in this case, been neglectful, and Charlie was looking, though that he did not know, where never man had been permitted to look with full knowledge since Time began. Above all, he was absolutely ignorant of the knowledge sold to me for five pounds; and he would retain that ignorance, for bank-clerks do not understand metempsychosis, and a sound commercial education does not include Greek. He would supply me—here I capered among the dumb gods of Egypt and laughed in their battered faces—with material to make my tale sure—so sure that the world would hail it as an impudent and vamped fiction. And I—I alone would know that it was absolutely and literally true. I—I alone held this jewel to my hand for the cutting and polishing! Therefore I danced again among the gods of the Egyptian court till a policeman saw me and took steps in my direction.

It remained now only to encourage Charlie to talk, and here there was no difficulty. But I had forgotten those accursed books of poetry. He came to me time after time, as useless as a surcharged phonograph—drunk on Byron, Shelley, or Keats. Knowing now what the boy had been in his past lives, and desperately anxious not to lose one word of his babble, I could not hide from him my respect and interest. He misconstrued both into respect for the present soul of Charlie Mears, to whom life was as new as it was to Adam, and interest in his readings; and stretched my patience to breaking point by reciting poetry—not his own now, but that of others. I wished every English poet blotted out of the memory of mankind. I blasphemed the mightiest names of song because they had drawn Charlie from the path of direct narrative, and would, later, spur him to imitate them; but I choked down my impatience until the first flood of enthusiasm should have spent itself and the boy returned to his dreams.

"What's the use of my telling you what *I* think, when these chaps wrote things for the angels to read?" he growled, one evening. "Why don't you write something like theirs?"

"I don't think you're treating me quite fairly," I said, speaking under strong restraint.

"I've given you the story," he said shortly, replunging into "Lara."

"But I want the details."

"The things I make up about that damned ship that you call a galley? They're quite easy. You can just make 'em up for yourself. Turn up the gas a little, I want to go on reading."

I could have broken the gas globe over his head for his amazing stupidity. I could indeed make up things for myself did I only know what Charlie did not know that he knew. But since the doors were shut behind me I could only wait his youthful pleasure and strive to keep him in good temper. One minute's want of guard might spoil a priceless revelation: now and again he would toss his books aside—he kept them in my rooms, for his mother would have been shocked at the waste of good money had she seen them—and launched into his sea-dreams. Again I cursed all the poets of England. The plastic mind of the bank-clerk had been overlaid, colored, and distorted by that which he had read, and the result as delivered was a confused tangle of other voices most like the mutter and hum through a City telephone in the busiest part of the day.

He talked of the galley—his own galley had he but known it—with illustrations borrowed from the "Bride of Abydos." He pointed the experiences of his hero with quotations from "The Corsair," and threw in deep and desperate moral reflections from "Cain" and "Manfred," expecting me to use them all. Only when the talk turned on Longfellow were the jarring cross-currents dumb, and I knew that Charlie was speaking the truth as he remembered it.

"What do you think of this?" I said one evening, as soon as I understood the medium in which his memory worked best, and, before he could expostulate, read him nearly the whole of "The Saga of King Olaf!"

He listened open-mouthed, flushed, his hands drumming on the back of the sofa where he lay, till I came to the Song of Einar Tamberskelver and the verse:—

"Einar then, the arrow taking
From the loosened string,
Answered, 'That was Norway breaking
'Neath thy hand, O King.' "

He gasped with pure delight of sound.

"That's better than Byron, a little?" I ventured.

"Better! Why it's *true!* How could he have known?"

I went back and repeated:—

" 'What was that?' said Olaf, standing
On the quarter-deck,
'Something heard I like the stranding
Of a shattered wreck.' "

"How could he have known how the ships crash and the oars rip out and go *z-zzp* all along the line? Why only the other night . . . But go back, please, and read 'The Skerry of Shrieks' again."

"No, I'm tired. Let's talk. What happened the other night?"

"I had an awful dream about that galley of ours. I dreamed I was drowned in a fight. You see we ran alongside another ship in harbor. The water was dead still except where our oars whipped it up. You know where I always sit in the galley?" He spoke haltingly at first, under a fine English fear of being laughed at.

"No. That's news to me," I answered meekly, my heart beginning to beat.

"On the fourth oar from the bow on the right side on the upper deck. There were four of us at that oar, all chained. I remember watching the water and trying to get my handcuffs off before the row began. Then we closed up on the other ship, and all their fighting men jumped over our bulwarks, and my bench broke and I was pinned down with the three other fellows on top of me, and the big oar jammed across our backs."

"Well?" Charlie's eyes were alive and alight. He was looking at the wall behind my chair.

"I don't know how we fought. The men were trampling all over my back, and I lay low. Then our rowers on the left side—tied to their oars, you know—began to yell and back water. I could hear the water sizzle, and we spun round like a cockchafer, and I knew, lying where I was, that there was a galley coming up bow-on to ram us on the left side. I could just lift up my head and see her sail over the bulwarks. We wanted to meet her bow to bow, but it was too late. We could only turn a little bit because the galley on our right had hooked herself on to us and stopped our moving. Then, by gum! there was a crash! Our left oars began to break as the other galley, the moving one y'know, stuck her nose into them. Then the lower-deck oars shot up through the deck planking, butt first, and one of them jumped clear up into the air and came down again close at my head."

"How was that managed?"

"The moving galley's bow was plunking them back through their own oar-holes, and I could hear no end of a shindy in the decks below. Then her nose caught us nearly in the middle, and we tilted sideways, and the fellows in the right-hand galley unhitched their hooks and ropes, and threw things on to our upper deck—arrows, and hot pitch or something that stung, and we went up and up and up on the left side, and the right side dipped, and I twisted my head round and saw the water stand still as it topped the right bulwarks, and then it curled over and crashed down on the whole lot of us on the right side, and I felt it hit my back, and I woke."

"One minute, Charlie. When the sea topped the bulwarks, what did it look like?" I had my reasons for asking. A man of my acquaintance had once gone down with a leaking ship in a still sea, and had seen the water-level pause for an instant ere it fell on the deck.

"It looked just like a banjo-string drawn tight, and it seemed to stay there for years," said Charlie.

Exactly! The other man had said, "It looked like a silver wire laid down along the bulwarks, and I thought it was never going to break." He had paid everything except the bare life for this little valueless piece of knowledge, and I had traveled ten thousand weary miles to meet him and take his knowledge at second hand. But Charlie, the bank-clerk on twenty-five shillings a week, who had never been out of sight of a made road, knew it all. It was no consolation to me that once in his lives he had been forced to die for his gains. I also must have died scores of times, but behind me, because I could have used my knowledge, the doors were shut.

"And then?" I said, trying to put away the devil of envy.

"The funny thing was, though, in all the row I didn't feel a bit astonished or frightened. It seemed as if I'd been in a good many fights, because I told my next man so when the row began. But that cad of an overseer on my deck wouldn't unloose our chains and give us a chance. He always said that we'd all be set free after a battle, but we never were; we never were." Charlie shook his head mournfully.

"What a scoundrel!"

"I should say he was. He never gave us enough to eat, and sometimes we were so thirsty that we used to drink salt-water. I can taste that salt-water still."

"Now tell me something about the harbor where the fight was fought."

"I didn't dream about that. I know it was a harbor, though; because we were tied up to a ring on a white wall and all the face of the stone under water was covered with wood to prevent our ram getting chipped when the tide made us rock."

"That's curious. Our hero commanded the galley, didn't he?"

"Didn't he just! He stood by the bows and shouted like a good 'un. He was the man who killed the overseer."

"But you were all drowned together, Charlie, weren't you?"

"I can't make that fit quite," he said, with a puzzled look. "The galley must have gone down with all hands, and yet I fancy that the hero went on living afterwards. Perhaps he climbed into the attacking ship. I wouldn't see that, of course. I was dead, you know."

He shivered slightly and protested that he could remember no more.

I did not press him further, but to satisfy myself that he lay in ignorance of the workings of his own mind, deliberately introduced him to Mortimer Collins's *Transmigration,* and gave him a sketch of the plot before he opened the pages.

"What rot it all is!" he said frankly, at the end of an hour. "I don't understand his nonsense about the Red Planet Mars and the King, and the rest of it. Chuck me the Longfellow again."

I handed him the book and wrote out as much as I could remember of his description of the sea-fight, appealing to him from time to time for confirmation of fact or detail. He would answer without raising his eyes from the book, as assuredly as though all his knowledge lay before him on the printed page. I spoke under the normal key of my voice that the current might not be broken, and I knew that he was not aware of what he was saying, for his thoughts were out on the sea with Longfellow.

"Charlie," I asked, "when the rowers on the galleys mutinied how did they kill their overseers?"

"Tore up the benches and brained 'em. That happened when a heavy sea was running. An overseer on the lower deck slipped from the center plank and fell among the rowers. They choked him to death against the side of the ship with their chained hands quite quietly, and it was too dark for the other overseer to see what had happened. When he asked, he was pulled down too and choked, and the lower deck fought their way up deck by deck, with the pieces of the broken benches banging behind 'em. How they howled!"

"And what happened after that?"

"I don't know. The hero went away—red hair and red beard and all. That was after he had captured our galley, I think."

The sound of my voice irritated him, and he motioned slightly with his left hand as a man does when interruption jars.

"You never told me he was red-headed before, or that he captured your galley," I said, after a discreet interval.

Charlie did not raise his eyes.

"He was as red as a red bear," said he abstractedly. "He came from the north; they said so in the galley when he looked for rowers—not slaves, but free men. Afterwards—years and years afterwards—news came from another ship, or else he came back—"

His lips moved in silence. He was rapturously retasting some poem before him.

"Where had he been, then?" I was almost whispering that the sentence might come gently to whichever section of Charlie's brain was working on my behalf.

"To the Beaches—the Long and Wonderful Beaches!" was the reply after a minute of silence.

"To Furdurstrandi?" I asked, tingling from head to foot.

"Yes, to Furdurstrandi," he pronounced the word in a new fashion. "And I too saw—" The voice failed.

"Do you know what you have said?" I shouted incautiously.

He lifted his eyes, fully roused now. "No!" he snapped. "I wish you'd let a chap go on reading. Hark to this:—

" 'But Othere, the old sea captain,
He neither paused nor stirred
  Till the king listened, and then
  Once more took up his pen
And wrote down every word.

" 'And to the King of the Saxons
In witness of the truth,
  Raising his noble head,
  He stretched his brown hand and said,
'Behold this walrus tooth.' "

"By Jove, what chaps those must have been, to go sailing all over the shop never knowing where they'd fetch the land! Hah!"

"Charlie," I pleaded, "if you'll only be sensible for a minute or two I'll make our hero in our tale every inch as good as Othere."

"Umph! Longfellow wrote that poem. I don't care about writing things any more. I want to read." He was thoroughly out of tune now, and raging over my own ill-luck, I left him.

Conceive yourself at the door of the world's treasure-house guarded by a child—an idle, irresponsible child playing knucklebones—on whose favor depends the gift of the key, and you will imagine one-half my torment. Till that evening Charlie had spoken nothing that might not lie within the experiences of a Greek galley-slave. But now, or there was no virtue in books, he had talked of some desperate adventure of the Vikings, of Thorfin Karlsefne's sailing to Wineland, which is America, in the ninth or tenth century. The battle in the harbor he had seen; and his own death he had described. But this was a much more startling plunge into the past. Was it possible that he had skipped half a dozen lives, and was then dimly remembering some episode of a thousand years later? It was a maddening jumble, and the worst of it was that Charlie Mears in his normal condition was the last person in the world to clear it up. I could only wait and watch, but I went to bed that night full of the wildest imaginings. There was nothing that was not possible if Charlie's detestable memory only held good.

I might rewrite the Saga of Thorfin Karlsefne as it had never been written before, might tell the story of the first discovery of America, myself the discoverer. But I was entirely at Charlie's mercy, and so long as there was a three-and-sixpenny Bohn volume within his reach Charlie would not tell. I dared not curse him openly; I hardly dared jog his memory, for I was dealing with the experiences of a thousand years ago, told through the mouth of a boy of today; and a boy of today is affected by every change of tone and gust of opinion, so that he must lie even when he most desires to speak the truth.

I saw no more of Charlie for nearly a week. When next I met him it was in Gracechurch Street with a bill-book chained to his waist. Business took him over London Bridge, and I accompanied him. He was very full of the importance of that book and magnified it. As we passed over the Thames we paused to look at a steamer unloading great slabs of white and brown marble. A barge drifted under the steamer's stern and a lonely ship's cow in that barge bellowed. Charlie's face changed from the face of the bank-clerk to that of an unknown and—though he would not have believed this—a much shrewder man. He flung out his arm across the parapet of the bridge and laughing very loudly, said:—

"When they heard *our* bulls bellow the Skraelings ran away!"

I waited only for an instant, but the barge and the cow had disappeared under the bows of the steamer before I answered.

"Charlie, what do you suppose are Skraelings?"

"Never heard of 'em before. They sound like a new kind of sea-gull. What a chap you are for asking questions!" he replied. "I have to go to the cashier of the Omnibus Company yonder. Will you wait for me and we can lunch somewhere together? I've a notion for a poem."

"No, thanks. I'm off. You're sure you know nothing about Skraelings?"

"Not unless he's been entered for the Liverpool Handicap." He nodded and disappeared in the crowd.

Now it is written in the Saga of Eric the Red or that of Thorfin

Karlsefne, that nine hundred years ago when Karlsefne's galleys came to Leif's booths, which Leif had erected in the unknown land called Markland, which may or may not have been Rhode Island, the Skraelings—and the Lord He knows who these may or may not have been—came to trade with the Vikings, and ran away because they were frightened at the bellowing of the cattle which Thorfin had brought with him in the ships. But what in the world could a Greek slave know of that affair? I wandered up and down among the streets trying to unravel the mystery, and the more I considered it the more baffling it grew. One thing only seemed certain, and that certainty took away my breath for the moment. If I came to full knowledge of anything at all, it would not be one life of the soul in Charlie Mears's body, but half a dozen—half a dozen several and separate existences spent on blue water in the morning of the world!

Then I reviewed the situation.

Obviously if I used my knowledge I should stand alone and unapproachable until all men were as wise as myself. That would be something, but, manlike, I was ungrateful. It seemed bitterly unfair that Charlie's memory should fail me when I needed it most. Great Powers Above—I looked up at them through the fog-smoke—did the Lords of Life and Death know what this meant to me? Nothing less than eternal fame of the best kind, that comes from One, and is shared by one alone. I would be content—remembering Clive, I stood astounded at my own moderation—with the mere right to tell one story, to work out one little contribution to the light literature of the day. If Charlie were permitted full recollection for one hour—for sixty short minutes—of existences that had extended over a thousand years—I would forgo all profit and honor from all that I should make of his speech. I would take no share in the commotion that would follow throughout the particular corner of the earth that calls itself "the world." The thing should be put forth anonymously. Nay, I would make other men believe that they had written it. They would hire bull-hided self-advertising Englishmen to bellow it abroad. Preachers would found a fresh conduct of life upon it, swearing that it was new and that they had lifted the fear of death from all mankind. Every Orientalist in Europe would patronize it discursively with Sanskrit and Pali texts. Terrible women would invent unclean variants of the men's belief for the elevation of their sisters. Churches and religions would war over it.

Between the hailing and restarting of an omnibus I foresaw the scuffles that would arise among half a dozen denominations all professing "the doctrine of the True Metempsychosis as applied to the world and the New Era"; and saw, too, the respectable English newspapers shying, like frightened kine, over the beautiful simplicity of the tale. The mind leaped forward a hundred—two hundred—a thousand years. I saw with sorrow that men would mutilate and garble the story; that rival creeds would turn it upside down till, at last, the western world which clings to the dread of death more closely than the hope of life, would set it aside as an interesting superstition and stampede after some faith so long forgotten that it seemed altogether new. Upon this I changed the terms of the bargain that I would make with the Lords of Life and Death. Only let me know, let me write, the story with sure knowledge that I wrote the truth, and I would burn the manuscript as a solemn sacrifice. Five minutes after the last line was written I would destroy it all. But I must be allowed to write it with absolute certainty.

There was no answer. The flaming colors of an Aquarium poster caught my eye, and I wondered whether it would be wise or prudent to lure Charlie into the hands of the professional mesmerist there, and whether, if he were under his power, he would speak of his past lives. If he did, and if people believed him . . . but Charlie would be frightened and flustered, or made conceited by the interviews. In either case he would begin to lie through fear or vanity. He was safest in my own hands.

"They are very funny fools, your English," said a voice at my elbow, and turning round I recognized a casual acquaintance, a young Bengali law student, called Grish Chunder, whose father had sent him to England to become civilized. The old man was a retired native official, and on an income of five pounds a month contrived to allow his son two hundred pounds a year, and the run of his teeth in a city where he could pretend to be the cadet of a royal house, and tell stories of the brutal Indian bureaucrats who ground the faces of the poor.

Grish Chunder was a young, fat, full-bodied Bengali, dressed with scrupulous care in frock coat, tall hat, light trousers, and tan gloves. But I had known him in the days when the brutal Indian Government paid for his university education, and he contributed cheap sedition to the *Sachi Durpan,* and intrigued with the wives of his fourteen-year-old schoolmates.

"That is very funny and very foolish," he said, nodding at the poster. "I am going down to the Northbrook Club. Will you come too?"

I walked with him for some time. "You are not well," he said. "What is there on your mind? You do not talk."

"Grish Chunder, you've been too well educated to believe in a God, haven't you?"

"Oah, yes, *here!* But when I go home I must conciliate popular superstition, and make ceremonies of purification, and my women will anoint idols."

"And hang up *tulsi* and feast the *purohit,* and take you back into caste again, and make a good *khuttri* of you again, you advanced Freethinker. And you'll eat *desi* food, and like it all, from the smell in the courtyard to the mustard oil over you."

"I shall very much like it," said Grish Chunder unguardedly. "Once a Hindu—always a Hindu. But I like to know what the English think they know."

"I'll tell you something that one Englishman knows. It's an old tale to you."

I began to tell the story of Charlie in English, but Grish Chunder put a question in the vernacular, and the history went forward naturally in the tongue best suited for its telling. After all, it could never have been told in English. Grish Chunder heard me, nodding from time to time, and then came up to my rooms, where I finished the tale.

"Beshak," he said philosophically. *"Lekin darwaza band hai.* (Without doubt; but the door is shut.) I have heard of this remembering of previous existences among my people. It is of course an old tale with us, but, to happen to an Englishman—a cow-fed *Mlechh*—an outcast. By Jove, that is *most* peculiar!"

"Outcast yourself, Grish Chunder! You eat cow-beef every day. Let's think the thing over. The boy remembers his incarnations."

"Does he know that?" said Grish Chunder quietly, swinging his legs as he sat on my table. He was speaking in his English now.

"He does not know anything. Would I speak to you if he did? Go on!"

"There is no going on at all. If you tell that to your friends they will say you are mad and put it in the papers. Suppose, now, you prosecute for libel."

"Let's leave that out of the question entirely. Is there any chance of his being made to speak?"

"There is a chance. Oah, yess! But *if* he spoke it would mean that all this world would end now—*instanto*—fall down on your head. These things are not allowed, you know. As I said, the door is shut."

"Not a ghost of a chance?"

"How can there be? You are a Christi-án, and it is forbidden to eat, in your books, of the Tree of Life, or else you would never die. How shall you all fear death if you all know what your friend does not know that he knows? I am afraid to be kicked, but I am not afraid to die, because I know what I know. You are not afraid to be kicked, but you are afraid to die. If you were not, by God! you English would be all over the shop in an hour, upsetting the balances of power, and making commotions. It would not be good. But no fear. He will remember a little and a little less, and he will call it dreams. Then he will forget altogether. When I passed my First Arts Examination in Calcutta that was all in the cram-book on Wordsworth. 'Trailing clouds of glory,' you know."

"This seems to be an exception to the rule."

"There are no exceptions to rules. Some are not so hard-looking as others, but they are all the same when you touch. If this friend of yours said so-and-so and so-and-so, indicating that he remembered all his lost lives, or one piece of a lost life, he would not be in the bank another hour. He would be what you called sack because he was mad, and they would send him to an asylum for lunatics. You can see that, my friend."

"Of course I can, but I wasn't thinking of him. His name need never appear in the story."

"Ah! I see. That story will never be written. You can try."

"I am going to."

"For your own credit and for the sake of money, *of* course?"

"No. For the sake of writing the story. On my honor that will be all."

"Even then there is no chance. You cannot play with the gods. It is a very pretty story now. As they say, let it go on that—I mean at that. Be quick; he will not last long."

"How do you mean?"

"What I say. He has never, so far, thought about a woman."

"Hasn't he, though!" I remembered some of Charlie's confidences.

"I mean no woman has thought about him. When that comes; *bus—hogya*—all up! I know. There are millions of women here. Housemaids, for instance. They kiss you behind doors."

I winced at the thought of my story being ruined by a housemaid. And yet nothing was more probable.

Grish Chunder grinned.

"Yes—also pretty girls—cousins of his house, and perhaps *not* of his house. One kiss that he gives back again and remembers will cure all this nonsense, or else—"

"Or else what? Remember he does not know that he knows."

"I know that. Or else, if nothing happens he will become immersed in the trade and the financial speculation like the rest. It must be so. You can see that it must be so. But the woman will come first, *I* think."

There was a rap at the door, and Charlie charged in impetuously. He had been released from office, and by the look in his eyes I could see that he had come over for a long talk; most probably with poems in his pockets. Charlie's poems were very wearying, but sometimes they led him to speak about the galley.

Grish Chunder looked at him keenly for a minute.

"I beg your pardon." Charlie said uneasily; "I didn't know you had any one with you."

"I am going," said Grish Chunder.

He drew me into the lobby as he departed.

"That is your man," he said quickly. "I tell you he will never speak all you wish. That is rot—bosh. But he would be most good to make to see things. Suppose now we pretend that it was only play"—I had never seen Grish Chunder so excited—"and pour the ink-pool into his hand. Eh, what do you think? I tell you that he could see *anything* that a man could see. Let me get the ink and the camphor. He is a seer and he will tell us very many things."

"He may be all you say, but I'm not going to trust him to your gods and devils."

"It will not hurt him. He will only feel a little stupid and dull when he wakes up. You have seen boys look into the ink-pool before."

"That is the reason why I am not going to see it any more. You'd better go, Grish Chunder."

He went, insisting far down the staircase that it was throwing away my only chance of looking into the future.

This left me unmoved, for I was concerned for the past, and no peering of hypnotized boys into mirrors and ink-pools would help me to that. But I recognised Grish Chunder's point of view and sympathized with it.

"What a big black brute that was!" said Charlie, when I returned to him. "Well, look here, I've just done a poem; did it instead of playing dominoes after lunch. May I read it?"

"Let me read it to myself."

"Then you miss the proper expression. Besides, you always make my things sound as if the rhymes were all wrong."

"Read it aloud, then. You're like the rest of 'em."

Charlie mouthed me his poem, and it was not much worse than the average of his verses. He had been reading his books faithfully, but he was not pleased when I told him that I preferred my Longfellow undiluted with Charlie.

Then we began to go through the manuscript line by line, Charlie parrying every objection and correction with:

"Yes, that may be better, but you don't catch what I'm driving at."

Charlie was, in one way at least, very like one kind of poet.

There was a pencil scrawl at the back of the paper, and "What's that?" I said.

"Oh, that's not poetry at all. It's some rot I wrote last night before I went to bed, and it was too much bother to hunt for rhymes; so I made it a sort of blank verse instead.

Here is Charlie's "blank verse":—

"We pulled for you when the wind was against us and the sails were low.

Will you never let us go?

We ate bread and onions when you took towns, or ran aboard quickly when you were beaten back by the foe,

The captains walked up and down the deck in fair weather singing songs, but we were below.

We fainted with our chins on the oars and you did not see that we were idle for we still swung to and fro.

Will you never let us go?

The salt made the oar-handles like shark-skin; our knees

were cut to the bone with salt cracks; our hair was stuck to our foreheads; and our lips were cut to our gums, and you whipped us because we could not row.

Will you never let us go?

But in a little time we shall run out of the portholes as the water runs along the oar-blade, and though you tell the others to row after us you will never catch us till you catch the oar-thresh and tie up the winds in the belly of the sail. Aho!

Will you never let us go?"

"H'm. What's oar-thresh, Charlie?"

"The water washed up by the oars. That's the sort of song they might sing in the galley y' know. Aren't you ever going to finish that story and give me some of the profits?"

"It depends on yourself. If you had only told me more about your hero in the first instance it might have been finished by now. You're so hazy in your notions."

"I only want to give you the general notion of it—the knocking about from place to place and the fighting and all that. Can't you fill in the rest yourself? Make the hero save a girl on a pirate-galley and marry her or do something."

"You're a really helpful collaborator. I suppose the hero went through some few adventures before he married."

"Well then, make him a very artful card—a low sort of man—a sort of political man who went about making treaties and breaking them—a black-haired chap who hid behind the mast when the fighting began."

"But you said the other day that he was red-haired."

"I couldn't have. Make him black-haired of course. You've no imagination."

Seeing that I had just discovered the entire principles upon which the half-memory falsely called imagination is based, I felt entitled to laugh, but forbore for the sake of the tale.

"You're right. *You're* the man with imagination. A black-haired chap in a decked ship," I said.

"No, an open ship—like a big boat."

This was maddening.

"Your ship has been built and designed, closed and decked in; you said so yourself," I protested.

"No, no, not that ship. That was open or half-decked because—By Jove, you're right. You made me think of the hero as a red-haired chap. Of course if he were red, the ship would be an open one with painted sails."

Surely, I thought, he would remember now that he had served in two galleys at least—in a three-decked Greek one under the black-haired "political man," and again in a Viking's open sea-serpent under the man "red as a red bear" who went to Markland. The devil prompted me to speak.

"Why, 'of course,' Charlie?" said I.

"I don't know. Are you making fun of me?"

The current was broken for the time being. I took up a note-book and pretended to make many entries in it.

"It's a pleasure to work with an imaginative chap like yourself," I said, after a pause. "The way that you've brought out the character of the hero is simply wonderful."

"Do you think so?" he answered, with a pleased flush. "I often tell myself that there's more in me than my mo—than people think."

"There's an enormous amount in you."

"Then, won't you let me send an essay on The Ways of Bank-Clerks to *Tit-Bits,* and get the guinea prize?"

"That wasn't exactly what I meant, old fellow: perhaps it would be better to wait a little and go ahead with the galley-story."

"Ah, but I shan't get the credit of that. *Tit-Bits* would publish my name and address if I win. What are you grinning at? They *would.*"

"I know it. Suppose you go for a walk. I want to look through my notes about our story."

Now this reprehensible youth who left me, a little hurt and put back, might for aught he or I knew have been one of the crew of the Argo—had been certainly slave or comrade to Thorfin Karlsefne. Therefore he was deeply interested in guinea competitions. Remembering what Grish Chunder had said I laughed aloud. The Lords of Life and Death would never allow Charlie Mears to speak with full knowledge of his pasts, and I must even piece out what he had told me with my own poor inventions while Charlie wrote of the ways of bank-clerks.

I got together and placed on one file all my notes; and the net result was not cheering. I read them a second time. There was nothing that might not have been compiled at second-hand from other people's books—except, perhaps, the story of the fight in the harbor. The adventures of a Viking had been written many times before; the history of a Greek galley-slave was no new thing, and though I wrote both, who could challenge or confirm the accuracy of my details? I might as well tell a tale of two thousand years hence. The Lords of Life and Death were as cunning as Grish Chunder had hinted. They would allow nothing to escape that might trouble or make easy the minds of men. Though I was convinced of this, yet I could not leave the tale alone. Exaltation followed reaction, not once, but twenty times in the next few weeks. My moods varied with the March sunlight and flying clouds. By night or in the beauty of a spring morning I perceived that I could write that tale and shift continents thereby. In the wet windy afternoons, I saw that the tale might indeed be written, but would be nothing more than a faked, false-varnished, sham-rusted piece of Wardour Street work in the end. Then I blessed Charlie in many ways—though it was no fault of his. He seemed to be busy with prize competitions, and I saw less and less of him as the weeks went by and the earth cracked and grew ripe to spring, and the buds swelled in their sheaths. He did not care to read or talk of what he had read, and there was a new ring of self-assertion in his voice. I hardly cared to remind him of the galley when we met; but Charlie alluded to it on every occasion, always as a story from which money was to be made.

"I think I deserve twenty-five percent, don't I, at least?" he said, with beautiful frankness. "I supplied all the ideas, didn't I?"

This greediness for silver was a new side in his nature. I assumed that it had been developed in the City, where Charlie was picking up the curious nasal drawl of the underbred City man.

"When the thing's done we'll talk about it. I can't make anything of it at present. Red-haired or black-haired heroes are equally difficult."

He was sitting by the fire staring at the red coals. "*I* can't understand what you find so difficult. It's all as clear as mud to me," he replied. A jet of gas puffed out between the bars, took light, and whistled softly. "Suppose we take the red-haired hero's adventures first, from the time that he came south to my galley and captured it and sailed to the Beaches."

I knew better now than to interrupt Charlie. I was out of reach of pen and paper, and dared not move to get them lest I should break the current. The gas-jet puffed and whinnied, Charlie's voice dropped almost to a whisper, and he told a tale of the sailing of an open galley to Furdurstrandi, of sunsets on the open sea, seen under the curve of the one sail evening after evening when the galley's beak was notched into the centre of the sinking disc, and "we sailed by that for we had no other guide," quoth Charlie. He spoke of a landing on an island and explorations in its woods, where the crew killed three men whom they found asleep under the pines. Their ghosts, Charlie said, followed the galley, swimming and choking in the water, and the crew cast lots and threw one of their number overboard as a sacrifice to the strange gods whom they had offended. Then they ate sea-weed when their provisions failed, and their legs swelled, and their leader, the red-haired man, killed two rowers who mutinied, and after a year spent among the woods they set sail for their own country, and a wind that never failed carried them back so safely that they all slept at night. This, and much more Charlie told. Sometimes the voice fell so low that I could not catch the words, though every nerve was on the strain. He spoke of their leader, the red-haired man, as a pagan speaks of his God; for it was he who cheered them and slew them impartially as he thought best for their needs; and it was he who steered them for three days among floating ice, each floe crowded with strange beasts that "tried to sail with us," said Charlie, "and we beat them back with the handles of the oars."

The gas-jet went out, a burnt coal gave way, and the fire settled with a tiny crash to the bottom of the grate. Charlie ceased speaking, and I said no word.

"By Jove!" he said at last, shaking his head. "I've been staring at the fire till I'm dizzy. What was I going to say?"

"Something about the galley-book."

"I remember now. It's twenty-five percent of the profits, isn't it?"

"It's anything you like when I've done the tale."

"I wanted to be sure of that. I must go now. I've—I've an appointment." And he left me.

Had not my eyes been held I might have known that that broken muttering over the fire was the swan-song of Charlie Mears. But I thought it the prelude to fuller revelation. At last and at last I should cheat the Lords of Life and Death!

When next Charlie came to me I received him with rapture. He was nervous and embarrassed, but his eyes were very full of light, and his lips a little parted.

"I've done a poem," he said; and then, quickly: "It's the best I've ever done. Read it." He thrust it into my hand and retreated to the window.

I groaned inwardly. It would be the work of half an hour to criticize—that is to say, praise—the poem sufficiently to please Charlie. Then I had good reason to groan, for Charlie, discarding his favorite centipede meters, had launched into shorter and choppier verse, and verse with a motive at the back of it. This is what I read:—

"The day is most fair, the cheery wind
Halloos behind the hill,
Where he bends the wood as seemeth good,
And the sapling to his will!
Riot, O wind; there is that in my blood
That would not have thee still!

"She gave me herself, O Earth, O Sky;
Gray sea, she is mine alone!
Let the sullen boulders hear my cry,
And rejoice tho' they be but stone!

"Mine! I have won her, O good brown earth,
Make merry! 'Tis hard on Spring;
Make merry; my love is doubly worth
All worship your fields can bring!
Let the hind that tills you feel my mirth
At the early harrowing!"

"Yes, it's the early harrowing, past a doubt," I said, with a dread at my heart. Charlie smiled, but did not answer.

"Red cloud of the sunset, tell it abroad;
I am victor. Greet me, O Sun,
Dominant master and absolute lord
Over the soul of one!"

"Well?" said Charlie, looking over my shoulder.

I thought it far from well, and very evil indeed, when he silently laid a photograph on the paper—the photograph of a girl with a curly head and a foolish slack mouth.

"Isn't it—isn't it wonderful?" he whispered, pink to the tips of his ears, wrapped in the rosy mystery of first love. "I didn't know; I didn't think—it came like a thunderclap."

"Yes. It comes like a thunderclap. Are you very happy, Charlie?"

"My God—she—she loves me!" He sat down repeating the last words to himself. I looked at the hairless face, the narrow shoulders already bowed by desk-work, and wondered when, where, and how he had loved in his past lives.

"What will your mother say?" I asked cheerfully.

"I don't care a damn what she says!"

At twenty the things for which one does not care a damn should, properly, be many, but one must not include mothers in the list. I told him this gently; and he described Her, even as Adam must have described to the newly-named beasts the glory and tenderness and beauty of Eve. Incidentally I learned that She was a tobacconist's assistant with a weakness for pretty dress, and had told him four or five times already that She had never been kissed by a man before.

Charlie spoke on and on, and on; while I, separated from him by thousands of years, was considering the beginnings of things. Now I understood why the Lords of Life and Death shut the doors so carefully behind us. It is that we may not remember our first and most beautiful wooings. Were this not so, our world would be without inhabitants in a hundred years.

"Now, about that galley-story," I said still more cheerfully, in a pause in the rush of the speech.

Charlie looked up as though he had been hit. "The galley—what galley? Good heavens, don't joke, man! This is serious! You don't know how serious it is!"

Grish Chunder was right. Charlie had tasted the love of woman that kills remembrance, and the finest story in the world would never be written.

The Children of the Zodiac

FROM MANY *INVENTIONS* (1893)

When Kipling wrote this mysterious and powerful story—it originally appeared in magazine form in November 1891—he was contemplating marriage, but hesitating, for he was suffering from a throat condition that he feared might prove to be cancer. He considered throat cancer to be "the family complaint." Charles Carrington therefore suggests that we should regard it as a parable reflecting his real-life situation at the time, and no doubt he is correct.

In my submission, though, it stands on its own merits, both as a fable concerning the human predicament and for the brilliance of its language and its images. I cannot forget the vision of the Ram bending his head to accept a wreath of wild garlic-leaves, nor the description of cancer at work on the body, "like the eating of a smothered fire into rotten timber"; nor, come to that, the reason why the Children laughed for the very first time.

And yet, at the end, it is a tale of triumph. As you'll see.

The attributes of two of the Houses from which death descends to the world are unexplained. We learn what fate attends those doomed to the Archer, the Fishes, the Scorpion and the Crab, but what of the Balance and the Waterman? I'll make a guess. I think the Balance must be the scales of justice, and its victims are those executed by law; and, given Kipling's Indian background, those whom the Waterman takes are lost to drought and the ensuing famine. But in the story, as it turned out, there was no call for direct reference to their respective attributes.

A cottar, by the way, was a man living in a cottage for which he paid by working in a landowner's fields.

The Children of the Zodiac

Though thou love her as thyself,
As a self of purer clay,
Though her parting dim the day,
Stealing grace from all alive,
  Heartily know
  When half Gods go
The Gods arrive.

EMERSON

Thousands of years ago, when men were greater than they are today, the Children of the Zodiac lived in the world. There were six Children of the Zodiac—the Ram, the Bull, Leo, the Twins, and the Girl; and they were afraid of the Six Houses which belonged to the Scorpion, the Balance, the Crab, the Fishes, the Archer, and the Waterman. Even when they first stepped down upon the earth and knew that they were immortal Gods, they carried this fear with them; and the fear grew as they became better acquainted with mankind and heard stories of the Six Houses. Men treated the Children as Gods and came to them with prayers and long stories of wrong, while the Children of the Zodiac listened and could not understand.

A mother would fling herself before the feet of the Twins, or the Bull, crying: "My husband was at work in the fields and the Archer shot him and he died; and my son will also be killed by the Archer. Help me!" The Bull would lower his huge head and answer: "What is that to me?" Or the Twins would smile and continue their play, for they could not understand why the water ran out of people's eyes. At other times a man and a woman would come to Leo or the Girl crying: "We two are newly married and we are very happy. Take these flowers." As they threw the flowers they would make mysterious sounds to show that they were happy, and Leo and the Girl wondered even more than the Twins why people shouted "Ha! ha! ha!" for no cause.

This continued for thousands of years by human reckoning, till on a day, Leo met the Girl walking across the hills and saw that she had changed entirely since he had last seen her. The Girl, looking at Leo, saw that he too had changed altogether. Then they decided that it would be well never to separate again, in case even more startling changes should occur when the one was not at hand to help the other. Leo kissed the Girl and all Earth felt that kiss, and the Girl sat down on a hill and the water ran out of her eyes; and this had never happened before in the memory of the Children of the Zodiac.

As they sat together a man and a woman came by, and the man said to the woman:

"What is the use of wasting flowers on those dull Gods? They will never understand, darling."

The Girl jumped up and put her arms round the woman, crying, "I understand. Give me the flowers and I will give you a kiss."

Leo said beneath his breath to the man: "What was the new name that I heard you give to your woman just now?"

The man answered, "Darling, of course."

"Why 'of course'?" said Leo; "and if of course, what does it mean?"

"It means 'very dear,' and you have only to look at your wife to see why."

"I see," said Leo; "you are quite right"; and when the man and the woman had gone on he called the Girl "darling wife"; and the Girl wept again from sheer happiness.

"I think," she said at last, wiping her eyes, "I think that we two have neglected men and women too much. What did you do with the sacrifices they made to you, Leo?"

"I let them burn," said Leo; "I could not eat them. What did you do with the flowers?"

"I let them wither. I could not wear them, I had so many of my own," said the Girl, "and now I am sorry."

"There is nothing to grieve for," said Leo; "we belong to each other."

As they were talking the years of men's life slipped by unnoticed, and presently the man and the woman came back, both white-headed, the man carrying the woman.

"We have come to the end of things," said the man quietly. "This that was my wife—"

"As I am Leo's wife," said the Girl quickly, her eyes staring.

"—was my wife, has been killed by one of your Houses." The man set down his burden, and laughed.

"Which House?" said Leo angrily, for he hated all the Houses equally.

"You are Gods, you should know," said the man. "We have lived together and loved one another, and I have left a good farm for my son. What have I to complain of except that I still live?"

As he was bending over his wife's body there came a whistling through the air, and he started and tried to run away, crying, "It is the arrow of the Archer. Let me live a little longer—only a little longer!" The arrow struck him and he died. Leo looked at the Girl and she looked at him, and both were puzzled.

"He wished to die," said Leo. "He said that he wished to die, and when Death came he tried to run away. He is a coward."

"No, he is not," said the Girl; "I think I feel what he felt. Leo, we must learn more about this for their sakes."

"For *their* sakes," said Leo, very loudly.

"Because *we* are never going to die," said the Girl and Leo together, still more loudly.

"Now sit you still here, darling wife," said Leo, "while I go to the Houses whom we hate, and learn how to make these men and women live as we do."

"And love as we do," said the Girl.

"I do not think they need to be taught that," said Leo, and he strode away very angry, with his lion-skin swinging from his shoulder, till he came to the House where the Scorpion lives in the darkness, brandishing his tail over his back.

"Why do you trouble the children of men?" said Leo, with his heart between his teeth.

"Are you so sure that I trouble the children of men alone?" said the Scorpion. "Speak to your brother the Bull, and see what he says."

"I come on behalf of the children of men," said Leo. "I have learned to love as they do, and I wish them to live as I—as we do."

"Your wish was granted long ago. Speak to the Bull. He is under my special care," said the Scorpion.

Leo dropped back to the earth again, and saw the great star Aldebaran, that is set in the forehead of the Bull, blazing very near to the earth. When he came up to it he saw that his brother the Bull, yoked to a countryman's plow, was toiling through a wet rice-field with his head bent down, and the sweat streaming from his flanks. The countryman was urging him forward with a goad.

"Gore that insolent to death," cried Leo, "and for the sake of our honor come out of the mire."

"I cannot," said the Bull, "the Scorpion has told me that some day, of which I cannot be sure, he will sting me where my neck is set on my shoulders, and that I shall die bellowing."

"What has that to do with this disgraceful work?" said Leo, standing on the dyke that bounded the wet field.

"Everything. This man could not plow without my help. He thinks that I am a stray beast."

"But he is a mud-crusted cottar with matted hair," insisted Leo. "We are not meant for his use."

"You may not be; I am. I cannot tell when the Scorpion may choose to sting me to death—perhaps before I have turned this furrow." The Bull flung his bulk into the yoke, and the plow tore through the wet ground behind him, and the countryman goaded him till his flanks were red.

"Do you like this?" Leo called down the dripping furrows.

"No," said the Bull over his shoulder as he lifted his hind legs from the clinging mud and cleared his nostrils.

Leo left him scornfully and passed to another country, where he found his brother the Ram in the center of a crowd of country people who were hanging wreaths round his neck and feeding him on freshly-plucked green corn.

"This is terrible," said Leo. "Break up that crowd and come away, my brother. Their hands are spoiling your fleece."

"I cannot," said the Ram. "The Archer told me that on some day of which I had no knowledge, he would send a dart through me, and that I should die in very great pain."

"What has that to do with this disgraceful show?" said Leo, but he did not speak as confidently as before.

"Everything in the world," said the Ram. "These people never saw a perfect sheep before. They think that I am a stray, and they will carry me from place to place as a model to all their flocks."

"But they are greasy shepherds; we are not intended to amuse them," said Leo.

"You may not be, I am," said the Ram. "I cannot tell when the Archer may choose to send his arrow at me—perhaps before the people a mile down the road have seen me." The Ram lowered his head that a yokel newly arrived might throw a wreath of wild garlic-leaves over it, and waited patiently while the farmers tugged his fleece.

"Do you like this?" cried Leo over the shoulders of the crowd.

"No," said the Ram, as the dust of the trampling feet made him sneeze, and he snuffed at the fodder piled before him.

Leo turned back intending to retrace his steps to the Houses, but as he was passing down a street he saw two small children, very dusty, rolling outside a cottage door, and playing with a cat. They were the Twins.

"What are you doing here?" said Leo, indignant.

"Playing," said the Twins calmly.

"Cannot you play on the banks of the Milky Way?" said Leo.

"We did," said they, "till the Fishes swam down and told us that some day they would come for us and not hurt us at all and carry us away. So now we are playing at being babies down here. The people like it."

"Do you like it?" said Leo.

"No," said the Twins, "but there are no cats in the Milky Way," and they pulled the cat's tail thoughtfully. A woman came out of the doorway and stood behind them, and Leo saw in her face a look that he had sometimes seen in the Girl's.

"She thinks that we are foundlings," said the Twins, and they trotted indoors to the evening meal.

Then Leo hurried as swiftly as possible to all the Houses one after another; for he could not understand the new trouble that had come to his brethren. He spoke to the Archer, and the Archer assured him that so far as that House was concerned Leo had nothing to fear. The Waterman, the Fishes, and the Scorpion gave the same answer. They knew nothing of Leo, and cared less. They were the Houses, and they were busied in killing men.

At last he came to that very dark House where Cancer the Crab lies so still that you might think he was asleep if you did not see the ceaseless play and winnowing motion of the feathery branches round his mouth. That movement never ceases. It is like the eating of a smothered fire into rotten timber in that it is noiseless and without haste.

Leo stood in front of the Crab, and the half darkness allowed him a glimpse of that vast blue-black back and the motionless eyes. Now and again he thought that he heard someone sobbing, but the noise was very faint.

"Why do you trouble the children of men?" said Leo. There was no answer, and against his will Leo cried, "Why do you trouble us? What have we done that you should trouble us?"

This time Cancer replied, "What do I know or care? You were born into my House, and at the appointed time I shall come for you."

"When is the appointed time?" said Leo, stepping back from the restless movement of the mouth.

"When the full moon fails to call the full tide," said the Crab, "I shall come for the one. When the other has taken the earth by the shoulders, I shall take that other by the throat."

Leo lifted his hand to the apple of his throat, moistened his lips, and recovering himself, said:

"Must I be afraid for two, then?"

"For two," said the Crab, "and as many more as may come after."

"My brother, the Bull, had a better fate," said Leo, sullenly; "he is alone."

A hand covered his mouth before he could finish the sentence, and he found the Girl in his arms. Womanlike, she had not stayed where Leo had left her, but had hastened off at once to know the worst, and passing all the other Houses, had come straight to Cancer.

"That is foolish," said the Girl, whispering. "I have been waiting in the dark for long and long before you came. *Then* I was afraid. But now—" She put her head down on his shoulder and sighed a sigh of contentment.

"I am afraid now," said Leo.

"That is on my account," said the Girl. "I know it is, because I am afraid for your sake. Let us go, husband."

They went out of the darkness together and came back to the Earth, Leo very silent, and the Girl striving to cheer him. "My brother's fate is the better one," Leo would repeat from time to time, and at last he said: "Let us each go our own way and live alone till we die. We were born into the House of Cancer, and he will come for us."

"I know; I know. But where shall I go? And where will you sleep in the evening? But let us try. I will stay here. Do you go on?"

Leo took six steps forward very slowly, and three long steps backward very quickly, and the third step set him again at the Girl's side. This time it was she who was begging him to go away and leave her, and he was forced to comfort her all through the night. That night decided them both never to leave each other for an instant, and when they had come to this decision they looked back at the darkness of the House of Cancer high above their heads, and with their arms round each other's necks laughed, "Ha! ha! ha!" exactly as the children of men laughed. And that was the first time in their lives that they had ever laughed.

Next morning they returned to their proper home, and saw the flowers and the sacrifices that had been laid before their doors by the villagers of the hills. Leo stamped down the fire with his heel, and the Girl flung the flower-wreaths out of sight, shuddering as she did so. When the villagers returned, as of custom, to see what had become of their offerings, they found neither roses nor burned flesh on the altars, but only a man and a woman, with frightened white faces, sitting hand in hand on the altar-steps.

"Are you not Virgo?" said a woman to the Girl. "I sent you flowers yesterday."

"Little sister," said the Girl, flushing to her forehead, "do not send any more flowers, for I am only a woman like yourself." The man and the woman went away doubtfully.

"Now, what shall we do?" said Leo.

"We must try to be cheerful, I think," said the Girl. "We know the very worst that can happen to us, but we do not know the best that love can bring us. We have a great deal to be glad of."

"The certainty of death," said Leo.

"All the children of men have that certainty also; yet they laughed long before we ever knew how to laugh. We must learn to laugh, Leo. We have laughed once already."

People who consider themselves Gods, as the Children of the Zodiac did, find it hard to laugh, because the Immortals know nothing worth laughter or tears. Leo rose up with a very heavy heart, and he and the Girl together went to and fro among men;

their new fear of death behind them. First they laughed at a naked baby attempting to thrust its fat toes into its foolish pink mouth; next they laughed at a kitten chasing her own tail; and then they laughed at a boy trying to steal a kiss from a girl, and getting his ears boxed. Lastly, they laughed because the wind blew in their faces as they ran down a hillside together, and broke panting and breathless into a knot of villagers at the bottom. The villagers laughed too at their flying clothes and wind-reddened faces; and in the evening gave them food and invited them to a dance on the grass, where everybody laughed through the mere joy of being able to dance.

That night Leo jumped up from the Girl's side crying: "Every one of those people we met just now will die—"

"So shall we," said the Girl sleepily. "Lie down again, dear." Leo could not see that her face was wet with tears.

But Leo was up and far across the fields, driven forward by the fear of death for himself and for the Girl, who was dearer to him than himself. Presently he came across the Bull drowsing in the moonlight after a hard day's work, and looking through half-shut eyes at the beautiful straight furrows that he had made.

"Ho!" said the Bull, "so you have been told these things too. Which of the Houses holds your death?"

Leo pointed upwards to the dark House of the Crab and groaned. "And he will come for the Girl too," he said.

"Well," said the Bull, "what will you do?"

Leo sat down on the dyke and said that he did not know.

"You cannot pull a plow," said the Bull, with a little touch of contempt. "I can, and that prevents me from thinking of the Scorpion."

Leo was angry and said nothing till the dawn broke, and the cultivator came to yoke the Bull to his work.

"Sing," said the Bull, as the stiff muddy ox-bow creaked and strained. "My shoulder is galled. Sing one of the songs that we sang when we thought we were all Gods together."

Leo stepped back into the cane-brake and lifted up his voice in a song of the Children of the Zodiac—the war-whoop of the young Gods who are afraid of nothing. At first he dragged the song along unwillingly, and then the song dragged him, and his voice rolled across the fields, and the Bull stepped to the tune, and the cultivator banged his flanks out of sheer light-heartedness, and the furrows rolled away behind the plow more and more swiftly. Then the Girl came across the fields looking for Leo and found him singing in the cane. She joined her voice to his, and the cultivator's wife brought her spinning into the open and listened with all her children round her. When it was time for the nooning, Leo and the Girl had sung themselves both thirsty and hungry, but the cultivator and his wife gave them rye-bread and milk, and many thanks, and the Bull found occasion to say: "You have helped me to do a full half-field more than I should have done. But the hardest part of the day is to come, brother."

Leo wished to lie down and brood over the words of the Crab. The Girl went away to talk to the cultivator's wife and baby, and the afternoon plowing began.

"Help us now," said the Bull. "The tides of the day are running down. My legs are very stiff. Sing if you never sang before."

"To a mud-spattered villager?" said Leo.

"He is under the same doom as ourselves. Are you a coward?" said the Bull. Leo flushed and began again with a sore throat and a bad temper. Little by little he dropped away from the songs of the Children and made up a song as he went along; and this was a thing he could never have done had he not met the Crab face to face. He remembered facts concerning cultivators, and bullocks, and rice-fields, that he had not particularly noticed before the interview, and he strung them all together, growing more interested as he sang, and he told the cultivator much more about himself and his work than the cultivator knew. The Bull grunted approval as he toiled down the furrows for the last time that day, and the song ended, leaving the cultivator with a very good opinion of himself in his aching bones. The Girl came out of the hut where she had been keeping the children quiet, and talking woman-talk to the wife, and they all ate the evening meal together.

"Now yours must be a very pleasant life," said the cultivator, "sitting as you do on a dyke all day and singing just what comes into your head. Have you been at it long, you two—gipsies?"

"Ah!" lowed the Bull from his byre. "That's all the thanks you will ever get from men, brother."

"No. We have only just begun it," said the Girl; "but we are going to keep to it as long as we live. Are we not, Leo?"

"Yes," said he, and they went away hand-in-hand.

"You can sing beautifully, Leo," said she, as a wife will to her husband.

"What were you doing?" said he.

"I was talking to the mother and the babies," she said. "You would not understand the little things that make us women laugh."

"And—and I am to go on with this—this gipsy-work?" said Leo.

"Yes, dear, and I will help you."

There is no written record of the life of Leo and of the Girl, so we cannot tell how Leo took to his new employment which he detested. We are only sure that the Girl loved him when and wherever he sang; even when, after the song was done, she went round with the equivalent of a tambourine, and collected the pence for the daily bread. There were times too when it was Leo's very hard task to console the Girl for the indignity of horrible praise that people gave him and her—for the silly wagging peacock feathers that they stuck in his cap, and the buttons and pieces of cloth that they sewed on his coat. Woman-like, she could advise and help to the end, but the meanness of the means revolted.

"What does it matter," Leo would say, "so long as the songs make them a little happier?" And they would go down the road and begin again on the old old refrain: that whatever came or did not come the children of men must not be afraid. It was heavy teaching at first, but in process of years Leo discovered that he could make men laugh and hold them listening to him even when the rain fell. Yet there were people who would sit down and cry softly, though the crowd was yelling with delight, and there were people who maintained that Leo made them do this; and the Girl would talk to them in the pauses of the performance and do her best to comfort them. People would die too, while Leo was talking, and singing, and laughing, for the Archer, and the Scorpion, and the Crab, and the other Houses were as busy as ever. Sometimes the crowd broke, and were frightened, and Leo strove to keep them steady by telling them that this was cowardly; and sometimes they mocked at the Houses that were killing them, and Leo explained that this was even more cowardly than running away.

In their wanderings they came across the Bull, or the Ram, or the Twins, but all were too busy to do more than nod to each other across the crowd, and go on with their work. As the years rolled on even that recognition ceased, for the Children of the

Zodiac had forgotten that they had ever been Gods working for the sake of men. The Star Aldebaran was crusted with caked dirt on the Bull's forehead, the Ram's fleece was dusty and torn, and the Twins were only babies fighting over the cat on the doorstep. It was then that Leo said: "Let us stop singing and making jokes." And it was then that the Girl said: "No—" but she did not know why she said "No" so energetically. Leo maintained that it was perversity, till she herself, at the end of a dusty day, made the same suggestion to him, and he said "most certainly not," and they quarreled miserably between the hedgerows, forgetting the meaning of the stars above them. Other singers and other talkers sprang up in the course of the years, and Leo, forgetting that there could never be too many of these, hated them for dividing the applause of the children of men, which he thought should be all his own. The Girl would grow angry too, and then the songs would be broken, and the jests fall flat for weeks to come, and the children of men would shout: "Go home, you two gipsies. Go home and learn something worth singing!"

After one of these sorrowful shameful days, the Girl, walking by Leo's side through the fields, saw the full moon coming up over the trees, and she clutched Leo's arm, crying: "The time has come now. Oh, Leo, forgive me!"

"What is it?" said Leo. He was thinking of the other singers.

"My husband!" she answered, and she laid his hand upon her breast, and the breast that he knew so well was hard as stone. Leo groaned, remembering what the Crab had said.

"Surely we were Gods once," he cried.

"Surely we are Gods still," said the Girl. "Do you not remember when you and I went to the house of the Crab and—were not very much afraid? And since then . . . we have forgotten what we were singing for—we sang for the pence, and, oh, we fought for them!—We, who are the Children of the Zodiac."

"It was my fault," said Leo.

"How can there be any fault of yours that is not mine too?" said the Girl. "My time has come, but you will live longer, and . . . " The look in her eyes said all she could not say.

"Yes, I will remember that we are Gods," said Leo.

It is very hard, even for a child of the Zodiac, who has forgotten his Godhead, to see his wife dying slowly and to know that he cannot help her. The Girl told Leo in those last months of all that she had said and done among the wives and the babies at the back of the roadside performances, and Leo was astonished that he knew so little of her who had been so much to him. When she was dying she told him never to fight for pence or quarrel with the other singers; and, above all, to go on with his singing immediately after she was dead.

Then she died, and after he had buried her he went down the road to a village that he knew, and the people hoped that he would begin quarreling with a new singer that had sprung up while he had been away. But Leo called him "my brother." The new singer was newly married—and Leo knew it—and when he had finished singing, Leo straightened himself and sang the "Song of the Girl," which he had made coming down the road. Every man who was married or hoped to be married, whatever his rank or color, understood that song—even the bride leaning on the new husband's arm understood it too—and presently when the song ended, and Leo's heart was bursting in him, the men sobbed. "That was a sad tale," they said at last, "now make us laugh." Because Leo had known all the sorrow that a man could know, including the full knowledge of his own fall who had once been a God—he, changing his song quickly, made the people laugh till they could laugh no more. They went away feeling ready for any trouble in reason, and they gave Leo more peacock feathers and pence than he could count. Knowing that pence led to quarrels and that peacock feathers were hateful to the Girl, he put them aside and went away to look for his brothers, to remind them that they too were Gods.

He found the Bull goring the undergrowth in a ditch, for the Scorpion had stung him, and he was dying, not slowly, as the Girl had died, but quickly.

"I know all," the Bull groaned, as Leo came up. "I had forgotten too, but I remember now. Go and look at the fields I plowed. The furrows are straight. I forgot that I was a God, but I drew the plow perfectly straight, for all that. And you, brother?"

"I am not at the end of the plowing," said Leo. "Does Death hurt?"

"No, but dying does," said the Bull, and he died. The cultivator who then owned him was much annoyed, for there was a field still unplowed.

It was after this that Leo made the "Song of the Bull" who had been a God and forgotten the fact, and he sang it in such a manner that half the young men in the world conceived that they too might be Gods without knowing it. A half of that half grew impossibly conceited, and died early. A half of the remainder strove to be Gods and failed, but the other half accomplished four times more work than they would have done under any other delusion.

Later, years later, always wandering up and down and making the children of men laugh, he found the Twins sitting on the bank of a stream waiting for the Fishes to come and carry them away. They were not in the least afraid, and they told Leo that the woman of the House had a real baby of her own, and that when that baby grew old enough to be mischievous he would find a well-educated cat waiting to have its tail pulled. Then the Fishes came for them, but all that the people saw was two children drowned in a brook; and though their foster-mother was very sorry, she hugged her own real baby to her breast and was grateful that it was only the foundlings.

Then Leo made the "Song of the Twins," who had forgotten that they were Gods and had played in the dust to amuse a foster-mother. That song was sung far and wide among the women. It caused them to laugh and cry and hug their babies closer to their hearts all in one breath; and some of the women who remembered the Girl said: "Surely that is the voice of Virgo. Only she could know so much about ourselves."

After those three songs were made, Leo sang them over and over again till he was in danger of looking upon them as so many mere words, and the people who listened grew tired, and there came back to Leo the old temptation to stop singing once and for all. But he remembered the Girl's dying words and persisted.

One of his listeners interrupted him as he was singing. "Leo," said he, "I have heard you telling us not to be afraid for the past forty years. Can you not sing something new now?"

"No," said Leo, "it is the only song that I am allowed to sing. You must not be afraid of the Houses, even when they kill you." The man turned to go, wearily, but there came a whistling through the air, and the arrow of the Archer was seen skimming low above the earth, pointing to the man's heart. He drew himself up, and stood still waiting till the arrow struck home.

"I die," he said quietly. "It is well for me, Leo, that you sang for forty years."

"Are you afraid?" said Leo, bending over him.

"I am a man, not a God," said the man. "I should have run

away but for your songs. My work is done, and I die without making a show of my fear."

"I am very well paid," said Leo to himself. "Now that I see what my songs are doing, I will sing better ones."

He went down the road, collected his little knot of listeners, and began the "Song of the Girl." In the middle of his singing he felt the cold touch of the Crab's claw on the apple of his throat. He lifted his hand, choked, and stopped for an instant.

"Sing on, Leo," said the crowd. "The old song runs as well as ever it did."

Leo went on steadily till the end with the cold fear at his heart. When his song was ended, he felt the grip on his throat tighten. He was old, he had lost the Girl, he knew that he was losing more than half his power to sing, he could scarcely walk to the diminishing crowds that waited for him, and could not see their faces when they stood about him. None the less, he cried angrily to the Crab:

"Why have you come for me *now?*"

"You were born under my care. How can I help coming for you?" said the Crab wearily. Every human being whom the Crab killed had asked that same question.

"But I was just beginning to know what my songs were doing," said Leo.

"Perhaps that is why," said the Crab, and the grip tightened.

"You said you would not come till I had taken the world by the shoulders," gasped Leo, falling back.

"I always keep my word. You have done that three times with three songs. What more do you desire?"

"Let me live to see the world know it," pleaded Leo. "Let me be sure that my songs—"

"Make men brave?" said the Crab. "Even then there would be one man who was afraid. The Girl was braver than you are. Come."

Leo was standing close to the restless, insatiable mouth.

"I forgot," said he simply. "The Girl was braver. But I am a God too, and I am not afraid."

"What is that to me?" said the Crab.

Then Leo's speech was taken from him and he lay still and dumb, watching Death till he died.

Leo was the last of the Children of the Zodiac. After his death there sprang up a breed of little mean men, whimpering and flinching and howling because the Houses killed them and theirs, who wished to live for ever without any pain. They did not increase their lives, but they increased their own torments miserably, and there were no Children of the Zodiac to guide them; and the greater part of Leo's songs were lost.

Only he had carved on the Girl's tombstone the last verse of the "Song of the Girl," which stands at the head of this story.

One of the children of men, coming thousands of years later, rubbed away the lichen, read the lines, and applied them to a trouble other than the one Leo meant. Being a man, men believed that he had made the verses himself; but they belong to Leo, the Child of the Zodiac, and teach, as he taught, that whatever comes or does not come we men must not be afraid.

The Bridge-Builders

FROM *THE DAY'S WORK* (1898)

This story was actually written in the autumn of 1892, while the Kiplings were living in Vermont. Some of the detail may have been contributed by RK's father, Lockwood Kipling, then on a visit to his son and daughter-in-law after his retirement. But RK, in his role as a reporter, had covered the building of railway bridges in India, and one suspects that Lockwood's part was confined to offering constructive criticism. Certainly the sense of the supernatural, even the divine, breaking into mundane affairs is pure RK. It runs clear through his work, from early ghost tales such as "The Phantom Rickshaw" to the item that closes this collection, "The Gardener."

Underpinning this story's argument is the concept that gods must die when their worshipers die. Even in the Christian tradition this idea was accepted by certain medieval mystics. In our own century L. Sprague de Camp has exploited it, notably in a charming story about how Pan was rescued by becoming a jazz clarinetist, and in my favorite sword-and-sorcery novel, *The Tritonian Ring*.

As to RK's acquaintance with opium: he wrote one curious short story—more exactly, a vignette—called "The Gate of the Hundred Sorrows," recounted in the first person by a European addicted to the Black Smoke, but though he may well have experimented with opium, like other inquisitive young men of his time, it is far more probable that he owed his subjective experience to being treated with it medicinally. It used to be, and until at least the 1930s it remained, a standard remedy in the British pharmacopoeia; how much more indispensable, then, must it have been in fever-haunted India.

At the start, a wealth of irony is condensed into three sets of initials. C.I.E. means Companion of the Order of the Indian Empire; C.S.I. means Companion of the Order of the Star of India; but C.E. simply stands for Civil Engineer.

There is some British railway (not railroad) usage: the "trolley" would have been what Americans call a handcar, and "sleepers" = U.S. ties.

Lascars (the word is Persian, originally = soldier, mercenary) were and are Asiatics serving on European ships; *serang* (also Persian) = commander—say bo'sun. A borrow-pit is what's left after you've dug out earth for, e.g., an embankment. The *Quetta* was a troopship that came to a sorry end. "Poojah" (more often *puja*) = an act of worship. Indigo is grown for the dark-blue dye that it yields. The *peepul* is the same tree RK elsewhere calls *pipal*; cf., "The Finances of the Gods." *Punchayet* = conference. *Kotwal* = chief constable, magistrate.

Lanka, where Hanuman hails from, was Ceylon in Kipling's day, but has now reverted to its former name, and with an honorific: Sri Lanka. A *lotah* is a brass or copper pot. *Tufan* = typhoon, a Malay-accented variant of Chinese words meaning "great wind." One *koss* = about 1¾ miles. And the dreams of Brahm, or Brahma, are, in Hindu cosmology, everything that we imagine to be real . . .

As to the gods:

Mother Gunga, who appears as a crocodile, is the Ganges personified. Shiva or Siva, whose mark the Bull bears, originated as a prince of demons, called "the favorable" to placate him, and became the Destroyer of the Hindu trinity. The elephant-headed god is Ganesh or Ganesha. Indra too was a demon in ancient Persia but in India became the god of warriors and of nature. Kali is a ferocious deity with a necklace of skulls; here she is present as a tigress. Hanuman is chief of the monkey people. Bhairon defines himself, and Krishna is defined, as is his parrot.

But so many tales are told about the Hindu gods, their legends exist in so many variations, and their incarnations and symbols are so numerous, that RK was able to pick the ones best suited to his purpose, without worrying about theological consistency any more than do the Hindus themselves.

The Bridge-Builders

The least that Findlayson, of the Public Works Department, expected was a C.I.E.; he dreamed of a C.S.I.: indeed his friends told him that he deserved more. For three years he had endured heat and cold, disappointment, discomfort, danger, and disease, with responsibility almost too heavy for one pair of shoulders; and day by day, through that time, the great Kashi Bridge over the Ganges had grown under his charge. Now, in less than three months, if all went well, His Excellency the Viceroy would open the bridge in state, an archbishop would bless it, the first train-load of soldiers would come over it, and there would be speeches.

Findlayson, C.E., sat in his trolley on a construction-line that ran along one of the main revetments—the huge stone-faced banks that flared away north and south for three miles on either side of the river—and permitted himself to think of the end. With its approaches, his work was one mile and three-quarters in length; a lattice-girder bridge, trussed with the Findlayson truss, standing on seven-and-twenty brick piers. Each one of those piers was twenty-four feet in diameter, capped with red Agra stone and sunk eighty feet below the shifting sand of the Ganges' bed. Above them ran the railway-line fifteen feet broad; above that, again, a cart-road of eighteen feet, flanked with footpaths. At either end rose towers of red brick, loopholed for musketry and pierced for big guns, and the ramp of the road was being pushed forward to their haunches. The raw earth-ends were crawling and alive with hundreds upon hundreds of tiny asses climbing out of the yawning borrow-pit below with sackfuls of stuff; and the hot afternoon air was filled with the noise of hooves, the rattle of the drivers' sticks, and the swish and roll-down of the dirt. The river was very low, and on the dazzling white sand between the three center piers stood squat cribs of railway-sleepers, filled within and daubed without with mud, to support the last of the girders as those were riveted up. In the little deep water left by the drought, an overhead-crane travelled to and fro along its spile-pier, jerking sections of iron into place, snorting and backing and grunting as an elephant grunts in the timber-yard. Riveters by the hundred swarmed about the lattice side-work and the iron roof of the railway-line, hung from invisible staging under the bellies of the girders, clustered round the throats of the piers, and rode on the overhang of the footpath-stanchions; their fire-pots and the spurts of flame that answered each hammer-stroke showing no more than pale yellow in the sun's glare. East and west and north and south the construction-trains rattled and shrieked up and down the embankments, the piled trucks of brown and white stone banging behind them till the side-boards were unpinned, and with a roar and a grumble a few thousand tons more material were thrown out to hold the river in place.

Findlayson, C.E., turned on his trolley and looked over the face of the country that he had changed for seven miles around. Looked back on the humming village of five thousand workmen; up-stream and down, along the vista of spurs and sand; across the river to the far piers, lessening in the haze; overhead to the guard-towers—and only he knew how strong those were—and with a sigh of contentment saw that his work was good. There stood his bridge before him in the sunlight, lacking only a few weeks' work on the girders of the three middle piers—his bridge, raw and ugly as original sin, but *pukka*—permanent—to endure when all memory of the builder, yea, even of the splendid Findlayson truss, had perished. Practically, the thing was done.

Hitchcock, his assistant, cantered along the line on a little switch-tailed Kabuli pony, who, through long practice, could have trotted securely over a trestle, and nodded to his chief.

"All but," said he, with a smile.

"I've been thinking about it," the senior answered. "Not half a bad job for two men, is it?"

"One—and a half. 'Gad, what a Cooper's Hill cub I was when I came on the works!" Hitchcock felt very old in the crowded experiences of the past three years, that had taught him power and responsibility.

"You *were* rather a colt," said Findlayson. "I wonder how you'll like going back to office work when this job's over."

"I shall hate it!" said the young man, and as he went on his eye followed Findlayson's, and he muttered, "Isn't it damned good?"

"I think we'll go up the service together," Findlayson said to himself. "You're too good a youngster to waste on another man. Cub thou wast; assistant thou art. Personal assistant, and at Simla, thou shalt be, if any credit comes to me out of the business!"

Indeed, the burden of the work had fallen altogether on Findlayson and his assistant, the young man whom he had chosen because of his rawness to break to his own needs. There were labor-contractors by the half-hundred—fitters and riveters, European, borrowed from the railway workshops, with perhaps twenty white and half-caste subordinates to direct, under direction, the bevies of workmen—but none knew better than these two, who trusted each other, how the underlings were not to be trusted. They had been tried many times in sudden crises—by slipping of booms, by breaking of tackle, failure of cranes, and the wrath of the river—but no stress had brought to light any man among them whom Findlayson and Hitchcock would have honored by working as remorselessly as they worked themselves. Findlayson thought it over from the beginning: the months of office work destroyed at a blow when the Government of India, at the last moment, added two feet to the width of the bridge, under the impression that bridges were cut out of paper, and so brought to ruin at least half an acre of calculations—and Hitchcock, new to disappointment, buried his head in his arms and wept; the heart-breaking delays over the filling of the contracts in England; the futile correspondences hinting at great wealth of commission if one, only one, rather doubtful consignment were passed; the war that followed the refusal; the careful, polite obstruction at the other end that followed the war, till young Hitchcock, putting one month's leave to another month, and borrowing ten days from Findlayson, spent his poor little savings of a year in a wild dash to London, and there, as his own tongue asserted and the later consignments proved, put the Fear of God into a man so great that he feared only Parliament, and said so till Hitchcock wrought with him across his own dinner-table, and—he feared the Kashi Bridge and all who spoke in its name. Then there was the cholera that came in the night to the village by the bridge-works; and after the cholera smote the smallpox. The fever they had always with them. Hitchcock had been appointed a magistrate of the third class with whipping powers, for the better government of the community, and Findlayson watched him wield his powers temperately, learning what to overlook and what to look after. It was a long, long reverie, and it covered storm, sudden freshets, death in every manner and shape, violent and awful rage against red tape half frenzying a mind that knows it should be busy on other things; drought, sanitation, finance; birth, wedding, burial, and riot in the village of twenty warring castes; argument, expostulation, persuasion, and the blank despair that a man goes to bed upon, thankful that his rifle is all in pieces in the gun-case. Behind everything rose the black frame of the Kashi Bridge—plate by plate, girder by girder, span by span—and each pier of it recalled Hitchcock, the all-round man, who had stood by his chief without failing from the very first to this last.

So the bridge was two men's work—unless one counted Peroo, as Peroo certainly counted himself. He was a Lascar, a Kharva from Bulsar, familiar with every port between Rockhampton and London, who had risen to the rank of *serang* on the British India boats, but wearying of routine musters and clean clothes had thrown up the service and gone inland, where men of his caliber were sure of employment. For his knowledge of tackle and the handling of heavy weights, Peroo was worth almost any price he might have chosen to put upon his services; but custom decreed the wage of the overhead-men, and Peroo was not within many silver pieces of his proper value. Neither running water nor extreme heights made him afraid; and, as an ex-*serang*, he knew how to hold authority. No piece of iron was so big or so badly placed that Peroo could not devise a tackle to lift it—a loose-ended, sagging arrangement, rigged with a scandalous amount of talking, but perfectly equal to the work in hand. It was Peroo who had saved the girder of Number Seven Pier from destruction when the new wire rope jammed in the eye of the crane, and the huge plate tilted in its slings, threatening to slide out sideways. Then the native workmen lost their heads with great shoutings, and Hitchcock's right arm was broken by a falling T-plate, and he buttoned it up in his coat and swooned, and came to and directed for four hours till Peroo, from the top of the crane, reported, "All's well," and the plate swung home. There was no one like Peroo, *serang,* to lash and guy and hold, to control the donkey-engines, to hoist a fallen locomotive craftily out of the borrow-pit into which it had tumbled; to strip and dive, if need be, to see how the concrete blocks round the piers stood the scouring of Mother Gunga, or to adventure up-stream on a monsoon night and report on the state of the embankment-facings. He would interrupt the field-councils of Findlayson and Hitchcock without fear, till his wonderful English, or his still more wonderful *lingua-franca,* half Portuguese and half Malay, ran out and he was forced to take string and show the knots that he would recommend. He controlled his own gang of tacklemen—mysterious relatives from Kutch Mandvi gathered month by month and tried to the uttermost. No consideration of family or kin allowed Peroo to keep weak hands or a giddy head on the pay-roll. "My honor is the honor of this bridge," he would say to the about-to-be-dismissed. "What do I care for your honor? Go and work on a steamer. That is all you are fit for."

The little cluster of huts where he and his gang lived centered round the tattered dwelling of a sea-priest—one who had never set foot on Black Water, but had been chosen as ghostly counselor by two generations of sea-rovers, all unaffected by port missions or those creeds which are thrust upon sailors by agencies along Thames' bank. The priest of the Lascars had nothing to do with their caste, or indeed with anything at all. He ate the offerings of his church, and slept and smoked, and slept again, "for," said Peroo, who had haled him a thousand miles inland, "he is a very holy man. He never cares what you eat so long as you do not eat beef, and that is good, because on land we worship Shiva, we Kharvas; but at sea on the Kumpani's boats we attend strictly to the orders of the *Burra Malum* (the first mate), and on this bridge we observe what Finlinson *Sahib* says."

Findlayson *Sahib* had that day given orders to clear the scaffolding from the guard-tower on the right bank, and Peroo with his mates was casting loose and lowering down the bamboo poles and planks as swiftly as ever they had whipped the cargo out of a coaster.

From his trolley he could hear the whistle of the *serang*'s silver pipe and the creak and clatter of the pulleys. Peroo was standing on the topmost coping of the tower, clad in the blue dungaree of his abandoned service, and as Findlayson motioned to him to be careful, for his was no life to throw away, he gripped the last pole, and, shading his eyes ship-fashion, answered with the long-drawn wail of the fo'c'sle look-out: *"Ham dekhta hai"* ("I am looking out"). Findlayson laughed, and then sighed. It was years since he had seen a steamer, and he was sick for home. As his trolley passed under the tower, Peroo descended by a rope, ape-fashion, and cried: "It looks well now, *Sahib*. Our bridge is all but done. What think you Mother Gunga will say when the rail runs over?"

"She has said little so far. It was never Mother Gunga that delayed us."

"There is always time for her; and none the less there has been delay. Has the *Sahib* forgotten last autumn's flood, when the stone-boats were sunk without warning—or only a half-day's warning?"

"Yes, but nothing save a big flood could hurt us now. The spurs are holding well on the west bank."

"Mother Gunga eats great allowances. There is always room for more stone on the revetments. I tell this to the *Chota Sahib*"—he meant Hitchcock—"and he laughs."

"No matter, Peroo. Another year thou wilt be able to build a bridge in thine own fashion."

The Lascar grinned. "Then it will not be in this way—with stonework sunk under water, as the *Quetta* was sunk. I like sus-sus-pen-sheen bridges that fly from bank to bank, with one big step, like a gang-plank. Then no water can hurt. When does the Lord *Sahib* come to open the bridge?"

"In three months, when the weather is cooler."

"Ho! ho! He is like the *Burra Malum*. He sleeps below while the work is being done. Then he comes upon the quarter-deck and touches with his finger, and says: 'This is not clean! Dam *jiboonwallah!*' "

"But the Lord *Sahib* does not call me a dam *jiboonwallah*, Peroo."

"No, *Sahib;* but he does not come on deck till the work is all finished. Even the *Burra Malum* of the *Nerbudda* said once at Tuticorin—"

"Bah! Go! I am busy."

"I, also!" said Peroo, with an unshaken countenance. "May I take the light dinghy now and row along the spurs?"

"To hold them with thy hands? They are, I think, sufficiently heavy."

"Nay, Sahib. It is thus. At sea, on the Black Water, we have room to be blown up and down without care. Here we have no room at all. Look you, we have put the river into a dock, and run her between stone sills."

Findlayson smiled at the "we."

"We have bitted and bridled her. She is not like the sea, that can beat against a soft beach. She is Mother Gunga—in irons." His voice fell a little.

"Peroo, thou hast been up and down the world more even than I. Speak true talk, now. How much dost thou in thy heart believe of Mother Gunga?"

"All that our priest says. London is London, *Sahib*. Sydney is Sydney, and Port Darwin is Port Darwin. Also Mother Gunga is Mother Gunga, and when I come back to her banks I know this and worship. In London I did *poojah* to the big temple by the river for the sake of the God within. . . . Yes, I will not take the cushions in the dinghy."

Findlayson mounted his horse and trotted to the shed of a bungalow that he shared with his assistant. The place had become home to him in the last three years. He had grilled in the heat, sweated in the rains, and shivered with fever under the rude thatch roof; the limewash beside the door was covered with rough drawings and formulas, and the sentry-path trodden in the matting of the verandah showed where he had walked alone. There is no eight-hour limit to an engineer's work, and the evening meal with Hitchcock was eaten booted and spurred: over their cigars they listened to the hum of the village as the gangs came up from the river-bed and the lights began to twinkle.

"Peroo has gone up the spurs in your dinghy. He's taken a couple of nephews with him, and he's lolling in the stern like a commodore," said Hitchcock.

"That's all right. He's got something on his mind. You'd think that ten years in the British India boats would have knocked most of his religion out of him."

"So it has," said Hitchcock, chuckling. "I overheard him the other day in the middle of a most atheistical talk with that fat old *guru* of theirs. Peroo denied the efficacy of prayer; and wanted the *guru* to go to sea and watch a gale out with him, and see if he could stop a monsoon."

"All the same, if you carried off his *guru* he'd leave us like a shot. He was yarning away to me about praying to the dome of St. Paul's when he was in London."

"He told me that the first time he went into the engine-room of a steamer, when he was a boy, he prayed to the low-pressure cylinder."

"Not half a bad thing to pray to, either. He's propitiating his own Gods now, and he wants to know what Mother Gunga will think of a bridge being run across her. Who's there?" A shadow darkened the doorway, and a telegram was put into Hitchcock's hand.

"She ought to be pretty well used to it by this time. Only a *tar*. It ought to be Ralli's answer about the new rivets. . . . Great Heavens!" Hitchcock jumped to his feet.

"What is it?" said the senior, and took the form. "*That's* what Mother Gunga thinks, is it," he said, reading. "Keep cool, young 'un. We've got all our work cut for us. Let's see. Muir wires, half an hour ago: '*Floods on the Ramgunga. Look out.*' Well, that gives us—one, two—nine and a half for the flood to reach Melipur Ghaut and seven's sixteen and a half to Latodi—say fifteen hours before it comes down to us."

"Curse that hill-fed sewer of a Ramgunga! Findlayson, this is two months before anything could have been expected, and the left bank is littered up with stuff still. Two full months before the time!"

"That's why it happens. I've only known Indian rivers for five and twenty years, and I don't pretend to understand. Here comes another *tar*." Findlayson opened the telegram. "Cockran, this time, from the Ganges Canal: '*Heavy rains here Bad.*' He might have saved the last word. Well, we don't want to know any more. We've got to work the gangs all night and clean up the river-bed. You'll take the east bank and work out to meet me in the middle. Get everything that floats below the bridge: we shall have quite enough river-craft coming down adrift anyhow, without letting the stone-boats ram the piers. What have you got on the east bank that needs looking after?"

"Pontoon, one big pontoon with the overhead crane on it. T'other overhead crane on the mended pontoon, with the cart-road rivets from Twenty to Twenty-three piers—two construction lines, and a turning-spur. The pile-work must take its chance," said Hitchcock.

"All right. Roll up everything you can lay hands on. We'll give the gang fifteen minutes more to eat their grub."

Close to the verandah stood a big night-gong, never used except for flood, or fire in the village. Hitchcock had called for a fresh horse, and was off to his side of the bridge when Findlayson took the cloth-bound stick and smote with the rubbing stroke that brings out the full thunder of the metal.

Long before the last rumble ceased every night-gong in the village had taken up the warning. To these were added the hoarse screaming of conchs in the little temples; the throbbing of drums and tomtoms; and from the European quarters, where the riveters lived, McCartney's bugle, a weapon of offense on Sundays and festivals, brayed desperately, calling to "Stables." Engine after engine toiling home along the spurs after her day's work whistled in answer till the whistles were answered from the far bank. Then the big gong thundered thrice for a sign that it was flood and not fire; conch, drum, and whistle echoed the call, and the village quivered to the sound of bare feet running upon soft earth. The order in all cases was to stand by the day's work and wait instructions. The gangs poured by in the dusk; men stopping to knot a loin-cloth or fasten a sandal; gang-foremen shouting to their subordinates as they ran or paused by the tool-issue sheds for bars and mattocks; locomotives creeping down their tracks wheel-deep in the crowd, till the brown torrent disappeared into the dusk of the river-bed, raced over the pilework, swarmed along the lattices, clustered by the cranes, and stood still, each man in his place.

Then the troubled beating of the gong carried the order to take up everything and bear it beyond high-water mark, and the flare-lamps broke out by the hundred between the webs of dull-iron as the riveters began a night's work racing against the flood that was to come. The girders of the three center piers—those that stood on the cribs—were all but in position. They needed just as many rivets as could be driven into them, for the flood would assuredly wash out the supports, and the iron-work would settle down on the caps of stone if they were not blocked at the ends. A hundred crowbars strained at the sleepers of the temporary line that fed the unfinished piers. It was heaved up in lengths, loaded into trucks, and backed up the bank beyond flood-level by the groaning locomotives. The tool-sheds on the sands melted away before the attack of shouting armies, and with them went the stacked ranks of Government stores, iron-bound boxes of rivets, pliers, cutters, duplicate parts of the riveting-machines, spare pumps, and chains. The big crane would be the last to be shifted, for she was hoisting all the heavy stuff up to the main structure of the bridge. The concrete blocks on the fleet of stone-boats were dropped overside, where there was any depth of water, to guard the piers, and the empty boats themselves were poled under the bridge downstream. It was here that Peroo's pipe shrilled loudest, for the first stroke of the big gong had brought back the dinghy at racing speed, and Peroo and his people were stripped to the waist, working for the honor and credit which are better than life.

"I knew she would speak," he cried. "*I* knew, but the telegraph gave us good warning. O sons of unthinkable begetting—children of unspeakable shame—are we here for the look of the thing?" It was two feet of wire rope frayed at the ends, and it did wonders as Peroo leaped from gunnel to gunnel, shouting the language of the sea.

Findlayson was more troubled for the stone-boats than anything else. McCartney, with his gangs, was blocking up the ends of the three doubtful spans, but boats adrift, if the flood chanced to be a high one, might endanger the girders; and there was a very fleet in the shrunken channels.

"Get them behind the swell of the guard-tower," he shouted to Peroo. "It will be dead-water there; get them below the bridge."

"*Accha!* [Very good.] *I* know. We are mooring them with wire rope," was the answer. "Heh! Listen to the *Chota Sahib*. He is working hard."

From across the river came an almost continuous whistling of locomotives, backed by the rumble of stone. Hitchcock at the last minute was spending a few hundred more trucks of Tarakee stone in reinforcing his spurs and embankments.

"The bridge challenges Mother Gunga," said Peroo, with a laugh. "But when *she* talks I know whose voice will be the loudest."

For hours the naked men worked, screaming and shouting under the lights. It was a hot, moonless night; the end of it was darkened by clouds and a sudden squall that made Findlayson very grave.

"She moves!" said Peroo, just before the dawn. "Mother Gunga is awake! Hear!" He dipped his hand over the side of a boat and the current mumbled on it. A little wave hit the side of a pier with a crisp slap.

"Six hours before her time," said Findlayson, mopping his forehead savagely. "Now we can't depend on anything. We'd better clear all hands out of the river-bed."

Again the big gong beat, and a second time there was the rushing of naked feet on earth and ringing iron; the clatter of tools ceased. In the silence, men heard the dry yawn of water crawling over thirsty sand.

Foreman after foreman shouted to Findlayson, who had posted himself by the guard-tower, that his section of the river-bed had been cleaned out, and when the last voice dropped Findlayson hurried over the bridge till the iron plating of the permanent way gave place to the temporary plank-walk over the three center piers, and there he met Hitchcock.

"All clear your side?" said Findlayson. The whisper rang in the box of latticework.

"Yes, and the east channel's filling now. We're utterly out of our reckoning. When is this thing down on us?"

"There's no saying. She's filling as fast as she can. Look!" Findlayson pointed to the planks below his feet, where the sand, burned and defiled by months of work, was beginning to whisper and fizz.

"What orders?" said Hitchcock.

"Call the roll—count stores—sit on your hunkers—and pray for the bridge. That's all I can think of. Good-night. Don't risk your life trying to fish out anything that may go downstream."

"Oh, I'll be as prudent as you are! 'Night. Heavens, how she's filling! Here's the rain in earnest!" Findlayson picked his way back to his bank, sweeping the last of McCartney's riveters before him. The gangs had spread themselves along the embankments, regardless of the cold rain of the dawn, and there they waited for the flood. Only Peroo kept his men together behind the swell of the guard-tower, where the stone-boats lay tied fore and aft with hawsers, wire-rope, and chains.

A shrill wail ran along the line, growing to a yell, half fear and half wonder: the face of the river whitened from bank to bank between the stone facings, and the far-away spurs went out in spouts of foam. Mother Gunga had come bank-high in haste, and a wall of chocolate-colored water was her messenger. There was a shriek above the roar of the water, the complaint of the spans coming down on their blocks as the cribs were whirled out from under their bellies. The stone-boats groaned and ground each other in the eddy that swung round the abutment, and their clumsy masts rose higher and higher against the dim sky-line.

"Before she was shut between these walls we knew what she would do. Now she is thus cramped God only knows what she will do!" said Peroo, watching the furious turmoil round the guard-tower. "*Ohé!* Fight, then! Fight hard, for it is thus that a woman wears herself out."

But Mother Gunga would not fight as Peroo desired. After the first down-stream plunge there came no more walls of water, but the river lifted herself bodily, as a snake when she drinks in midsummer, plucking and fingering along the revetments, and banking up behind the piers till even Findlayson began to recalculate the strength of his work.

When day came the village gasped. "Only last night," men said, turning to each other, "it was as a town in the river-bed! Look now!"

And they looked and wondered afresh at the deep water, the racing water that licked the throat of the piers. The farther bank was veiled by rain, into which the bridge ran out and vanished; the spurs upstream were marked by no more than eddies and spoutings, and downstream the pent river, once freed of her guide-lines, had spread like a sea to the horizon. Then hurried by, rolling in the water, dead men and oxen together, with here and there a patch of thatched roof that melted when it touched a pier.

"Big flood," said Peroo, and Findlayson nodded. It was as big a flood as he had any wish to watch. His bridge would stand what was upon her now, but not very much more; and if by any of a thousand chances there happened to be a weakness in the embankments, Mother Gunga would carry his honor to the sea with the other raffle. Worst of all, there was nothing to do except to sit still; and Findlayson sat still under his macintosh till his helmet became pulp on his head, and his boots were over-ankle in mire. He took no count of time, for the river was marking the hours, inch by inch and foot by foot, along the embankment, and he listened, numb and hungry, to the straining of the stone-boats, the hollow thunder under the piers, and the hundred noises that make the full note of a flood. Once a dripping servant brought him food, but he could not eat; and once he thought that he heard a faint toot from a locomotive across the river, and then he smiled. The bridge's failure would hurt his assistant not a little, but Hitchcock was a young man with his big work yet to do. For himself the crash meant everything—everything that made a hard life worth the living. They would say, the men of his own profession—he remembered the half-pitying things that he himself had said when Lockhart's big water-works burst and broke down in brick heaps and sludge, and Lockhart's spirit broke in him and he died. He remembered what he himself had said when the Sumao Bridge went out in the big cyclone by the sea; and most he remembered poor Hartopp's face three weeks later, when the shame had marked it. His bridge was twice the size of Hartopp's, and it carried the Findlayson truss as well as the new pier-shoe—the Findlayson bolted shoe. There were no excuses in his service. Government might listen, perhaps, but his own kind would judge him by his bridge, as that stood or fell. He went over it in his head, plate by plate, span by span, brick by brick, pier by pier, remembering, comparing, estimating, and recalculating, lest there should be any mistake; and through the long hours and through the flights of formulas that danced and wheeled before him a cold fear would come to pinch his heart. His side of the sum was beyond question; but what man knew Mother Gunga's arithmetic? Even as he was making all sure by the multiplication-table, the river might be scooping pot-holes to the very bottom of any one of those eighty-foot piers that carried his reputation. Again a servant came to him with food, but his mouth was dry, and he could only drink and return to the decimals in his brain. And the river was still rising. Peroo, in a mat shelter-coat, crouched at his feet, watching now his face and now the face of the river, but saying nothing.

At last the Lascar rose and floundered through the mud towards the village, but he was careful to leave an ally to watch the boats.

Presently he returned, most irreverently driving before him the priest of his creed—a fat old man, with a grey beard that whipped the wind with the wet cloth that blew over his shoulder. Never was seen so lamentable a *guru*.

"What good are offerings and little kerosene lamps and dry

grain," shouted Peroo, "if squatting in the mud is all that thou canst do? Thou hast dealt long with the Gods when they were contented and well-wishing. Now they are angry. Speak to them!"

"What is a man against the wrath of Gods?" whined the priest, cowering as the wind took him. "Let me go to the temple, and I will pray there."

"Son of a pig, pray *here!* Is there no return for salt fish and curry powder and dried onions? Call aloud! Tell Mother Gunga we have had enough. Bid her be still for the night. I cannot pray, but I have served in the Kumpani's boats, and when men did not obey my orders I—" A flourish of the wire-rope colt rounded the sentence, and the priest, breaking from his disciple, fled to the village.

"Fat pig!" said Peroo. "After all that we have done for him! When the flood is down I will see to it that we get a new *guru*. Finlinson *Sahib,* it darkens for night now, and since yesterday nothing has been eaten. Be wise, *Sahib*. No man can endure watching and great thinking on an empty belly. Lie down, *Sahib*. The river will do what the river will do."

"The bridge is mine; I cannot leave it."

"Wilt thou hold it up with thy hands, then?" said Peroo, laughing. "I was troubled for my boats and sheers *before* the flood came. Now we are in the hands of the Gods. The *Sahib* will not eat and lie down? Take these, then. They are meat and good toddy together, and they kill all weariness, besides the fever that follows the rain. I have eaten nothing else to-day at all."

He took a small tin tobacco-box from his sodden waist-belt and thrust it into Findlayson's hand, saying, "Nay, do not be afraid. It is no more than opium—clean Malwa opium!"

Findlayson shook two or three of the dark-brown pellets into his hand, and hardly knowing what he did, swallowed them. The stuff was at least a good guard against fever—the fever that was creeping upon him out of the wet mud—and he had seen what Peroo could do in the stewing mists of autumn on the strength of a dose from the tin box.

Peroo nodded with bright eyes. "In a little—in a little the *Sahib* will find that he thinks well again. I too will—" He dived into his treasure-box, resettled the rain-coat over his head, and squatted down to watch the boats. It was too dark now to see beyond the first pier, and the night seemed to have given the river new strength. Findlayson stood with his chin on his chest, thinking. There was one point about one of the piers—the Seventh—that he had not fully settled in his mind. The figures would not shape themselves to the eye except one by one and at enormous intervals of time. There was a sound, rich and mellow in his ears, like the deepest note of a double-bass—an entrancing sound upon which he pondered for several hours, as it seemed. Then Peroo was at his elbow, shouting that a wire hawser had snapped and the stone-boats were loose. Findlayson saw the fleet open and swing out fanwise to a long-drawn shriek of wire straining across gunnels.

"A tree hit them. They will all go," cried Peroo. "The main hawser has parted. What does the *Sahib* do?"

An immensely complex plan had suddenly flashed into Findlayson's mind. He saw the ropes running from boat to boat in straight lines and angles—each rope a line of white fire. But there was one rope which was the master-rope. He could see that rope. If he could pull it once, it was absolutely and mathematically certain that the disordered fleet would reassemble itself in the backwater behind the guard-tower. But why, he wondered, was Peroo clinging so desperately to his waist as he hastened down the bank? It was necessary to put the Lascar aside, gently and slowly, because it was necessary to save the boats, and, further, to demonstrate the extreme ease of the problem that looked so difficult. And then—but it was of no conceivable importance—a wire rope raced through his hand, burning it, the high bank disappeared, and with it all the slowly dispersing factors of the problem. He was sitting in the rainy darkness—sitting in a boat that spun like a top, and Peroo was standing over him.

"I had forgotten," said the Lascar slowly, "that to those fasting and unused the opium is worse than any wine. Those who die in Gunga go to the Gods. Still, I have no desire to present myself before such great ones. Can the *Sahib* swim?"

"What need? He can fly—fly as swiftly as the wind," was the thick answer.

"He is mad!" muttered Peroo under his breath. "And he threw me aside like a bundle of dung-cakes. Well, he will not know his death. The boat cannot live an hour here even if she strike nothing. It is not good to look at death with a clear eye."

He refreshed himself again from the tin box, squatted down in the bows of the reeling, pegged, and stitched craft, staring through the mist at the nothing that was there. A warm drowsiness crept over Findlayson, the Chief Engineer, whose duty was with his bridge. The heavy raindrops struck him with a thousand tingling little thrills, and the weight of all time since time was made hung heavy on his eyelids. He thought and perceived that he was perfectly secure, for the water was so solid that a man could surely step out upon it, and, standing still with his legs apart to keep his balance—this was the most important point—would be borne with great and easy speed to the shore. But yet a better plan came to him. It needed only an exertion of will for the soul to hurl the body ashore as wind drives paper; to waft it kite-fashion to the bank. Thereafter—the boat spun dizzily—suppose the high wind got under the freed body? Would it tower up like a kite and pitch headlong on the far-away sands, or would it duck about beyond control through all eternity? Findlayson gripped the gunnel to anchor himself, for it seemed that he was on the edge of taking the flight before he had settled all his plans. Opium has more effect on the white man than the black. Peroo was only comfortably indifferent to accidents. "She cannot live," he grunted. "Her seams open already. If she were even a dinghy with oars we could have ridden it out; but a box with holes is no good. Finlinson *Sahib,* she fills."

"*Accha!* I am going away. Come thou also."

In his mind Findlayson had already escaped from the boat, and was circling high in air to find a rest for the sole of his foot. His body—he was really sorry for its gross helplessness—lay in the stern, the water rushing about its knees.

"How very ridiculous!" he said to himself, from his eyrie; "that—is Findlayson—chief of the Kashi Bridge. The poor beast is going to be drowned, too. Drowned when it's close to shore. I'm—I'm on shore already. Why doesn't it come along?"

To his intense disgust, he found his soul back in his body again, and that body spluttering and choking in deep water. The pain of the reunion was atrocious, but it was necessary, also, to fight for the body. He was conscious of grasping wildly at wet sand, and striding prodigiously, as one strides in a dream, to keep foot-hold in the swirling water, till at last he hauled himself clear of the hold of the river, and dropped, panting, on wet earth.

"Not this night," said Peroo in his ear. "The Gods have protected us." The Lascar moved his feet cautiously, and they rustled among dried stumps. "This is some island of last year's indigo crop," he went on. "We shall find no men here; but have great care, Sahib; all the snakes of a hundred miles have been flooded out. Here comes the lightning, on the heels of the wind. Now we shall be able to look; but walk carefully."

Findlayson was far and far beyond any fear of snakes, or indeed any merely human emotion. He saw, after he had rubbed the water from his eyes, with an immense clearness, and trod, so it seemed to himself, with world-encompassing strides. Somewhere in the night of time he had built a bridge—a bridge that spanned illimitable levels of shining seas; but the Deluge had swept it away, leaving this one island under heaven for Findlayson and his companion, sole survivors of the breed of man.

An incessant lightning, forked and blue, showed all that there was to be seen on the little patch in the flood—a clump of thorn, a clump of swaying creaking bamboos, and a grey gnarled *peepul* overshadowing a Hindoo shrine, from whose dome floated a tattered red flag. The holy man whose summer resting-place it was had long since abandoned it, and the weather had broken the red-daubed image of his God. The two men stumbled, heavy-limbed and heavy-eyed, over the ashes of a brick-set cooking-place, and dropped down under the shelter of the branches, while the rain and river roared together.

The stumps of the indigo crackled, and there was a smell of cattle, as a huge and dripping Brahminee Bull shouldered his way under the tree. The flashes revealed the trident mark of Shiva on his flank, the insolence of head and hump, the luminous stag-like eyes, the brow crowned with a wreath of sodden marigold blooms, and the silky dewlap that nigh swept the ground. There was a noise behind him of other beasts coming up from the flood-line through the thicket, a sound of heavy feet and deep breathing.

"Here be more beside ourselves," said Findlayson, his head against the tree-pole, looking through half-shut eyes, wholly at ease.

"Truly," said Peroo thickly, "and no small ones."

"What are they, then? I do not see clearly."

"The Gods. Who else? Look!"

"Ah, true! The Gods surely—the Gods." Findlayson smiled as his head fell forward on his chest. Peroo was eminently right. After the Flood, who should be alive in the land except the Gods that made it—the Gods to whom his village prayed nightly—the

Gods who were in all men's mouths and about all men's ways? He could not raise his head or stir a finger for the trance that held him, and Peroo was smiling vacantly at the lightning.

The Bull paused by the shrine, his head lowered to the damp earth. A green Parrot in the branches preened his wet wings and screamed against the thunder as the circle under the tree filled with the shifting shadows of beasts. There was a Black-buck at the Bull's heels—such a buck as Findlayson in his far-away life upon earth might have seen in dreams—a buck with a royal head, ebon back, silver belly, and gleaming straight horns. Beside him, her head bowed to the ground, the green eyes burning under the heavy brows, with restless tail switching the dead grass, paced a Tigress, full-bellied and deep-jowled.

The Bull crouched beside the shrine, and there leaped from the darkness a monstrous grey Ape, who seated himself man-wise in the place of the fallen image, and the rain spilled like jewels from the hair of his neck and shoulders.

Other shadows came and went behind the circle, among them a drunken Man flourishing staff and drinking-bottle. Then a hoarse bellow broke out from near the ground. "The flood lessens even now," it cried. "Hour by hour the water falls, and their bridge still stands!"

"My bridge," said Findlayson to himself. "That must be very old work now. What have the Gods to do with my bridge?"

His eyes rolled in the darkness following the roar. A Crocodile—the blunt-nosed, ford-haunting *Mugger* of the Ganges—draggled herself before the beasts, lashing furiously to right and left with her tail.

"They have made it too strong for me. In all this night I have only torn away a handful of planks. The walls stand! The towers stand! They have chained my flood, and my river is not free any more. Heavenly Ones, take this yoke away! Give me clear water between bank and bank! It is I, Mother Gunga, that speak. The Justice of the Gods! Deal me the Justice of the Gods!"

"What said I?" whispered Peroo. "This is in truth a *Punchayet* of the Gods. Now we know that all the world is dead, save you and I, *Sahib*."

The Parrot screamed and fluttered again, and the Tigress, her ears flat to her head, snarled wickedly.

Somewhere in the shadow a great trunk and gleaming tusks

swayed to and fro, and a low gurgle broke the silence that followed on the snarl.

"We be here," said a deep voice, "the Great Ones. One only and very many. Shiv, my father, is here, with Indra. Kali has spoken already. Hanuman listens also."

"Kashi is without her *Kotwal* to-night," shouted the Man with the drinking-bottle, flinging his staff to the ground, while the island rang to the baying of hounds. "Give her the Justice of the Gods."

"Ye were still when they polluted my waters," the great Crocodile bellowed. "Ye made no sign when my river was trapped between the walls. I had no help save my own strength, and that failed—the strength of Mother Gunga failed—before their guard-towers. What could I do? I have done everything. Finish now, Heavenly Ones!"

"I brought the death; I rode the spotted sickness from hut to hut of their workmen, and yet they would not cease." A nose-slitten, hide-worn Ass, lame, scissor-legged, and galled, limped forward. "I cast the death at them out of my nostrils, but they would not cease."

Peroo would have moved, but the opium lay heavy upon him.

"Bah!" he said, spitting. "Here is Sitala herself; *Mata*—the small-pox. Has the *Sahib* a handkerchief to put over his face?"

"Small help! They fed me the corpses for a month, and I flung them out on my sand-bars, but their work went forward. Demons they are, and sons of demons! And ye left Mother Gunga alone for their fire-carriage to make a mock of. The Justice of the Gods on the bridge-builders!"

The Bull turned the cud in his mouth and answered slowly, "If the Justice of the Gods caught all who made a mock of holy things, there would be many dark altars in the land, mother."

"But this goes beyond a mock," said the Tigress, darting forward a griping paw. "Thou knowest, Shiv, and ye too, Heavenly Ones; ye know that they have defiled Gunga. Surely they must come to the Destroyer. Let Indra judge."

The Buck made no movement as he answered, "How long has this evil been?"

"Three years, as men count years," said the *Mugger,* close pressed to the earth.

"Does Mother Gunga die, then, in a year, that she is so anxious to see vengeance now? The deep sea was where she runs but yesterday, and tomorrow the sea shall cover her again as the Gods count that which men call time. Can any say that this their bridge endures till to-morrow?" said the Buck.

There was a long hush, and in the clearing of the storm the full moon stood up above the dripping trees.

"Judge ye, then," said the River sullenly. "I have spoken my shame. The flood falls still. I can do no more."

"For my own part"—it was the voice of the great Ape seated within the shrine—"it pleases me well to watch these men, remembering that I also builded no small bridge in the world's youth."

"They say, too," snarled the Tiger, "that these men came of the wreck of thy armies, Hanuman, and therefore thou hast aided—"

"They toil as my armies toiled in Lanka, and they believe that their toil endures. Indra is too high, but Shiv, thou knowest how the land is threaded with their fire-carriages."

"Yea, I know," said the Bull. "Their Gods instructed them in the matter."

A laugh ran round the circle.

"Their Gods! What should their Gods know? They were born yesterday, and those that made them are scarcely yet cold," said the *Mugger*. "Tomorrow their Gods will die."

"Ho!" said Peroo. "Mother Gunga talks good talk. I told that to the padre-*sahib* who preached on the *Mombassa,* and he asked the *Burra Malum* to put me in irons for a great rudeness."

"Surely they make these things to please their Gods," said the Bull again.

"Not altogether," the Elephant rolled forth. "It is for the profit of my *mahajuns*—my fat money-lenders that worship me at each new year, when they draw my image at the head of the account-books. I, looking over their shoulders by lamplight, see that the names in the books are those of men in far places—for all the towns are drawn together by the fire-carriage, and the money comes and goes swiftly, and the account-books grow as fat as—myself. And I, who am Ganesh of Good Luck, I bless my peoples."

"They have changed the face of the land—which is my land. They have killed and made new towns on my banks," said the *Mugger*.

"It is but the shifting of a little dirt. Let the dirt dig in the dirt if it pleases the dirt," answered the Elephant.

"But afterwards?" said the Tiger. "Afterwards they will see that Mother Gunga can avenge no insult, and they fall away from her first, and later from us all, one by one. In the end, Ganesh, we are left with naked altars."

The drunken Man staggered to his feet, and hiccupped vehemently in the face of the assembled Gods.

"Kali lies. My sister lies. Also this my stick is the *Kotwal* of Kashi, and he keeps tally of my pilgrims. When the time comes to worship Bhairon—and it is always time—the fire-carriages move one by one, and each bears a thousand pilgrims. They do not come afoot any more, but rolling upon wheels, and my honor is increased."

"Gunga, I have seen thy bed at Pryag black with the pilgrims," said the Ape, leaning forward, "and but for the fire-carriage they would have come slowly and in fewer numbers. Remember."

"They come to me always," Bhairon went on thickly. "By day and night they pray to me, all the Common People in the fields and the roads. Who is like Bhairon today? What talk is this of changing faiths? Is my staff *Kotwal* of Kashi for nothing? He keeps the tally, and he says that never were so many altars as today, and the fire-carriage serves them well. Bhairon am I—Bhairon of the Common People, and the chiefest of the Heavenly Ones today. Also my staff says—"

"Peace, thou!" lowed the Bull. "The worship of the schools is mine, and they talk very wisely, asking whether I be one or many, as is the delight of my people, and ye know what I am. Kali, my wife, thou knowest also."

"Yea, I know," said the Tigress, with lowered head.

"Greater am I than Gunga also. For ye know who moved the minds of men that they should count Gunga holy among the rivers. Who die in that water—ye know how men say—come to us without punishment, and Gunga knows that the fire-carriage has borne to her scores upon scores of such anxious ones; and Kali knows that she has held her chiefest festivals among the pilgrimages that are fed by the fire-carriage. Who smote at Pooree, under the Image there, her thousands in a day and a night, and bound the sickness to the wheels of the fire-carriages, so that it ran from one end of the land to the other? Who but Kali? Before the fire-carriage came it was a heavy toil. The fire-carriages have served thee well, Mother of Death. But I speak for mine own altars, who am not Bhairon of the Common Folk, but Shiv. Men go to and fro, making words and telling talk of strange Gods, and I listen. Faith follows faith among my people in the schools, and I have no anger; for when the words are said, and the new talk is ended, to Shiv men return at the last."

"True. It is true," murmured Hanuman. "To Shiv and to the others, mother, they return. I creep from temple to temple in the North, where they worship one God and His Prophet; and presently my image is alone within their shrines."

"Small thanks," said the Buck, turning his head slowly. "I am that One and His Prophet also."

"Even so, father," said Hanuman. "And to the South I go who am the oldest of the Gods as men know the Gods, and presently I touch the shrines of the new faith and the Woman whom we know is hewn twelve-armed, and still they call her Mary."

"Small thanks, brother," said the Tigress. "I am that Woman."

"Even so, sister; and I go West among the fire-carriages, and stand before the bridge-builders in many shapes, and because of me they change their faiths and are very wise. Ho! ho! I am the builder of bridges indeed—bridges between this and that, and each bridge leads surely to Us in the end. Be content, Gunga. Neither these men nor those that follow them mock thee at all."

"Am I alone, then, Heavenly Ones? Shall I smooth out my flood lest unhappily I bear away their walls? Will Indra dry my springs in the hills and make me crawl humbly between their wharfs? Shall I bury me in the sand ere I offend?"

"And all for the sake of a little iron bar with the fire-carriage atop. Truly, Mother Gunga is always young!" said Ganesh the Elephant. "A child had not spoken more foolishly. Let the dirt dig in the dirt ere it return to the dirt. I know only that my people grow rich and praise me. Shiv has said that the men of the schools do not forget; Bhairon is content for his crowd of the Common People: and Hanuman laughs."

"Surely I laugh," said the Ape. "My altars are few beside those of Ganesh or Bhairon, but the fire-carriages bring me new worshipers from beyond the Black Water—the men who believe that their God is toil. I run before them beckoning, and they follow Hanuman."

"Give them the toil that they desire, then," said the River. "Make a bar across my flood and throw the water back upon the bridge. Once thou wast strong in Lanka, Hanuman. Stoop and lift my bed."

"Who gives life can take life." The Ape scratched in the mud with a long forefinger. "And yet, who would profit by the killing? Very many would die."

There came up from the water a snatch of a love-song such as the boys sing when they watch their cattle in the noon heats of late spring. The Parrot screamed joyously, sidling along his branch with lowered head as the song grew louder, and in a patch of clear moonlight stood revealed the young herd, the darling of the Gopis, the idol of dreaming maids and of mothers ere their children are born—Krishna the Well-beloved. He stooped to knot up his long wet hair, and the Parrot fluttered to his shoulder.

"Fleeting and singing, and singing and fleeting," hiccupped Bhairon. "Those make thee late for the council, brother."

"And then?" said Krishna, with a laugh, throwing back his head. "Ye can do little without me or Karma here." He fondled the Parrot's plumage and laughed again. "What is this sitting and talking together? I heard Mother Gunga roaring in the dark, and so came quickly from a hut where I lay warm. And what have ye done to Karma, that he is so wet and silent? And what does Mother Gunga here? Are the heavens full that ye must come paddling in the mud beast-wise? Karma, what do they do?"

"Gunga has prayed for a vengeance on the bridge-builders, and Kali is with her. Now she bids Hanuman whelm the bridge, that her honor may be made great," cried the Parrot. "I waited here, knowing that thou wouldst come, O my master!"

"And the Heavenly Ones said nothing? Did Gunga and the Mother of Sorrows out-talk them? Did none speak for my people?"

"Nay," said Ganesh, moving uneasily from foot to foot; "I said it was but dirt at play, and why should we stamp it flat?"

"I was content to let them toil—well content," said Hanuman.

"What had I to do with Gunga's anger?" said the Bull.

"I am Bhairon of the Common Folk, and this my staff is *Kotwal* of all Kashi. I spoke for the Common People."

"Thou?" The young God's eyes sparkled.

"Am I not the first of the Gods in their mouths today?" returned Bhairon, unabashed. "For the sake of the Common People I said—very many wise things which I have now forgotten—but this my staff—"

Krishna turned impatiently, saw the *Mugger* at his feet, and kneeling, slipped an arm round the cold neck. "Mother," he said gently, "get thee to thy flood again. The matter is not for thee, What harm shall thy honor take of this live dirt? Thou hast given them their fields new year after year, and by thy flood they are made strong. They come all to thee at the last. What need to slay them now? Have pity, mother, for a little—and it is only for a little."

"If it be only for a little——" the slow beast began.

"Are they Gods, then?" Krishna returned with a laugh, his eyes looking into the dull eyes of the River. "Be certain that it is only for a little. The Heavenly Ones have heard thee, and presently justice will be done. Go now, mother, to the flood again. Men and cattle are thick on the waters—the banks fall—the villages melt because of thee."

"But the bridge—the bridge stands." The *Mugger* turned grunting into the undergrowth as Krishna rose.

"It is ended," said the Tigress, viciously. "There is no more justice from the Heavenly Ones. Ye have made shame and sport of Gunga, who asked no more than a few score lives."

"Of *my* people—who lie under the leaf-roofs of the village yonder—of the young girls, and the young men who sing to them in the dark—of the child that will be born next morn—of that which was begotten tonight," said Krishna. "And when all is done, what profit? Tomorrow sees them at work. Ay, if ye swept the bridge out from end to end they would begin anew. Hear me! Bhairon is drunk always. Hanuman mocks his people with new riddles."

"Nay, but they are very old ones," the Ape said, laughing.

"Shiv hears the talk of the schools and the dreams of the holy men; Ganesh thinks only of his fat traders; but I—I live with these my people, asking for no gifts, and so receiving them hourly."

"And very tender art thou of thy people," said the Tigress.

"They are my own. The old women dream of me, turning in their sleep; the maids look and listen for me when they go to fill their *lotahs* by the river. I walk by the young men waiting without the gates at dusk, and I call over my shoulder to the white-beards. Ye know, Heavenly Ones, that I alone of us all walk upon the earth continually, and have no pleasure in our heavens so long as a green blade springs here, or there are two voices at twilight in the standing crops. Wise are ye, but ye live far off, forgetting whence ye came. So do I not forget. And the fire-carriage feeds your shrines, ye say? And the fire-carriages bring a thousand pilgrimages where but ten came in the old years? True. That is true today."

"But tomorrow they are dead, brother," said Ganesh.

"Peace!" said the Bull, as Hanuman leaned forward again. "And tomorrow, beloved—what of tomorrow?"

"This only. A new word creeping from mouth to mouth among the Common Folk—a word that neither man nor God can lay hold of—an evil word—a little lazy word among the Common Folk, saying (and none know who set that word afoot) that they weary of ye, Heavenly Ones."

The Gods laughed together softly. "And then, beloved?" they said.

"And to cover that weariness they, my people, will bring to thee, Shiv, and to thee, Ganesh, at first greater offerings and a louder noise of worship. But the word has gone abroad, and, after, they will pay fewer dues to your fat Brahmins. Next they will forget your altars, but so slowly that no man can say how his forgetfulness began."

"I knew—I knew! I spoke this also, but they would not hear," said the Tigress. "We should have slain—we should have slain!"

"It is too late now. Ye should have slain at the beginning, when the men from across the water had taught our folk nothing. Now my people see their work, and go away thinking. They do not think of the Heavenly Ones altogether. They think of the fire-carriage and the other things that the bridge-builders have done, and when your priests thrust forward hands asking alms, they give unwillingly a little. That is the beginning, among one or two, or five or ten—for I, moving among my people, know what is in their hearts."

"And the end, Jester of the Gods? What shall the end be?" said Ganesh.

"The end shall be as it was in the beginning, O slothful son of Shiv! The flame shall die upon the altars and the prayer upon the tongue till ye become little Gods again—Gods of the jungle—names that the hunters of rats and noosers of dogs whisper in the thicket and among the caves—rag-Gods, pot Godlings of the tree, and the village-mark, as ye were at the beginning. That is the end, Ganesh, for thee, and for Bhairon—Bhairon of the Common People."

"It is very far away," grunted Bhairon. "Also, it is a lie."

"Many women have kissed Krishna. They told him this to cheer their own hearts when the grey hairs came, and he has told us the tale," said the Bull, below his breath.

"Their Gods came, and we changed them. I took the Woman and made her twelve-armed. So shall we twist all their Gods," said Hanuman.

"Their Gods! This is no question of their Gods—one or three—man or woman. The matter is with the people. *They* move, and not the Gods of the bridge-builders," said Krishna.

"So be it. I have made a man worship the fire-carriage as it stood still breathing smoke, and he knew not that he worshiped me," said Hanuman the Ape. "They will only change a little the names of their Gods. I shall lead the builders of the bridges as of old; Shiv shall be worshiped in the schools by such as doubt and despise their fellows; Ganesh shall have his *mahajuns,* and Bhairon the donkey-drivers, the pilgrims, and the sellers of toys. Beloved, they will do no more than change the names, and that we have seen a thousand times."

"Surely they will do no more than change the names," echoed Ganesh: but there was an uneasy movement among the Gods.

"They will change more than the names. Me alone they cannot kill, so long as maiden and man meet together or the spring follows the winter rains. Heavenly Ones, not for nothing have I walked upon the earth. My people know not now what they know; but I, who live with them, I read their hearts. Great Kings, the beginning of the end is born already. The fire-carriages shout the names of new Gods that are *not* the old under new names. Drink now and eat greatly! Bathe your faces in the smoke of the altars before they grow cold! Take dues and listen to the cymbals and the drums, Heavenly Ones, while yet there are flowers and songs. As men count time the end is far off; but as we who know reckon it is today. I have spoken."

The young God ceased, and his brethren looked at each other long in silence.

"This I have not heard before," Peroo whispered in his companion's ear. "And yet sometimes, when I oiled the brasses in the engine-room of the *Goorkha,* I have wondered if our priests were so wise—so wise. The day is coming, *Sahib*. They will be gone by the morning."

A yellow light broadened in the sky, and the tone of the river changed as the darkness withdrew.

Suddenly the Elephant trumpeted aloud as though man had goaded him.

"Let Indra judge. Father of all, speak thou! What of the things we have heard? Has Krishna lied indeed? Or——"

"Ye know," said the Buck, rising to his feet. "Ye know the Riddle of the Gods. When Brahm ceases to dream the Heavens and the Hells and Earth disappear. Be content. Brahm dreams still. The dreams come and go, and the nature of the dreams changes, but still Brahm dreams. Krishna has walked too long upon earth, and yet I love him the more for the tale he has told. The Gods change, beloved—all save One!"

"Ay, all save one that makes love in the hearts of men," said Krishna, knotting his girdle. "It is but a little time to wait, and ye shall know if I lie."

"Truly it is but a little time, as thou sayest, and we shall know. Get thee to thy huts again, beloved, and make sport for the young things, for still Brahm dreams. Go, my children! Brahm dreams—and till He wakes the Gods die not."

"Whither went they?" said the Lascar, awestruck, shivering a little with the cold.

"God knows!" said Findlayson. The river and the island lay in full daylight now, and there was never mark of hoof or pug on the wet earth under the *peepul*. Only a parrot screamed in the branches, bringing down showers of water-drops as he fluttered his wings.

"Up! We are cramped with cold! Has the opium died out? Canst thou move, *Sahib?*"

Findlayson staggered to his feet and shook himself. His head swam and ached, but the work of the opium was over, and, as he sluiced his forehead in a pool, the Chief Engineer of the Kashi Bridge was wondering how he had managed to fall upon the island, what chances the day offered of return, and, above all, how his work stood.

"Peroo, I have forgotten much. I was under the guard-tower watching the river; and then—— Did the flood sweep us away?"

"No. The boats broke loose, *Sahib,* and" (if the *Sahib* had forgotten about the opium, decidedly Peroo would not remind him) "in striving to retie them, so it seemed to me—but it was dark—a rope caught the *Sahib* and threw him upon a boat. Considering that we two, with Hitchcock *Sahib,* built, as it were, that bridge, I came also upon the boat, which came riding on horseback, as it were, on the nose of this island, and so, splitting, cast us ashore. I made a great cry when the boat left the wharf, and without doubt Hitchcock *Sahib* will come for us. As for the bridge, so many have died in the building that it cannot fall."

A fierce sun, that drew out all the smell of the sodden land, had followed the storm, and in that clear light there was no room for a man to think of dreams of the dark. Findlayson stared upstream, across the blaze of moving water, till his eyes ached. There was no sign of any bank to the Ganges, much less of a bridge-line.

"We came down far," he said. "It was wonderful that we were not drowned a hundred times."

"That was the least of the wonder, for no man dies before his time. I have seen Sydney, I have seen London, and twenty great ports, but"—Peroo looked at the damp, discolored shrine under the *peepul*—"never man has seen that we saw here."

"What?"

"Has the *Sahib* forgotten; or do we black men only see the Gods?"

"There was a fever upon me." Findlayson was still looking uneasily across the water. "It seemed that the island was full of beasts and men talking, but I do not remember. A boat could live in this water now, I think."

"Oho! Then it *is* true. 'When Brahm ceases to dream, the Gods die.' Now I know, indeed, what he meant. Once, too, the *guru* said as much to me; but then I did not understand. Now I am wise."

"What?" said Findlayson over his shoulder.

Peroo went on as if he were talking to himself. "Six—seven—ten monsoons since, I was watch on the fo'c'sle of the *Rewah*—the Kumpani's big boat—and there was a big *tufan,* green and black water beating; and I held fast to the life-lines, choking under the waters. Then I thought of the Gods—of Those whom we saw tonight"—he stared curiously at Findlayson's back, but the white man was looking across the flood. "Yes, I say of Those whom we saw this night past, and I called upon Them to protect me. And while I prayed, still keeping my look-out, a big wave came and threw me forward upon the ring of the great black bow-anchor, and the *Rewah* rose high and high, leaning towards the left-hand side, and the water drew away from beneath her nose, and I lay upon my belly, holding the ring, and looking down into those great deeps. Then I thought, even in the face of death, if I lose hold I die, and for me neither the *Rewah* nor my place by the galley where the rice is cooked, nor Bombay, nor Calcutta, nor even London, will be any more for me. 'How shall I be sure,' I said, 'that the Gods to whom I pray will abide at all?' This I thought, and the *Rewah* dropped her nose as a hammer falls, and all the sea came in and slid me backwards along the fo'c'sle and over the break of the fo'c'sle, and I very badly bruised my shin against the donkey-engine: but I did not die, and I have seen the Gods. They are good for live men, but for the dead— They have spoken Themselves. Therefore, when I come to the village I will beat the *guru* for talking riddles which are no riddles. When Brahm ceases to dream, the Gods go."

"Look upstream. The light blinds. Is there smoke yonder?"

Peroo shaded his eyes with his hands. "He is a wise man and quick. Hitchcock *Sahib* would not trust a rowboat. He has borrowed the *Rao Sahib*'s steam-launch, and comes to look for us. I have always said that there should have been a steam-launch on the bridge-works for us."

The territory of the *Rao* of Baraon lay within ten miles of the bridge; and Findlayson and Hitchcock had spent a fair portion of their scanty leisure in playing billiards and shooting Black-buck with the young man. He had been bear-led by an English tutor of sporting tastes for some five or six years, and was now royally wasting the revenues accumulated during his minority by the Indian Government. His steam-launch, with its silver-plated rails, striped silk awning, and mahogany decks, was a new toy which Findlayson had found horribly in the way when the *Rao* came to look at the bridge-works.

"It's great luck," murmured Findlayson, but he was none the less afraid, wondering what news might be of the bridge.

The gaudy blue and white funnel came downstream swiftly. They could see Hitchcock in the bows, with a pair of opera-glasses, and his face was unusually white. Then Peroo hailed, and the launch made for the tail of the island. The *Rao Sahib,* in tweed shooting-suit and a seven-hued turban, waved his royal hand, and Hitchcock shouted. But he need have asked no questions, for Findlayson's first demand was for his bridge.

"All serene! 'Gad, I never expected to see you again, Findlayson. You're seven koss down-stream. Yes, there's not a stone shifted anywhere; but how are you? I borrowed the *Rao Sahib*'s launch, and he was good enough to come along. Jump in."

"Ah, Finlinson, you are very well, eh? That was most unprecedented calamity last night, eh? My royal palace, too, it leaks like the devil, and the crops will also be short all about my country. Now you shall back her out, Hitchcock. I—I do not understand steam-engines. You are wet? You are cold, Finlinson? I have some things to eat here, and you will take a good drink."

"I'm immensely grateful, *Rao Sahib*. I believe you've saved my life. How did Hitchcock—"

"Oho! His hair was upon end. He rode to me in the middle of the night and woke me up in the arms of Morphus. I was most truly concerned, Finlinson, so I came too. My head-priest he is very angry just now. We will go quick, Mister Hitchcock. I am due to attend at twelve forty-five in the state temple, where we sanctify some new idol. If not so I would have asked you to spend the day with me. They are dam-bore, these religious ceremonies, Finlinson, eh?"

Peroo, well known to the crew, had possessed himself of the wheel, and was taking the launch craftily up-stream. But while he steered he was, in his mind, handling two feet of partially untwisted wire-rope; and the back upon which he beat was the back of his *guru*.

The Sing-Song of Old Man Kangaroo

FROM *JUST SO STORIES* (1902)

All his life Kipling was immensely fond of children. His surviving daughter described him as a wonderful father, full of jokes and stories and ideas for games—and not just games: he invented forms of play that would help their later education. (By the time his son and daughter were seven and eight they had already enacted the excerpt from *A Midsummer Night's Dream* that gave rise to *Puck of Pook's Hill*, with RK playing Bottom in a paper donkey-head.)

Young readers who discover Kipling's work usually first chance across either *The Jungle Book* or *Just So Stories*. In my case it was the latter. I was mesmerized by them, and delighted by the illustrations—RK's own, which he complained about not being allowed to color from his children's paint-box. Here's one of my favorites. It demonstrates his talent for exploiting snippets of detail to the full (he visited Australia only once, and that briefly, yet his astonishing memory stored a wealth of local information), and what is more, it stands up on the page and shouts about its origin as a tale devised for his children. It positively *clamors* to be recited aloud!

Spinifex is a kind of Australian grass. A dingo is an Australian wild dog. "Ti-tree," according to *Chambers Twentieth Century Dictionary*, is an error; it should be tea-tree, though it has nothing to do with tea the drink. Mulga is the Australian acacia. The Flinders is a mountain range called after an explorer of that name.

The Sing-Song of Old Man Kangaroo

Not always was the Kangaroo as now we do behold him, but a Different Animal with four short legs. He was grey and he was woolly, and his pride was inordinate: he danced on an outcrop in the middle of Australia, and he went to the Little God Nqa.

He went to Nqa at six before breakfast, saying, "Make me different from all other animals by five this afternoon."

Up jumped Nqa from his seat on the sand-flat and shouted, "Go away!"

He was grey and he was woolly, and his pride was inordinate; he danced on a rock-ledge in the middle of Australia, and he went to the Middle God Nquing.

He went to Nquing at eight after breakfast, saying, "Make me different from all other animals; make me, also, wonderfully popular by five this afternoon."

Up jumped Nquing from his burrow in the spinifex and shouted, "Go away!"

He was grey and he was woolly, and his pride was inordinate: he danced on a sandbank in the middle of Australia, and he went to the Big God Nqong.

He went to Nqong at ten before dinner-time, saying, "Make me different from all other animals; make me popular and wonderfully run after by five this afternoon."

Up jumped Nqong from his bath in the salt-pan and shouted, "Yes, I will!"

Nqong called Dingo—Yellow-Dog Dingo—always hungry, dusty in the sunshine, and showed him Kangaroo. Nqong said, "Dingo! Wake up, Dingo! Do you see that gentleman dancing on an ashpit? He wants to be popular and very truly run after. Dingo, make him so!"

Up jumped Dingo—Yellow-Dog Dingo—and said, "What, *that* cat-rabbit?"

Off ran Dingo—Yellow-Dog Dingo—always hungry, grinning like a coal-scuttle,—ran after Kangaroo.

Off went the proud Kangaroo on his four little legs like a bunny.

This, O Beloved of mine, ends the first part of the tale!

He ran through the desert; he ran through the mountains; he ran through the salt-pans; he ran through the reed-beds; he ran through the blue gums; he ran through the spinifex; he ran till his front legs ached.

He had to!

Still ran Dingo—Yellow-Dog Dingo—always hungry, grinning like a rat-trap, never getting nearer, never getting farther,—ran after Kangaroo.

He had to!

Still ran Kangaroo—Old Man Kangaroo. He ran through the ti-trees; he ran through the mulga; he ran through the long grass; he ran through the short grass; he ran through the Tropics of Capricorn and Cancer; he ran till his hind legs ached.

He had to!

Still ran Dingo—Yellow-Dog Dingo—hungrier and hungrier, grinning like a horse-collar, never getting nearer, never getting farther; and they came to the Wollgong River.

Now, there wasn't any bridge, and there wasn't any ferry-boat, and Kangaroo didn't know how to get over; so he stood on his legs and hopped.

He had to!

He hopped through the Flinders; he hopped through the Cinders; he hopped through the deserts in the middle of Australia. He hopped like a Kangaroo.

First he hopped one yard; then he hopped three yards; then he hopped five yards; his legs growing stronger; his legs growing longer. He hadn't any time for rest or refreshment, and he wanted them very much.

Still ran Dingo—Yellow-Dog Dingo—very much bewildered, very much hungry, and wondering what in the world or out of it made Old Man Kangaroo hop.

For he hopped like a cricket; like a pea in a saucepan; or a new rubber ball on a nursery floor.

He had to!

He tucked up his front legs; he hopped on his hind legs; he stuck out his tail for a balance-weight behind him; and he hopped through the Darling Downs.

He had to!

Still ran Dingo—Tired-Dog Dingo—hungrier and hungrier, very much bewildered, and wondering when in the world or out of it would Old Man Kangaroo stop.

Then came Nqong from his bath in the salt-pans, and said, "It's five o'clock."

Down sat Dingo—Poor-Dog Dingo—always hungry, dusty in the sunshine; hung out his tongue and howled.

Down sat Kangaroo—Old Man Kangaroo—stuck out his tail like a milking-stool behind him, and said, "Thank goodness *that's* finished!"

Then said Nqong, who is always a gentleman, "Why aren't you grateful to Yellow-Dog Dingo? Why don't you thank him for all he has done for you?"

Then said Kangaroo—Tired Old Kangaroo—"He's chased me out of the homes of my childhood; he's chased me out of my regular meal-times; he's altered my shape so I'll never get it back; and he's played Old Scratch with my legs."

Then said Nqong, "Perhaps I'm mistaken, but didn't you ask me to make you different from all other animals, as well as to make you very truly sought after? And now it is five o'clock."

"Yes," said Kangaroo. "I wish that I hadn't. I thought you would do it by charms and incantations, but this is a practical joke."

"Joke!" said Nqong, from his bath in the blue gums. "Say that again and I'll whistle up Dingo and run your hind legs off."

"No," said the Kangaroo. "I must apologize. Legs are legs, and you needn't alter 'em so far as I am concerned. I only meant to explain to Your Lordliness that I've had nothing to eat since morning, and I'm very empty indeed."

"Yes," said Dingo—Yellow-Dog Dingo,—"I am just in the same situation. I've made him different from all other animals; but what may I have for my tea?"

Then said Nqong from his bath in the salt-pan, "Come and ask me about it tomorrow, because I'm going to wash."

So they were left in the middle of Australia, Old Man Kangaroo and Yellow-Dog Dingo, and each said, "That's *your* fault."

"They"

FROM *TRAFFICS AND DISCOVERIES* (1904)

Kipling was an enthusiastic motorist in the days when cars were few and far between. No doubt the marvelous descriptions of landscape with which the story opens are based on his explorations of his own beloved Sussex.

This is another ghost story. But it is totally unconventional. One might call it a ghost story in reverse. Most of the genre are about assaults by malevolent spirits such as one would seek to exorcise. Who but Kipling—perhaps because he had so tragically lost his eldest child—would have conceived of a woman whose home was haunted . . . *because that was what she wanted most?*

The "hamlet which stands godmother to the capital of the United States" is Washington in West Sussex—rather more than a hamlet now, with a population well over a thousand. Tithe-barns were built to store the parson's share of the corn-harvest. The West Coast is of course that of Africa. The word "nigger" was less offensive in RK's day than in ours—indeed, conventional, deriving as it does from the Spanish word for black. But RK was strict about confining its use to black Africans and their descendants in the New World. In "On the City Wall" (in *Soldiers Three*), wanting to sum up the repulsive personality of an English officer, he says, "The Captain was not a nice man. He called all natives 'niggers,' which, besides being extreme bad form, shows gross ignorance."

A tax cart was small and light, attracting little or no tax: hence, the best that poor countryfolk could afford. The tonneau is the rear part of the car's body; it would probably have had a door hinged to open at the back.

"They"

One view called me to another; one hill top to its fellow, half across the county, and since I could answer at no more trouble than the snapping forward of a lever, I let the county flow under my wheels. The orchid-studded flats of the East gave way to the thyme, ilex, and grey grass of the Downs; these again to the rich cornland and fig-trees of the lower coast, where you carry the beat of the tide on your left hand for fifteen level miles; and when at last I turned inland through a huddle of rounded hills and woods I had run myself clean out of my known marks. Beyond that precise hamlet which stands godmother to the capital of the United States, I found hidden villages where bees, the only things awake, boomed in eighty-foot lindens that overhung grey Norman churches; miraculous brooks diving under stone bridges built for heavier traffic than would ever vex them again; tithe-barns larger than their churches, and an old smithy that cried out aloud how it had once been a hall of the Knights of the Temple. Gipsies I found on a common where the gorse, bracken, and heath fought it out together up a mile of Roman road; and a little farther on I disturbed a red fox rolling dog-fashion in the naked sunlight.

As the wooded hills closed about me I stood up in the car to take the bearings of that great Down whose ringed head is a landmark for fifty miles across the low countries. I judged that the lie of the country would bring me across some westward-running road that went to his feet, but I did not allow for the confusing veils of the woods. A quick turn plunged me first into a green cutting brim-full of liquid sunshine, next into a gloomy tunnel where last year's dead leaves whispered and scuffled about my tires. The strong hazel stuff meeting overhead had not been cut for a couple of generations at least, nor had any axe helped the moss-cankered oak and beech to spring above them. Here the road changed frankly into a carpeted ride on whose brown velvet spent primrose-clumps showed like jade, and a few sickly, white-stalked blue-bells nodded together. As the slope favored I shut off the power and slid over the whirled leaves, expecting every moment to meet a keeper; but I only heard a jay, far off, arguing against the silence under the twilight of the trees.

Still the track descended. I was on the point of reversing and working my way back on the second speed ere I ended in some swamp, when I saw sunshine through the tangle ahead and lifted the brake.

It was down again at once. As the light beat across my face my fore-wheels took the turf of a great still lawn from which sprang horsemen ten feet high with levelled lances, monstrous peacocks, and sleek round-headed maids of honor—blue, black, and glistening—all of clipped yew. Across the lawn—the marshaled woods besieged it on three sides—stood an ancient house of lichened and weather-worn stone, with mullioned windows and roofs of rose-red tile. It was flanked by semi-circular walls, also rose-red, that closed the lawn on the fourth side, and at their feet a box hedge grew man-high. There were doves on the roof about the slim brick chimneys, and I caught a glimpse of an octagonal dove-house behind the screening wall.

Here, then, I stayed; a horseman's green spear laid at my breast; held by the exceeding beauty of that jewel in that setting.

"If I am not packed off for a trespasser, or if this knight does not ride a wallop at me," thought I, "Shakespeare and Queen Elizabeth at least must come out of that half-open garden door and ask me to tea."

A child appeared at an upper window, and I thought the little thing waved a friendly hand. But it was to call a companion, for presently another bright head showed. Then I heard a laugh among the yew-peacocks, and turning to make sure (till then I had been watching the house only) I saw the silver of a fountain behind a hedge thrown up against the sun. The doves on the roof cooed to the cooing water; but between the two notes I caught the utterly happy chuckle of a child absorbed in some light mischief.

The garden door—heavy oak sunk deep in the thickness of the wall—opened further: a woman in a big garden hat set her foot slowly on the time-hollowed stone step and as slowly walked across the turf. I was forming some apology when she lifted up her head and I saw that she was blind.

"I heard you," she said. "Isn't that a motor car?"

"I'm afraid I've made a mistake in my road. I should have turned off up above—I never dreamed—" I began.

"But I'm very glad. Fancy a motor car coming into the garden! It will be such a treat—" She turned and made as though looking about her. "You—you haven't seen any one, have you—perhaps?"

"No one to speak to, but the children seemed interested at a distance."

"Which?"

"I saw a couple up at the window just now, and I think I heard a little chap in the grounds."

"Oh, lucky you!" she cried, and her face brightened. "I hear them, of course, but that's all. You've seen them and heard them?"

"Yes," I answered. "And if I know anything of children, one of them's having a beautiful time by the fountain yonder. Escaped, I should imagine."

"You're fond of children?"

I gave her one or two reasons why I did not altogether hate them.

"Of course, of course," she said. "Then you understand. Then you won't think it foolish if I ask you to take your car through the gardens, once or twice—quite slowly. I'm sure they'd like to see it. They see so little, poor things. One tries to make their life pleasant, but—" she threw out her hands towards the woods. "We're so out of the world here."

"That will be splendid," I said. "But I can't cut up your grass."

She faced to the right. "Wait a minute," she said. "We're at the South gate, aren't we? Behind those peacocks there's a flagged path. We call it the Peacocks' Walk. You can't see it from here, they tell me, but if you squeeze along by the edge of the wood you can turn at the first peacock and get on to the flags."

It was sacrilege to wake that dreaming house-front with the clatter of machinery, but I swung the car to clear the turf, brushed along the edge of the wood and turned in on the broad stone path where the fountain-basin lay like one star-sapphire.

"May I come too?" she cried. "No, please don't help me. They'll like it better if they see me."

She felt her way lightly to the front of the car, and with one foot on the step she called: "Children, oh, children! Look and see what's going to happen!"

The voice would have drawn lost souls from the Pit, for the yearning that underlay its sweetness, and I was not surprised to hear an answering shout behind the yews. It must have been the child by the fountain, but he fled at our approach, leaving a little toy boat in the water. I saw the glint of his blue blouse among the still horsemen.

Very disposedly we paraded the length of the walk and at her request backed again. This time the child had got the better of his panic, but stood far off and doubting.

"The little fellow's watching us," I said. "I wonder if he'd like a ride."

"They're very shy still. Very shy. But, oh, lucky you to be able to see them! Let's listen."

I stopped the machine at once, and the humid stillness, heavy with the scent of box, cloaked us deep. Shears I could hear where some gardener was clipping; a mumble of bees and broken voices that might have been the doves.

"Oh, unkind!" she said wearіedly.

"Perhaps they're only shy of the motor. The little maid at the window looks tremendously interested."

"Yes?" She raised her head. "It was wrong of me to say that. They are really fond of me. It's the only thing that makes life worth living—when they're fond of you, isn't it? I daren't think what the place would be without them. By the way, is it beautiful?"

"I think it is the most beautiful place I have ever seen."

"So they all tell me. I can feel it, of course, but that isn't quite the same thing."

"Then have you never—?" I began, but stopped abashed.

"Not since I can remember. It happened when I was only a few months old, they tell me. And yet I must remember something, else how could I dream about colors? I see light in my dreams, and colors, but I never see *them*. I only hear them just as I do when I'm awake."

"It's difficult to see faces in dreams. Some people can, but most of us haven't the gift," I went on, looking up at the window where the child stood all but hidden.

"I've heard that too," she said. "And they tell me that one never sees a dead person's face in a dream. Is that true?"

"I believe it is—now I come to think of it."

"But how is it with yourself—yourself?" The blind eyes turned towards me.

"I have never seen the faces of my dead in any dream," I answered.

"Then it must be as bad as being blind."

The sun had dipped behind the woods and the long shades were possessing the insolent horsemen one by one. I saw the light die from off the top of a glossy-leaved lance and all the brave hard green turn to soft black. The house, accepting another day at end, as it had accepted an hundred thousand gone, seemed to settle deeper into its rest among the shadows.

"Have you ever wanted to?" she said after the silence.

"Very much sometimes," I replied. The child had left the window as the shadows closed upon it.

"Ah! So've I, but I don't suppose it's allowed. . . . Where d'you live?"

"Quite the other side of the county—sixty miles and more, and I must be going back. I've come without my big lamp."

"But it's not dark yet. I can feel it."

"I'm afraid it will be by the time I get home. Could you lend me someone to set me on my road at first? I've utterly lost myself."

"I'll send Madden with you to the cross-roads. We are so out of the world, I don't wonder you were lost! I'll guide you round to the front of the house; but you will go slowly, won't you, till you're out of the grounds? It isn't foolish, do you think?"

"I promise you I'll go like this," I said, and let the car start herself down the flagged path.

We skirted the left wing of the house, whose elaborately cast lead guttering alone was worth a day's journey; passed under a great rose-grown gate in the red wall, and so round to the high front of the house which in beauty and stateliness as much excelled the back as that all others I had seen.

"Is it so very beautiful?" she said wistfully when she heard my raptures. "And you like the lead-figures too? There's the old azalea garden behind. They say that this place must have been made for children. Will you help me out, please? I should like to come with you as far as the cross-roads, but I mustn't leave them. Is that you, Madden? I want you to show this gentleman the way to the cross-roads. He has lost his way but—he has seen them."

A butler appeared noiselessly at the miracle of old oak that must be called the front door, and slipped aside to put on his hat. She stood looking at me with open blue eyes in which no sight lay, and I saw for the first time that she was beautiful.

"Remember," she said quietly, "if you are fond of them you will come again," and disappeared within the house.

The butler in the car said nothing till we were nearly at the lodge gates, where catching a glimpse of a blue blouse in a shrubbery I swerved amply lest the devil that leads little boys to play should drag me into child-murder.

"Excuse me," he asked of a sudden, "but why did you do that, Sir?"

"The child yonder."

"Our young gentleman in blue?"

"Of course."

"He runs about a good deal. Did you see him by the fountain, Sir?"

"Oh, yes, several times. Do we turn here?"

"Yes, Sir. And did you 'appen to see them upstairs too?"

"At the upper window? Yes."

"Was that before the mistress come out to speak to you, Sir?"

"A little before that. Why d'you want to know?"

He paused a little. "Only to make sure that—that they had seen the car, Sir, because with children running about, though I'm sure you're driving particularly careful, there might be an accident. That was all, Sir. Here are the crossroads. You can't miss your way from now on. Thank you, Sir, but that isn't *our* custom, not with—"

"I beg your pardon," I said, and thrust away the British silver.

"Oh, it's quite right with the rest of 'em as a rule. Goodbye, Sir."

He retired into the armor-plated conning tower of his caste and walked away. Evidently a butler solicitous for the honour of his house, and interested, probably through a maid, in the nursery.

Once beyond the signposts at the cross-roads I looked back, but the crumpled hills interlaced so jealously that I could not see where the house had lain. When I asked its name at a cottage along the road, the fat woman who sold sweetmeats there gave me to understand that people with motor cars had small right to live—much less to "go about talking like carriage folk." They were not a pleasant-mannered community.

When I retraced my route on the map that evening I was little wiser. Hawkin's Old Farm appeared to be the Survey title of the place, and the old County Gazetteer, generally so ample, did not allude to it. The big house of those parts was Hodnington Hall, Georgian with early Victorian embellishments, as an atrocious steel engraving attested. I carried my difficulty to a neighbor—a deep-rooted tree of that soil—and he gave me a name of a family which conveyed no meaning.

A month or so later—I went again, or it may have been that my car took the road of her own volition. She over-ran the fruitless Downs, threaded every turn of the maze of lanes below the hills, drew through the high-walled woods, impenetrable in their full leaf, came out at the cross-roads where the butler had left me, and a little farther on developed an internal trouble which forced me to turn her in on a grass way-waste that cut into a summer-silent hazel wood. So far as I could make sure by the sun and a six-inch Ordnance map, this should be the road flank of that wood which I had first explored from the heights above. I made a mighty serious business of my repairs and a glittering shop of my repair kit, spanners, pump, and the like, which I spread out orderly upon a rug. It was a trap to catch all childhood, for on such a day, I argued, the children would not be far off. When I paused in my work I listened, but the wood was so full of the noises of summer (though the birds had mated) that I could not at first distinguish these from the tread of small cautious feet stealing across the dead leaves. I rang my bell in an alluring manner, but the feet fled, and I repented, for to a child a sudden noise is very real terror. I must have been at work half an hour when I heard in the wood the voice of the blind woman crying: "Children, oh, children! Where are you?" and the stillness made slow to close on the perfection of that cry. She came towards me, half feeling her way between the tree boles, and though a child it seemed clung to her skirt, it swerved into the leafage like a rabbit as she drew nearer.

"Is that you?" she said, "from the other side of the county?"

"Yes, it's me from the other side of the county."

"Then why didn't you come through the upper woods? They were there just now."

"They were here a few minutes ago. I expect they knew my car had broken down, and came to see the fun."

"Nothing serious, I hope? How do cars break down?"

"In fifty different ways. Only mine has chosen the fifty-first."

She laughed merrily at the tiny joke, cooed with delicious laughter, and pushed her hat back.

"Let me hear," she said.

"Wait a moment," I cried, "and I'll get you a cushion."

She set her foot on the rug all covered with spare parts, and stooped above it eagerly. "What delightful things!" The hands through which she saw glanced in the chequered sunlight. "A box here—another box! Why you've arranged them like playing shop!"

"I confess now that I put it out to attract them. I don't need half those things really."

"How nice of you! I heard your bell in the upper wood. You say they were here before that?"

"I'm sure of it. Why are they so shy? That little fellow in blue who was with you just now ought to have got over his fright. He's been watching me like a Red Indian."

"It must have been your bell," she said. "I heard one of them go past me in trouble when I was coming down. They're shy—so shy even with me." She turned her face over her shoulder and cried again: "Children, oh, children! Look and see!"

"They must have gone off together on their own affairs," I suggested, for there was a murmur behind us of lowered voices broken by the sudden squeaking giggles of childhood. I returned to my tinkerings and she leaned forward, her chin on her hand, listening interestedly.

"How many are they?" I said at last. The work was finished, but I saw no reason to go.

Her forehead puckered a little in thought. "I don't quite know," she said simply. "Sometimes more—sometimes less. They come and stay with me because I love them, you see."

"That must be very jolly," I said, replacing a drawer, and as I spoke I heard the inanity of my answer.

"You—you aren't laughing at me," she cried. "I—I haven't any of my own. I never married. People laugh at me sometimes about them because—because—"

"Because they're savages," I returned. "It's nothing to fret for. That sort laugh at everything that isn't in their own fat lives."

"I don't know. How should I? I only don't like being laughed at about *them*. It hurts; and when one can't see. . . . I don't want to seem silly," her chin quivered like a child's as she spoke, "but we blindies have only one skin, I think. Everything outside hits straight at our souls. It's different with you. You've such good defenses in your eyes—looking out—before anyone can really pain you in your soul. People forget that with us."

I was silent reviewing that inexhaustible matter—the more than inherited (since it is also carefully taught) brutality of the Christian peoples, beside which the mere heathendom of the West Coast nigger is clean and restrained. It led me a long distance into myself.

"Don't do that!" she said of a sudden, putting her hands before her eyes.

"What?"

She made a gesture with her hand.

"That! It's—it's all purple and black. Don't! That color hurts."

"But, how in the world do you know about colors?" I exclaimed, for here was a revelation indeed.

"Colors as colors?" she asked.

"No. *Those* Colors which you saw just now."

"You know as well as I do," she laughed, "else you wouldn't have asked that question. They aren't in the world at all. They're in *you*—when you went so angry."

"D'you mean a dull purplish patch, like port wine mixed with ink?" I said.

"I've never seen ink or port wine, but the colors aren't mixed. They are separate—all separate."

"Do you mean black streaks and jags across the purple?"

She nodded. "Yes—if they are like this," and zig-zagged her finger again, "but it's more red than purple—that bad color."

"And what are the colors at the top of the—whatever you see?"

Slowly she leaned forward and traced on the rug the figure of the Egg itself.

"I see them so," she said, pointing with a grass stem, "white, green, yellow, red, purple, and when people are angry or bad, black across the red—as you were just now."

"Who told you anything about it—in the beginning?" I demanded.

"About the colors? No one. I used to ask what colors were

when I was little—in table-covers and curtains and carpets, you see—because some colors hurt me and some made me happy. People told me; and when I got older that was how I saw people." Again she traced the outline of the Egg which it is given to very few of us to see.

"All by yourself?" I repeated.

"All by myself. There wasn't anyone else. I only found out afterwards that other people did not see the Colors."

She leaned against the tree-bole plaiting and unplaiting chance-plucked grass stems. The children in the wood had drawn nearer. I could see them with the tail of my eye frolicking like squirrels.

"Now I am sure you will never laugh at me," she went on after a long silence. "Nor at *them.*"

"Goodness! No!" I cried, jolted out of my train of thought. "A man who laughs at a child—unless the child is laughing too—is a heathen!"

"I didn't mean that, of course. You'd never laugh *at* children, but I thought—I used to think—that perhaps you might laugh about *them.* So now I beg your pardon. . . . What are you going to laugh at?"

I had made no sound, but she knew.

"At the notion of your begging my pardon. If you had done your duty as a pillar of the State and a landed proprietress you ought to have summoned me for trespass when I barged through your woods the other day. It was disgraceful of me—inexcusable."

She looked at me, her head against the tree trunk—long and steadfastly—this woman who could see the naked soul.

"How curious," she half whispered. "How very curious."

"Why, what have I done?"

"You don't understand . . . and yet you understood about the Colors. Don't you understand?"

She spoke with a passion that nothing had justified, and I faced her bewilderedly as she rose. The children had gathered themselves in a roundel behind a bramble bush. One sleek head bent over something smaller, and the set of the little shoulders told me that fingers were on lips. They, too, had some child's tremendous secret. I alone was hopelessly astray there in the broad sunlight.

"No," I said, and shook my head as though the dead eyes could note. "Whatever it is, I don't understand yet. Perhaps I shall later—if you'll let me come again."

"You will come again," she answered. "You will surely come again and walk in the wood."

"Perhaps the children will know me well enough by that time to let me play with them—as a favor. You know what children are like."

"It isn't a matter of favor but of right," she replied, and while I wondered what she meant, a disheveled woman plunged round the bend of the road, loose-haired, purple, almost lowing with agony as she ran. It was my rude, fat friend of the sweetmeat shop. The blind woman heard and stepped forward. "What is it, Mrs. Madehurst?" she asked.

The woman flung her apron over her head and literally groveled in the dust, crying that her grandchild was sick to death, that the local doctor was away fishing, that Jenny the mother was at her wits' end, and so forth, with repetitions and bellowings.

"Where's the next nearest doctor?" I asked between paroxysms.

"Madden will tell you. Go round to the house and take him with you. I'll attend to this. Be quick!" She half supported the fat woman into the shade. In two minutes I was blowing all the horns of Jericho under the front of the House Beautiful, and Madden, in the pantry, rose to the crisis like a butler and a man.

A quarter of an hour at illegal speeds caught us a doctor five miles away. Within the half-hour we had decanted him, much interested in motors, at the door of the sweetmeat shop, and drew up the road to await the verdict.

"Useful things, cars," said Madden, all man and no butler. "If I'd had one when mine took sick she wouldn't have died."

"How was it?" I asked.

"Croup. Mrs. Madden was away. No one knew what to do. I drove eight miles in a tax cart for the doctor. She was choked when we came back. This car'd ha' saved her. She'd have been close on ten now."

"I'm sorry," I said. "I thought you were rather fond of children from what you told me going to the cross-roads the other day."

"Have you seen 'em again, Sir—this mornin'?"

"Yes, but they're well broke to cars. I couldn't get any of them within twenty yards of it."

He looked at me carefully as a scout considers a stranger—not as a menial should lift his eyes to his divinely appointed superior.

"I wonder why," he said just above the breath that he drew.

We waited on. A light wind from the sea wandered up and down the long lines of the woods, and the wayside grasses, whitened already with summer dust, rose and bowed in sallow waves.

A woman, wiping the suds off her arms, came out of the cottage next the sweetmeat shop.

"I've be'n listenin' in de back-yard," she said cheerily. "He says Arthur's unaccountable bad. Did ye hear him shruck just now? Unaccountable bad. I reckon t'will come Jenny's turn to walk in de wood nex' week along, Mr. Madden."

"Excuse me, Sir, but your lap-robe is slipping," said Madden deferentially. The woman started, dropped a curtsey, and hurried away.

"What does she mean by 'walking in the wood'?" I asked.

"It must be some saying they use hereabouts. I'm from Norfolk myself," said Madden. "They're an independent lot in this county. She took you for a chauffeur, Sir."

I saw the Doctor come out of the cottage followed by a draggle-tailed wench who clung to his arm as though he could make treaty for her with Death. "Dat sort," she wailed—"dey're just as much to us dat has 'em as if dey was lawful born. Just as much—just as much! An' God he'd be just as pleased if you saved 'un, Doctor. Don't take it from me. Miss Florence will tell ye de very same. Don't leave 'im, Doctor!"

"I know, I know," said the man; "but he'll be quiet for a while now. We'll get the nurse and the medicine as fast as we can." He signaled me to come forward with the car, and I strove not to be privy to what followed; but I saw the girl's face, blotched and frozen with grief, and I felt the hand without a ring clutching at my knees when we moved away.

The Doctor was a man of some humor, for I remember he claimed my car under the Oath of Æsculapius, and used it and me without mercy. First we convoyed Mrs. Madehurst and the blind woman to wait by the sick bed till the nurse should come. Next we invaded a neat county town for prescriptions (the Doctor said the trouble was cerebro-spinal meningitis), and when the County Institute, banked and flanked with scared market cattle, reported itself out of nurses for the moment we literally flung ourselves loose upon the county. We conferred with the owners of great houses—magnates at the ends of overarching avenues whose big-boned womenfolk strode away from their tea-tables to listen to the imperious Doctor. At last a white-haired lady sitting under a cedar of Lebanon and surrounded by a court of magnificent Borzois—all hostile to motors—gave the Doctor, who received them as from a princess, written orders which we bore many miles at top speed, through a park, to a French nunnery, where we took over in exchange a pallid-faced and trembling Sister. She knelt at the bottom of the tonneau telling her beads without pause till, by short cuts of the Doctor's invention, we had her to the sweetmeat shop once more. It was a long afternoon crowded with mad episodes that rose and dissolved like the dust of our wheels; cross-sections of remote and incomprehensible lives through which we raced at right angles; and I went home in the dusk, wearied out, to dream of the clashing horns of cattle; round-eyed nuns walking in a garden of graves; pleasant tea-parties beneath shaded trees; the carbolic-scented, grey-painted corridors of the County Institute; the steps of shy children in the wood, and the hands that clung to my knees as the motor began to move.

I had intended to return in a day or two, but it pleased Fate to hold me from that side of the county, on many pretexts, till the elder and the wild rose had fruited. There came at last a brilliant day, swept clear from the south-west, that brought the hills within hand's reach—a day of unstable airs and high filmy clouds. Through no merit of my own I was free, and set the car for the third time on that known road. As I reached the crest of the Downs I felt the soft air change, saw it glaze under the sun; and, looking down at the sea, in that instant beheld the blue of the Channel turn through polished silver and dulled steel to dingy pewter. A laden collier hugging the coast steered outward for deeper water, and, across copper-colored haze, I saw sails rise one by one on the anchored fishing-fleet. In a deep dene behind me an eddy of sudden wind drummed through sheltered oaks, and spun aloft the first dry sample of autumn leaves. When I reached the beach road the sea-fog fumed over the brickfields, and the tide was telling all the groins of the gale beyond Ushant. In less than an hour summer England vanished in chill grey. We were again the shut island of the North, all the ships of the world bellowing at our perilous gates; and between their outcries ran the piping of bewildered gulls. My cap dripped moisture, the folds of the rug held it in pools or sluiced it away in runnels, and the salt-rime stuck to my lips.

Inland the smell of autumn loaded the thickened fog among the trees, and the drip became a continuous shower. Yet the late flowers—mallow of the wayside, scabious of the field, and dahlia of the garden—showed gay in the mist, and beyond the sea's breath there was little sign of decay in the leaf. Yet in the villages the house doors were all open, and bare-legged, bare-headed children sat at ease on the damp doorsteps to shout "pip-pip" at the stranger.

I made bold to call at the sweetmeat shop, where Mrs. Madehurst met me with a fat woman's hospitable tears. Jenny's child, she said, had died two days after the nun had come. It was, she felt, best out of the way, even though insurance offices, for reasons which she did not pretend to follow, would not willingly insure such stray lives. "Not but what Jenny didn't tend to Arthur as though he'd come all proper at de end of de first year—like Jenny herself." Thanks to Miss Florence, the child had been buried with a pomp which, in Mrs. Madehurst's opinion, more than covered the small irregularity of its birth. She described the coffin, within and without, the glass hearse, and the evergreen lining of the grave.

"But how's the mother?" I asked.

"Jenny? Oh, she'll get over it. I've felt dat way with one or two o' my own. She'll get over. She's walkin' in de wood now."

"In this weather?"

Mrs. Madehurst looked at me with narrowed eyes across the counter.

"I dunno but it opens de 'eart like. Yes, it opens de 'eart. Dat's where losin' and bearin' comes so alike in de long run, we do say."

Now the wisdom of the old wives is greater than that of all the Fathers, and this last oracle sent me thinking so extendedly as I went up the road, that I nearly ran over a woman and a child at the wooded corner by the lodge gates of the House Beautiful.

"Awful weather!" I cried, as I slowed dead for the turn.

"Not so bad," she answered placidly out of the fog. "Mine's used to 'un. You'll find yours indoors, I reckon."

Indoors, Madden received me with professional courtesy, and kind inquiries for the health of the motor, which he would put under cover.

I waited in a still, nut-brown hall, pleasant with late flowers and warmed with a delicious wood fire—a place of good influence and great peace. (Men and women may sometimes, after great effort, achieve a creditable lie; but the house, which is their temple, cannot say anything save the truth of those who have lived in it.) A child's cart and a doll lay on the black-and-white floor, where a rug had been kicked back. I felt that the children had only just hurried away—to hide themselves, most like—in the many turns of the great adzed staircase that climbed statelily out of the hall, or to crouch at gaze behind the lions and roses of the carven gallery above. Then I heard her voice above me, singing as the blind sing—from the soul:—

"In the pleasant orchard-closes."

And all my early summer came back at the call.

"In the pleasant orchard-closes,
God bless all our gains say we—
But may God bless all our losses,
Better suits with our degree."

She dropped the marring fifth line, and repeated—

"Better suits with our degree!"

I saw her lean over the gallery, her linked hands white as pearl against the oak.

"Is that you—from the other side of the county?" she called.

"Yes, me—from the other side of the county," I answered, laughing.

"What a long time before you had to come here again." She ran down the stairs, one hand lightly touching the broad rail. "It's two months and four days. Summer's gone!"

"I meant to come before, but Fate prevented."

"I knew it. Please do something to that fire. They won't let me play with it, but I can feel it's behaving badly. Hit it!"

I looked on either side of the deep fireplace, and found but a half-charred hedge-stake with which I punched a black log into flame.

"It never goes out, day or night," she said, as though explaining. "In case any one comes in with cold toes, you see."

"It's even lovelier inside than it was out," I murmured. The red light poured itself along the age-polished dusky panels till the Tudor roses and lions of the gallery took color and motion. An old eagle-topped convex mirror gathered the picture into its mysterious heart, distorting afresh the distorted shadows, and curving the gallery lines into the curves of a ship. The day was shutting down in half a gale as the fog turned to stringy scud. Through the uncurtained mullions of the broad window I could see valiant horsemen of the lawn rear and recover against the wind that taunted them with legions of dead leaves.

"Yes, it must be beautiful," she said. "Would you like to go over it? There's still light enough upstairs."

I followed her up the unflinching, wagon-wide staircase to the gallery whence opened the thin fluted Elizabethan doors.

"Feel how they put the latch low down for the sake of the children." She swung a light door inward.

"By the way, where are they?" I asked. "I haven't even heard them to-day."

She did not answer at once. Then, "I can only hear them," she replied softly. "This is one of their rooms—everything ready, you see."

She pointed into a heavily-timbered room. There were little low gate tables and children's chairs. A doll's house, its hooked front half open, faced a great dappled rocking-horse, from whose padded saddle it was but a child's scramble to the broad window-seat overlooking the lawn. A toy gun lay in a corner beside a gilt wooden cannon.

"Surely they've only just gone," I whispered. In the failing light a door creaked cautiously. I heard the rustle of a frock and the patter of feet—quick feet through a room beyond.

"I heard that," she cried triumphantly. "Did you? Children, oh, children! Where are you?"

The voice filled the walls that held it lovingly to the last perfect note, but there came no answering shout such as I had heard in the garden. We hurried on from room to oak-floored room; up a step here, down three steps there; among a maze of passages; always mocked by our quarry. One might as well have tried to work an unstopped warren with a single ferret. There were bolt-holes innumerable—recesses in walls, embrasures of deep slitten windows now darkened, whence they could start up behind us; and abandoned fireplaces, six feet deep in the masonry, as well as the tangle of communicating doors. Above all, they had the twilight for their helper in our game. I had caught one or two joyous chuckles of evasion, and once or twice had seen the silhouette of a child's frock against some darkening window at the end of a passage; but we returned empty-handed to the gallery, just as a middle-aged woman was setting a lamp in its niche.

"No, I haven't seen her either this evening, Miss Florence," I heard her say, "but that Turpin he says he wants to see you about his shed."

"Oh, Mr. Turpin must want to see me very badly. Tell him to come to the hall, Mrs. Madden."

I looked down into the hall whose only light was the dulled fire, and deep in the shadow I saw them at last. They must have slipped down while we were in the passages, and now thought themselves perfectly hidden behind an old gilt leather screen. By child's law, my fruitless chase was as good as an introduction, but since I had taken so much trouble I resolved to force them to come forward later by the simple trick, which children detest, of pretending not to notice them. They lay close, in a little huddle, no more than shadows except when a quick flame betrayed an outline.

"And now we'll have some tea," she said. "I believe I ought to have offered it you at first, but one doesn't arrive at manners somehow when one lives alone and is considered—h'm—peculiar." Then with very pretty scorn, "Would you like a lamp to see to eat by?"

"The firelight's much pleasanter, I think." We descended into that delicious gloom and Madden brought tea.

I took my chair in the direction of the screen ready to surprise or be surprised as the game should go, and at her permission, since a hearth is always sacred, bent forward to play with the fire.

"Where do you get these beautiful short faggots from?" I asked idly. "Why, they are tallies!"

"Of course," she said. "As I can't read or write I'm driven back on the early English tally for my accounts. Give me one and I'll tell you what it meant."

I passed her an unburned hazel-tally, about a foot long, and she ran her thumb down the nicks.

"This is the milk-record for the home farm for the month of

April last year, in gallons," said she. "I don't know what I should have done without tallies. An old forester of mine taught me the system. It's out of date now for every one else; but my tenants respect it. One of them's coming now to see me. Oh, it doesn't matter. He has no business here out of office hours. He's a greedy, ignorant man—very greedy or—he wouldn't come here after dark."

"Have you much land then?"

"Only a couple of hundred acres in hand, thank goodness. The other six hundred are nearly all let to folk who knew my folk before me, but this Turpin is quite a new man—and a highway robber."

"But are you sure I shan't be—?"

"Certainly not. You have the right. He hasn't any children."

"Ah, the children!" I said, and slid my low chair back till it nearly touched the screen that hid them. "I wonder whether they'll come out for me."

There was a murmur of voices—Madden's and a deeper note—at the low, dark side door, and a ginger-headed, canvas-gaitered giant of the unmistakable tenant-farmer type stumbled or was pushed in.

"Come to the fire, Mr. Turpin," she said.

"If—if you please, Miss, I'll—I'll be quite as well by the door." He clung to the latch as he spoke like a frightened child. Of a sudden I realized that he was in the grip of some almost overpowering fear.

"Well?"

"About that new shed for the young stock—that was all. These first autumn storms settin' in . . . but I'll come again, Miss." His teeth did not chatter much more than the door latch.

"I think not," she answered levelly. "The new shed—m'm. What did my agent write you on the 15th?"

"I—fancied p'raps that if I came to see you—ma—man to man like, Miss. But——"

His eyes rolled into every corner of the room wide with horror. He half opened the door through which he had entered, but I noticed it shut again—from without and firmly.

"He wrote what I told him," she went on. "You are overstocked already. Dunnett's Farm never carried more than fifty bullocks—even in Mr. Wright's time. And *he* used cake. You've sixty-seven and you don't cake. You've broken the lease in that respect. You're dragging the heart out of the farm."

"I'm—I'm getting some minerals—superphosphates—next week. I've as good as ordered a truck-load already. I'll go down to the station tomorrow about 'em. Then I can come and see you man to man like, Miss, in the daylight. . . . That gentleman's not going away, is he?" He almost shrieked.

I had only slid the chair a little farther back, reaching behind me to tap on the leather of the screen, but he jumped like a rat.

"No. Please attend to me, Mr. Turpin." She turned in her chair and faced him with his back to the door. It was an old and sordid little piece of scheming that she forced from him—his plea for the new cow-shed at his landlady's expense, that he might with the covered manure pay his next year's rent out of the valuation after, as she made clear, he had bled the enriched pastures to the bone. I could not but admire the intensity of his greed, when I saw him out-facing for its sake whatever terror it was that ran wet on his forehead.

I ceased to tap the leather—was, indeed, calculating the cost of the shed—when I felt my relaxed hand taken and turned softly between the soft hands of a child. So at last I had triumphed. In a moment I would turn and acquaint myself with those quick-footed wanderers. . . .

The little brushing kiss fell in the center of my palm—as a gift on which the fingers were, once, expected to close: as the all-faithful half-reproachful signal of a waiting child not used to neglect even when grown-ups were busiest—a fragment of the mute code devised very long ago.

Then I knew. And it was as though I had known from the first day when I looked across the lawn at the high window.

I heard the door shut. The woman turned to me in silence, and I felt that she knew.

What time passed after this I cannot say. I was roused by the fall of a log, and mechanically rose to put it back. Then I returned to my place in the chair very close to the screen.

"Now you understand," she whispered, across the packed shadows.

"Yes, I understand—now. Thank you."

"I—I only hear them." She bowed her head in her hands. "I have no right, you know—no other right. I have neither borne nor lost—neither borne nor lost!"

"Be very glad then," said I, for my soul was torn open within me.

"Forgive me!"

She was still, and I went back to my sorrow and my joy.

"It was because I loved them so," she said at last, brokenly. "*That* was why it was, even from the first—even before I knew that they—they were all I should ever have. And I loved them so!"

She stretched out her arms to the shadows and the shadows within the shadow.

"They came because I loved them—because I needed them. I—I must have made them come. Was that wrong, think you?"

"No—no."

"I—I grant you that the toys and—and all that sort of thing were nonsense, but—but I used to so hate empty rooms myself when I was little." She pointed to the gallery. "And the passages all empty. . . . And how could I ever bear the garden door shut? Suppose—"

"Don't! For pity's sake, don't!" I cried. The twilight had brought a cold rain with gusty squalls that plucked at the leaded windows.

"And the same thing with keeping the fire in all night. *I* don't think it so foolish—do you?"

I looked at the broad brick hearth, saw, through tears I believe, that there was no unpassable iron on or near it, and bowed my head.

"I did all that and lots of other things—just to make believe. Then they came. I heard them, but I didn't know that they were not mine by right till Mrs. Madden told me——"

"The butler's wife? What?"

"One of them—I heard—she saw. And knew. Hers! *Not* for me. I didn't know at first. Perhaps I was jealous. Afterwards, I began to understand that it was only because I loved them, not because— . . . Oh, you *must* bear or lose," she said piteously. "There is no other way—and yet they love me. They must! Don't they?"

There was no sound in the room except the lapping voices of the fire, but we two listened intently, and she at least took comfort from what she heard. She recovered herself and half rose. I sat still in my chair by the screen.

"Don't think me a wretch to whine about myself like this, but—but I'm all in the dark, you know, and *you* can see."

In truth I could see, and my vision confirmed me in my resolve, though that was like the very parting of spirit and flesh. Yet a little longer I would stay since it was the last time.

"You think it is wrong, then?" she cried sharply, though I had said nothing.

"Not for you. A thousand times no. For you it is right. . . . I am grateful to you beyond words. For me it would be wrong. For me only. . . ."

"Why?" she said, but passed her hand before her face as she had done at our second meeting in the wood. "Oh, I see," she went on simply as a child. "For you it would be wrong." Then with a little indrawn laugh, "and, d'you remember, I called you lucky—once—at first. You who must never come here again!"

She left me to sit a little longer by the screen, and I heard the sound of her feet die out along the gallery above.

The House Surgeon

FROM *ACTIONS AND REACTIONS* (1909)

This comes from the first of Kipling's books to be published after he was awarded the Nobel Prize for literature.

It is, I suppose, a horror story, with—unusually for that genre—a happy ending. What happens on the way to that ending is another matter. My nape always tingles at the dinner-table scene, when "the other thing" comes bringing with it "aching, helpless grief" . . .

RK was somewhat secretive about his own religious convictions, but despite his disguising himself herein behind the mask of his narrator, one suspects he must have felt considerable contempt for the rigid Protestantism of the Moultrie sisters, who were so rude about both the Catholic practice of praying for the souls of the dead and the taste of the Jewish family that had bought their old home.

It may seem surprising that L. Maxwell McLeod, bearing as he does a Scottish patronymic, should turn out to be a Jew. In fact this was not uncommon. During the last century one of the largest Jewish communities in Britain was in Dundee. Fleeing persecution in Eastern Europe, individuals and families made their way to Baltic ports whence, if they could afford it, they took ship for America. If they had insufficient funds (or, legend says, if they were cheated by captains who lied about the port at which they were put ashore), they settled for Scotland where, as in other countries, they adopted local names.

"Spelicans" are more usually called spillikins: little sticks used in the game also known as jackstraws. (When visiting the "stately home" Penshurst Place, Kent, in the spring of 1989, I found in the Toy Museum there a set of miniature rakes, hoes, ladders, and so forth, under the registered trade-name "Spellicans" with two *l*'s, dating from the right period, so presumably what RK had run across.) A hydro is a spa, a center for hydropathic treatment. A bath-chair (strictly, Bath chair, from the English city of that name) was a conveyance for invalids usually built of wickerwork, with a large wheel either side and a small one in front that could be steered with a lever by the occupant.

Friar's Balsam is "a tincture of benzoin, storax, tolu and aloes" *(Chambers Twentieth Century Dictionary)*; its vapors relieve a sore throat. It would have been added to the water in the bronchitis kettle, a long-spouted vessel somewhat resembling a watering-can. "Groovy" is used in a sense now obsolete; we would refer to a one-track mind. And a fly was a light horse-drawn carriage.

The House Surgeon

On an evening after Easter Day, I sat at a table in a homeward-bound steamer's smoking-room, where half a dozen of us told ghost stories. As our party broke up, a man, playing Patience in the next alcove, said to me: "I didn't quite catch the end of that last story about the Curse on the family's first-born."

"It turned out to be drains," I explained. "As soon as new ones were put into the house the Curse was lifted, I believe. I never knew the people myself."

"Ah! I've had *my* drains up twice; I'm on gravel too."

"You don't mean to say you've a ghost in your house? Why didn't you join our party?"

"Any more orders, gentlemen, before the bar closes?" the steward interrupted.

"Sit down again and have one with me," said the Patience player. "No, it isn't a ghost. Our trouble is more depression than anything else."

"How interesting! Then it's nothing any one can see?"

"It's—it's nothing worse than a little depression. And the odd part is that there hasn't been a death in the house since it was built—in 1863. The lawyer said so. That decided me—my good lady, rather—and he made me pay an extra thousand for it."

"How curious. Unusual, too!" I said.

"Yes, ain't it? It was built for three sisters—Moultrie was the name—three old maids. They all lived together; the eldest owned it. I bought it from her lawyer a few years ago, and if I've spent a pound on the place first and last, I must have spent five thousand. Electric light, new servants' wing, garden—all that sort of thing. A man and his family ought to be happy after so much expense, ain't it?" He looked at me through the bottom of his glass.

"Does it affect your family much?"

"My good lady—she's a Greek by the way—and myself are middle-aged. We can bear up against depression; but it's hard on my little girl. I say little; but she's twenty. We send her visiting to escape it. She almost lived at hotels and hydros last year, but that isn't pleasant for her. She used to be a canary—a perfect canary—always singing. You ought to hear her. She doesn't sing now. That sort of thing's unwholesome for the young, ain't it?"

"Can't you get rid of the place?" I suggested.

"Not except at a sacrifice, and we are fond of it. Just suits us three. We'd love it if we were allowed."

"What do you mean by not being allowed?"

"I mean because of the depression. It spoils everything."

"What's it like exactly?"

"I couldn't very well explain. It must be seen to be appreciated, as the auctioneers say. Now, I was much impressed by the story you were telling just now."

"It wasn't true," I said.

"My tale is true. If you would do me the pleasure to come down and spend a night at my little place, you'd learn more than you would if I talked till morning. Very likely 'twouldn't touch your good self at all. You might be—immune, ain't it? On the other hand, if this influenza-influence *does* happen to affect you, why, I think it will be an experience."

While he talked he gave me his card, and I read his name was L. Maxwell McLeod, Esq., of Holmescroft. A City address was tucked away in a corner.

"My business," he added, "used to be furs. If you are interested in furs—I've given thirty years of my life to 'em."

"You're very kind," I murmured.

"Far from it, I assure you. I can meet you next Saturday afternoon anywhere in London you choose to name, and I'll be only too happy to motor you down. It ought to be a delightful run at this time of year—the rhododendrons will be out. I mean it. You don't know how truly I mean it. Very probably—it won't affect you at all. And—I think I may say I have the finest collection of narwhal tusks in the world. All the best skins and horns have to go through London, and L. Maxwell McLeod, he knows where they come from, and where they go to. That's his business."

For the rest of the voyage up-channel Mr. McLeod talked to me of the assembling, preparation, and sale of the rarer furs; and told me things about the manufacture of fur-lined coats which quite shocked me. Somehow or other, when we landed on Wednesday, I found myself pledged to spend that week-end with him at Holmescroft.

On Saturday he met me with a well-groomed motor, and ran me out in an hour-and-a-half to an exclusive residential district of dustless roads and elegantly designed country villas, each standing in from three to five acres of perfectly appointed land. He told me land was selling at eight hundred pounds the acre, and the new golf links, whose Queen Anne pavilion we passed, had cost nearly twenty-four thousand pounds to create.

Holmescroft was a large, two-storied, low, creeper-covered residence. A verandah at the south side gave on to a garden and two tennis courts, separated by a tasteful iron fence from a most park-like meadow of five or six acres, where two Jersey cows grazed. Tea was ready in the shade of a promising copper beech, and I could see groups on the lawn of young men and maidens appropriately clothed, playing lawn tennis in the sunshine.

"A pretty scene, ain't it?" said Mr. McLeod. "My good lady's sitting under the tree, and that's my little girl in pink on the far court. But I'll take you to your room, and you can see 'em all later."

He led me through a wide parquet-floored hall furnished in pale lemon, with huge cloisonné vases, an ebonised and gold grand piano, and banks of pot flowers in Benares brass bowls, up a pale oak staircase to a spacious landing, where there was a green velvet settee trimmed with silver. The blinds were down, and the light lay in parallel lines on the floors.

He showed me my room, saying cheerfully: "You may be a little tired. One often is without knowing it after a run through traffic. Don't come down till you feel quite restored. We shall all be in the garden."

My room was rather close, and smelt of perfumed soap. I threw up the window at once, but it opened so close to the floor and worked so clumsily that I came within an ace of pitching out, where I should certainly have ruined a rather lopsided laburnum below. As I set about washing off the journey's dust, I began to feel a little tired. But, I reflected, I had not come down here in this weather and among these new surroundings to be depressed, so I began to whistle.

And it was just then that I was aware of a little grey shadow, as it might have been a snowflake seen against the light, floating at an immense distance in the background of my brain. It annoyed me, and I shook my head to get rid of it. Then my brain telegraphed that it was the forerunner of a swift-striding gloom which there was yet time to escape if I would force my thoughts away from it, as a man leaping for life forces his body forward and away from the fall of a wall. But the gloom overtook me before I could take in the meaning of the message. I moved toward the bed, every nerve already aching with the foreknowledge of the pain that was to be dealt it, and sat down, while my amazed and angry soul dropped, gulf by gulf, into that horror of great darkness which is spoken of in the Bible, and which, as auctioneers say, must be experienced to be appreciated.

Despair upon despair, misery upon misery, fear after fear, each causing their distinct and separate woe, packed in upon me for an unrecorded length of time, until at last they blurred together, and I heard a click in my brain like the click in the ear when one descends in a diving bell, and I knew that the pressures were equalized within and without, and that, for the moment, the worst was at an end. But I knew also that at any moment the darkness might come down anew; and while I dwelt on this speculation precisely as a man torments a raging tooth with his tongue, it ebbed away into the little grey shadow on the brain of its first coming, and once more I heard my brain, which knew what would recur, telegraph to every quarter for help, release, or diversion.

The door opened, and McLeod reappeared. I thanked him politely, saying I was charmed with my room, anxious to meet Mrs. McLeod, much refreshed with my wash, and so on and so forth. Beyond a little stickiness at the corners of my mouth, it seemed to me that I was managing my words admirably, the while that I myself cowered at the bottom of unclimbable pits. McLeod laid his hand on my shoulder, and said: "You've got it now already, ain't it?"

"Yes," I answered, "it's making me sick!"

"It will pass off when you come outside. I give you my word it will then pass off. Come!"

I shambled out behind him, and wiped my forehead in the hall.

"You mustn't mind," he said. "I expect the run tired you. My good lady is sitting there under the copper beech."

She was a fat woman in an apricot-colored gown, with a heavily powdered face, against which her black long-lashed eyes showed like currants in dough. I was introduced to many fine ladies and gentlemen of those parts. Magnificently appointed landaus and covered motors swept in and out of the drive, and the air was gay with the merry outcries of the tennis players.

As twilight drew on they all went away, and I was left alone with Mr. and Mrs. McLeod, while tall men-servants and maid-servants took away the tennis and tea things. Miss McLeod had walked a little down the drive with a light-haired young man, who apparently knew everything about every South American railway stock. He had told me at tea that these were the days of financial specialization.

"I think it went off beautifully, my dear," said Mr. McLeod to his wife; and to me: "You feel all right now, ain't it? Of course you do."

Mrs. McLeod surged across the gravel. Her husband skipped nimbly before her into the south verandah, turned a switch, and all Holmescroft was flooded with light.

"You can do that from your room also," he said as they went in. "There is something in money, ain't it?"

Miss McLeod came up behind me in the dusk. "We have not yet been introduced," she said, "but I suppose you are staying the night?"

"Your father was kind enough to ask me," I replied.

She nodded. "Yes, *I* know; and you know too, don't you? I saw your face when you came to shake hands with mamma. You felt the depression very soon. It is simply frightful in that bedroom sometimes. What do you think it is—bewitchment? In Greece, where I was a little girl, it might have been; but not in England, do you think? Or *do* you?"

"I don't know what to think," I replied. "I never felt anything like it. Does it happen often?"

"Yes, sometimes. It comes and goes."

"Pleasant!" I said, as we walked up and down the gravel at the lawn edge. "What has been your experience of it?"

"That is difficult to say, but—sometimes that—that depression is like as it were"—she gesticulated in most un-English fashion—"a light. Yes, like a light turned into a room—only a light of blackness, do you understand?—into a happy room. For sometimes we are so happy, all we three,—so very happy. Then this blackness, it is turned on us just like—ah, I know what I mean now—like the head-lamp of a motor, and we are eclipsed. And there is another thing—"

The dressing gong roared, and we entered the over-lighted hall. My dressing was a brisk athletic performance, varied with outbursts of song—careful attention paid to articulation and expression. But nothing happened. As I hurried downstairs, I thanked Heaven that nothing had happened.

Dinner was served breakfast fashion; the dishes were placed on the sideboard over heaters, and we helped ourselves.

"We always do this when we are alone, so we talk better," said Mr. McLeod.

"And we are always alone," said the daughter.

"Cheer up, Thea. It will all come right," he insisted.

"No, papa." She shook her dark head. "Nothing is right while *it* comes."

"It is nothing that we ourselves have ever done in our lives—that I will swear to you," said Mrs. McLeod suddenly. "And we have changed our servants several times. So we know it is not *them*."

"Never mind. Let us enjoy ourselves while we can," said Mr. McLeod, opening the champagne.

But we did not enjoy ourselves. The talk failed. There were long silences.

"I beg your pardon," I said, for I thought some one at my elbow was about to speak.

"Ah! That is the other thing!" said Miss McLeod. Her mother groaned.

We were silent again, and, in a few seconds it must have been, a live grief beyond words—not ghostly dread or horror, but aching, helpless grief—overwhelmed us, each, I felt, according to his or her nature, and held steady like the beam of a burning-glass. Behind that pain I was conscious there was a desire on somebody's part to explain something on which some tremendously important issue hung.

Meantime I rolled bread pills and remembered my sins; McLeod considered his own reflection in a spoon; his wife seemed to be praying, and the girl fidgeted desperately with hands and feet, till the darkness passed on—as though the malignant rays of a burning glass had been shifted from us.

"There," said Miss McLeod, half rising. "Now you see what makes a happy home. Oh, sell it—sell it, father mine, and let us go away!"

"But I've spent thousands on it. You shall go to Harrogate next week, Thea dear."

"I'm only just back from hotels. I am *so* tired of packing."

"Cheer up, Thea. It is over. You know it does not often come here twice in the same night. I think we shall dare now to be comfortable."

He lifted a dish-cover, and helped his wife and daughter. His face was lined and fallen like an old man's after debauch, but his hand did not shake, and his voice was clear. As he worked to restore us by speech and action, he reminded me of a grey-muzzled collie herding demoralized sheep.

After dinner we sat round the dining-room fire—the drawing-room might have been under the Shadow for aught we knew—talking with the intimacy of gipsies by the wayside, or of wounded comparing notes after a skirmish. By eleven o'clock the three between them had given me every name and detail they could recall that in any way bore on the house, and what they knew of its history.

We went to bed in a fortifying blaze of electric light. My one fear was that the blasting gust of depression would return—the surest way, of course, to bring it. I lay awake till dawn, breathing quickly and sweating lightly, beneath what De Quincey inadequately describes as "the oppression of inexpiable guilt." Now as soon as the lovely day was broken, I fell into the most terrible of all dreams—that joyous one in which all past evil has not only been wiped out of our lives, but has never been committed; and in the very bliss of our assured innocence, before our loves shriek and change countenance, we wake to the day we have earned.

It was a coolish morning, but we preferred to breakfast in the south verandah. The forenoon we spent in the garden, pretending to play games that come out of boxes, such as croquet and clock golf. But most of the time we drew together and talked. The young man who knew all about South American railways took Miss McLeod for a walk in the afternoon, and at five McLeod thoughtfully whirled us all up to dine in town.

"Now, don't say you will tell the Psychological Society, and that you will come again," said Miss McLeod, as we parted. "Because I know you will not."

"You should not say that," said her mother. "You should say, 'Good-bye, Mr. Perseus. Come again.' "

"Not him!" the girl cried. "He has seen the Medusa's head!"

Looking at myself in the restaurant's mirrors, it seemed to me that I had not much benefited by my week-end. Next morning I wrote out all my Holmescroft notes at fullest length, in the hope that by so doing I could put it all behind me. But the experience worked on my mind, as they say certain imperfectly understood rays work on the body.

I am less calculated to make a Sherlock Holmes than any man I know, for I lack both method and patience, yet the idea of following up the trouble to its source fascinated me. I had no theory to go on, except a vague idea that I had come between two poles of a discharge, and had taken a shock meant for some one else. This was followed by a feeling of intense irritation. I waited cautiously on myself, expecting to be overtaken by horror of the supernatural, but my self persisted in being humanly indignant, exactly as though it had been the victim of a practical joke. It was in great pains and upheavals—that I felt in every fiber—but its dominant idea, to put it coarsely, was to get back a bit of its own. By this I knew that I might go forward if I could find the way.

After a few days it occurred to me to go to the office of Mr. J. M. M. Baxter—the solicitor who had sold Holmescroft to McLeod. I explained I had some notion of buying the place. Would he act for me in the matter?

Mr. Baxter, a large, greyish, throaty-voiced man, showed no enthusiasm. "I sold it to Mr. McLeod," he said. "It 'ud scarcely do for me to start on the running-down tack now. But I can recommend—"

"I know he's asking an awful price," I interrupted, "and atop of it he wants an extra thousand for what he calls your clean bill of health."

Mr. Baxter sat up in his chair. I had all his attention.

"Your guarantee with the house. Don't you remember it?"

"Yes, yes. That no death had taken place in the house since it was built. I remember perfectly."

He did not gulp as untrained men do when they lie, but his jaws moved stickily, and his eyes, turning towards the deed boxes on the wall, dulled. I counted seconds, one, two, three—one, two, three—up to ten. A man, I knew, can live through ages of mental depression in that time.

"I remember perfectly." His mouth opened a little as though it had tasted old bitterness.

"Of course *that* sort of thing doesn't appeal to me," I went on. "*I* don't expect to buy a house free from death."

"Certainly not. No one does. But it was Mr. McLeod's fancy—his wife's rather, I believe; and since we could meet it—it was my duty to my clients—at whatever cost to my own feelings—to make him pay."

"That's really why I came to you. I understood from him you knew the place well."

"Oh yes. Always did. It originally belonged to some connections of mine."

"The Misses Moultrie, I suppose. How interesting! They must have loved the place before the country round about was built up."

"They were very fond of it indeed."

"I don't wonder. So restful and sunny. I don't see how they could have brought themselves to part with it."

Now it is one of the most constant peculiarities of the English that in polite conversation—and I had striven to be polite—no one ever does or sells anything for mere money's sake.

"Miss Agnes—the youngest—fell ill" (he spaced his words a little), "and, as they were very much attached to each other, that broke up the home."

"Naturally. I fancied it must have been something of that kind. One doesn't associate the Staffordshire Moultries" (my Demon of Irresponsibility at that instant created 'em), "with—with being hard up."

"I don't know whether we're related to them," he answered importantly. "We may be, for our branch of the family comes from the Midlands."

I give this talk at length, because I am so proud of my first attempt at detective work. When I left him, twenty minutes later, with instructions to move against the owner of Holmescroft with a view to purchase, I was more bewildered than any Doctor Watson at the opening of a story.

Why should a middle-aged solicitor turn plover's egg color and drop his jaw when reminded of so innocent and festal a matter as that no death had ever occurred in a house that he had sold? If I knew my English vocabulary at all, the tone in which he said the youngest sister "fell ill" meant that she had gone out of her mind. That might explain his change of countenance, and it was just possible that her demented influence still hung about Holmescroft; but the rest was beyond me.

I was relieved when I reached McLeod's City office, and could tell him what I had done—not what I thought.

McLeod was quite willing to enter into the game of the pretended purchase, but did not see how it would help if I knew Baxter.

"He's the only living soul I can get at who was connected with Holmescroft," I said.

"Ah! Living soul is good," said McLeod. "At any rate our little girl will be pleased that you are still interested in us. Won't you come down some day this week?"

"How is it there now?" I asked.

He screwed up his face. "Simply frightful!" he said. "Thea is at Droitwich."

"I should like it immensely, but I must cultivate Baxter for the present. You'll be sure and keep him busy your end, won't you?"

He looked at me with quiet contempt. "Do not be afraid. I shall be a good Jew. I shall be my own solicitor."

Before a fortnight was over, Baxter admitted ruefully that

McLeod was better than most firms in the business. We buyers were coy, argumentative, shocked at the price of Holmescroft, inquisitive, and cold by turns, but Mr. McLeod the seller easily met and surpassed us; and Mr. Baxter entered every letter, telegram, and consultation at the proper rates in a cinematograph-film of a bill. At the end of a month he said it looked as though McLeod, thanks to him, were really going to listen to reason. I was many pounds out of pocket, but I had learned something of Mr. Baxter on the human side. I deserved it. Never in my life have I worked to conciliate, amuse, and flatter a human being as I worked over my solicitor.

It appeared that he golfed. Therefore, I was an enthusiastic beginner, anxious to learn. Twice I invaded his office with a bag (McLeod lent it) full of the spelicans needed in this detestable game, and a vocabulary to match. The third time the ice broke, and Mr. Baxter took me to his links, quite ten miles off, where in a maze of tramway lines, railroads, and nursery-maids, we skelped our divoted way round nine holes like barges plunging through head seas. He played vilely and had never expected to meet any one worse; but as he realized my form, I think he began to like me, for he took me in hand by the two hours together. After a fortnight he could give me no more than a stroke a hole, and when, with this allowance, I once managed to beat him by one, he was honestly glad, and assured me that I should be a golfer if I stuck to it. I was sticking to it for my own ends, but now and again my conscience pricked me; for the man was a nice man. Between games he supplied me with odd pieces of evidence, such as that he had known the Moultries all his life, being their cousin, and that Miss Mary, the eldest, was an unforgiving woman who would never let bygones be. I naturally wondered what she might have against him; and somehow connected him unfavourably with mad Agnes.

"People ought to forgive and forget," he volunteered one day between rounds. "Specially where, in the nature of things, they can't be sure of their deductions. Don't you think so?"

"It all depends on the nature of the evidence on which one forms one's judgment," I answered.

"Nonsense!" he cried. "I'm lawyer enough to know that there's nothing in the world so misleading as circumstantial evidence. Never was."

"Why? Have you ever seen men hanged on it?"

"Hanged? People have been supposed to be eternally lost on it," his face turned grey again. "I don't know how it is with you, but my consolation is that God must know. He *must!* Things that seem on the face of 'em like murder, or say suicide, may appear different to God. Heh?"

"That's what the murderer and the suicide can always hope—I suppose."

"I have expressed myself clumsily as usual. The facts as God knows 'em—may *be* different—even after the most clinching evidence. I've always said that—both as a lawyer and a man, but some people won't—I don't want to judge 'em—we'll say they can't—believe it; whereas *I* say there's always a working chance—a certainty—that the worst hasn't happened." He stopped and cleared his throat. "Now, let's come on! This time next week I shall be taking my holiday."

"What links?" I asked carelessly, while twins in a perambulator got out of our line of fire.

"A potty little nine-hole affair at a Hydro in the Midlands. My cousins stay there. Always will. Not but what the fourth and the seventh holes take some doing. You could manage it, though," he said encouragingly. "You're doing much better. It's only your approach shots that are weak."

"You're right. I can't approach for nuts! I shall go to pieces while you're away—with no one to coach me," I said mournfully.

"I haven't taught you anything," he said, delighted with the compliment.

"I owe all I've learned to you, anyhow. When will you come back?"

"Look here," he began. "I don't know your engagements, but I've no one to play with at Burry Mills. Never have. Why couldn't you take a few days off and join me there? I warn you it will be rather dull. It's a throat and gout place—baths, massage, electricity, and so forth. But the fourth and the seventh holes really take some doing."

"I'm for the game," I answered valiantly, Heaven well knowing that I hated every stroke and word of it.

"That's the proper spirit. As their lawyer I must ask you not to say anything to my cousins about Holmescroft. It upsets 'em. Always did. But speaking as man to man, it would be very pleasant for me if you could see your way to—"

I saw it as soon as decency permitted, and thanked him sincerely. According to my now well-developed theory he had certainly misappropriated his aged cousins' monies under power of attorney, and had probably driven poor Agnes Moultrie out of her wits, but I wished that he was not so gentle, and good-tempered, and innocent-eyed.

Before I joined him at Burry Mills Hydro, I spent a night at Holmescroft. Miss McLeod had returned from her Hydro, and first we made very merry on the open lawn in the sunshine over the manners and customs of the English resorting to such places. She knew dozens of Hydros, and warned me how to behave in them, while Mr. and Mrs. McLeod stood aside and adored her.

"Ah! That's the way she always comes back to us," he said. "Pity it wears off so soon, ain't it? You ought to hear her sing 'With mirth, thou pretty bird.' "

We had the house to face through the evening, and there we neither laughed nor sang. The gloom fell on us as we entered, and did not shift till ten o'clock, when we crawled out, as it were, from beneath it.

"It has been bad this summer," said Mrs. McLeod in a whisper after we realized that we were freed. "Sometimes I think the house will get up and cry out—it is so bad."

"How?"

"Have you forgotten what comes after the depression?"

So then we waited about the small fire, and the dead air in the room presently filled and pressed down upon us with the sensation (but words are useless here) as though some dumb and bound power were striving against gag and bond to deliver its soul of an articulate word. It passed in a few minutes, and I fell to thinking about Mr. Baxter's conscience and Agnes Moultrie, gone mad in the well-lit bedroom that waited me. These reflections secured me a night during which I rediscovered how, from purely mental causes, a man can be physically sick; but the sickness was bliss compared to my dreams when the birds waked. On my departure, McLeod gave me a beautiful narwhal's horn, much as a nurse gives a child sweets for being brave at a dentist's.

"There's no duplicate of it in the world," he said, "else it would have come to old Max McLeod," and he tucked it into the motor. Miss McLeod on the far side of the car whispered, "Have you found out anything, Mr. Perseus?"

I shook my head.

"Then I shall be chained to my rock all my life," she went on. "Only don't tell papa."

I supposed she was thinking of the young gentleman who specialized in South American rails, for I noticed a ring on the third finger of her left hand.

I went straight from that house to Burry Mills Hydro, keen for the first time in my life on playing golf, which is guaranteed to occupy the mind. Baxter had taken me a room communicating with his own, and after lunch introduced me to a tall, horse-headed elderly lady of decided manners, whom a white-haired maid pushed along in a bath-chair through the park-like grounds of the Hydro. She was Miss Mary Moultrie, and she coughed and cleared her throat just like Baxter. She suffered—she told me it was the Moultrie caste-mark—from some obscure form of chronic bronchitis, complicated with spasm of the glottis; and, in a dead flat voice, with a sunken eye that looked and saw not, told me what washes, gargles, pastilles, and inhalations she had proved most beneficial. From her I was passed on to her younger sister, Miss Elizabeth, a small and withered thing with twitching lips, victim, she told me, to very much the same sort of throat, but secretly devoted to another set of medicines. When she went away with Baxter and the bath-chair, I fell across a major of the Indian army with gout in his glassy eyes, and a stomach which he had taken all round the Continent. He laid everything before me; and him I escaped only to be confided in by a matron with a tendency to follicular tonsilitis and eczema. Baxter waited hand and foot on his cousins till five o'clock, trying, as I saw, to atone for his treatment of the dead sister. Miss Mary ordered him about like a dog.

"I warned you it would be dull," he said when we met in the smoking-room.

"It's tremendously interesting," I said. "But how about a look round the links?"

"Unluckily damp always affects my eldest cousin. I've got to buy her a new bronchitis-kettle. Arthurs broke her old one yesterday."

We slipped out to the chemist's shop in the town, and he bought a large glittering tin thing whose workings he explained.

"I'm used to this sort of work. I come up here pretty often," he said. "I've the family throat too."

"You're a good man," I said. "A very good man."

He turned towards me in the evening light among the beeches, and his face was changed to what it might have been a generation before.

"You see," he said huskily, "there was the youngest—Agnes. Before she fell ill, you know. But she didn't like leaving her sisters. Never would." He hurried on with his odd-shaped load and left me among the ruins of my black theories. The man with that face had done Agnes Moultrie no wrong.

We never played our game. I was waked between two and three in the morning from my hygienic bed by Baxter in an ulster over orange and white pyjamas, which I should never have suspected from his character.

"My cousin has had some sort of a seizure," he said. "Will you come? I don't want to wake the doctor. Don't want to make a scandal. Quick!"

So I came quickly, and led by the white-haired Arthurs in a jacket and petticoat, entered a double-bedded room reeking with steam and Friar's Balsam. The electrics were all on. Miss Mary—I knew her by her height—was at the open window, wrestling with Miss Elizabeth, who gripped her round the knees. Her hand was at her throat, which was streaked with blood.

"She's done it. She's done it too!" Miss Elizabeth panted. "Hold her! Help me!"

"Oh, I say! Women don't cut their throats," Baxter whispered.

"My God! Has she cut her throat?" the maid cried, and with no warning rolled over in a faint. Baxter pushed her under the wash-basins, and leaped to hold the gaunt woman who crowed and whistled as she struggled towards the window. He took her by the shoulder, and she struck out wildly.

"All right! She's only cut her hand," he said. "Wet towel—quick!"

While I got that he pushed her backward. Her strength seemed almost as great as his. I swabbed at her throat when I could, and found no mark; then helped him to control her a little. Miss Elizabeth leaped back to bed, wailing like a child.

"Tie up her hand somehow," said Baxter. "Don't let it drip about the place. She"—he stepped on broken glass in his slippers, "she must have smashed a pane."

Miss Mary lurched towards the open window again, dropped

on her knees, her head on the sill, and lay quiet, surrendering the cut hand to me.

"What did she do?" Baxter turned towards Miss Elizabeth in the far bed.

"She was going to throw herself out of the window," was the answer. "I stopped her, and sent Arthurs for you. Oh, we can never hold up our heads again!"

Miss Mary writhed and fought for breath. Baxter found a shawl which he threw over her shoulders.

"Nonsense!" said he. "That isn't like Mary"; but his face worked when he said it.

"You wouldn't believe about Aggie, John. Perhaps you will now!" said Miss Elizabeth. "I *saw* her do it, and she's cut her throat too!"

"She hasn't," I said. "It's only her hand."

Miss Mary suddenly broke from us with an indescribable grunt, flew, rather than ran, to her sister's bed, and there shook her as one furious schoolgirl would shake another.

"No such thing," she croaked. "How dare you think so, you wicked little fool?"

"Get into bed, Mary," said Baxter. "You'll catch a chill."

She obeyed, but sat up with the grey shawl round her lean shoulders, glaring at her sister. "I'm better now," she crowed. "Arthurs let me sit out too long. Where's Arthurs? The kettle."

"Never mind Arthurs," said Baxter. "*You* get the kettle." I hastened to bring it from the side table. "Now Mary, as God sees you, tell me what you've done."

His lips were dry, and he could not moisten them with his tongue.

Miss Mary applied herself to the mouth of the kettle, and between indraws of steam said: "The spasm came on just now, while I was asleep. I was nearly choking to death. So I went to the window. I've done it often before, without waking any one. Bessie's such an old maid about drafts. I tell you I was choking to death. I couldn't manage the catch, and I nearly fell out. That window opens too low. I cut my hand trying to save myself. Who has tied it up in this filthy handkerchief? I wish you had had my throat, Bessie. I never was nearer dying!" She scowled on us all impartially, while her sister sobbed.

From the bottom of the bed we heard a quivering voice: "Is she dead? Have they took her away? Oh, I never could bear the sight o' blood!"

"Arthurs," said Miss Mary, "you are an hireling. Go away!"

It is my belief that Arthurs crawled out on all fours, but I was busy picking up broken glass from the carpet.

Then Baxter, seated by the side of the bed, began to cross-examine in a voice I scarcely recognized. No one could for an instant have doubted the genuine rage of Miss Mary against her sister, her cousin, or her maid; and that the doctor should have been called in—for she did me the honor of calling me doctor—was the last drop. She was choking with her throat; had rushed to the window for air; had near pitched out, and in catching at the window bars had cut her hand. Over and over she made this clear to the intent Baxter. Then she turned on her sister and tongue-lashed her savagely.

"You mustn't blame me," Miss Bessie faltered at last. "You know what we think of night and day."

"I'm coming to that," said Baxter. "Listen to me. What *you* did, Mary, misled four people into thinking you—you meant to do away with yourself."

"Isn't one suicide in the family enough? Oh God, help and pity us! You *couldn't* have believed that!" she cried.

"The evidence was complete. Now, don't you think," Baxter's finger wagged under her nose—"*can't* you think that poor Aggie did the same thing at Holmescroft when she fell out of the window?"

"She had the same throat," said Miss Elizabeth. "Exactly the same symptoms. Don't you remember, Mary?"

"Which was her bedroom?" I asked of Baxter in an undertone.

"Over the south verandah, looking on to the tennis lawn."

"I nearly fell out of that very window when I was at Holmescroft—opening it to get some air. The sill doesn't come much above your knees," I said.

"You hear that, Mary? Mary, do you hear what this gentleman says? Won't you believe that what nearly happened to you must have happened to poor Aggie that night? For God's sake—for her sake—Mary, *won't* you believe?"

There was a long silence while the steam kettle puffed.

"If I could have proof—if I could have proof," said she, and broke into most horrible tears.

Baxter motioned to me, and I crept away to my room, and lay

awake till morning, thinking more specially of the dumb Thing at Holmescroft which wished to explain itself. I hated Miss Mary as perfectly as though I had known her for twenty years, but I felt that, alive or dead, I should not like her to condemn me.

Yet at mid-day, when I saw Miss Mary in her bath-chair, Arthurs behind and Baxter and Miss Elizabeth on either side, in the park-like grounds of the Hydro, I found it difficult to arrange my words.

"Now that you know all about it," said Baxter aside, after the first strangeness of our meeting was over, "it's only fair to tell you that my poor cousin did not die in Holmescroft at all. She was dead when they found her under the window in the morning. Just dead."

"Under that laburnum outside the window?" I asked, for I suddenly remembered the crooked evil thing.

"Exactly. She broke the tree in falling. But no death has ever taken place *in* the house, so far as we were concerned. You can make yourself quite easy on that point. Mr. McLeod's extra thousand for what you called the 'clean bill of health' was something towards my cousins' estate when we sold. It was my duty as their lawyer to get it for them—at any cost to my own feelings."

I know better than to argue when the English talk about their duty. So I agreed with my solicitor.

"Their sister's death must have been a great blow to your cousins," I went on. The bath-chair was behind me.

"Unspeakable," Baxter whispered. "They brooded on it day and night. No wonder. If their theory of poor Aggie making away with herself was correct, she was eternally lost!"

"Do you believe that she made away with herself?"

"No, thank God! Never have! And after what happened to Mary last night, I see perfectly what happened to poor Aggie. She had the family throat too. By the way, Mary thinks you are a doctor. Otherwise she wouldn't like your having been in her room."

"Very good. Is she convinced now about her sister's death?"

"She'd give anything to be able to believe it, but she's a hard woman, and brooding along certain lines makes one groovy. I have sometimes been afraid for her reason—on the religious side, don't you know. Elizabeth doesn't matter. Brain of a hen. Always had."

Here Arthurs summoned me to the bath-chair, and the ravaged face, beneath its knitted Shetland wool hood, of Miss Mary Moultrie.

"I need not remind you, I hope, of the seal of secrecy—absolute secrecy—in your profession," she began. "Thanks to my cousin's and my sister's stupidity, you have found out—" she blew her nose.

"Please don't excite her, sir," said Arthurs at the back.

"But, my dear Miss Moultrie, I only know what I've seen, of course, but it seems to me that what you thought was a tragedy in your sister's case, turns out, on your own evidence, so to speak, to have been an accident—a dreadfully sad one—but absolutely an accident."

"Do you believe that too?" she cried. "Or are you only saying it to comfort me?"

"I believe it from the bottom of my heart. Come down to Holmescroft for an hour—for half an hour—and satisfy yourself."

"Of what? You don't understand. I see the house every day—every night. I am always there in spirit—waking or sleeping. I couldn't face it in reality."

"But you must," I said. "If you go there in the spirit the greater need for you to go there in the flesh. Go to your sister's room once more, and see the window—I nearly fell out of it myself. It's—it's awfully low and dangerous. That would convince you," I pleaded.

"Yet Aggie had slept in that room for years," she interrupted.

"You've slept in your room here for a long time, haven't you? But you nearly fell out of the window when you were choking."

"That is true. That is one thing true," she nodded. "And I might have been killed as—perhaps—Aggie was killed."

"In that case your own sister and cousin and maid would have said you had committed suicide, Miss Moultrie. Come down to Holmescroft, and go over the place just once."

"You are lying," she said quite quietly. "You don't want me to come down to see a window. It is something else. I warn you we are Evangelicals. We don't believe in prayers for the dead. 'As the tree falls—' "

"Yes. I daresay. But you persist in thinking that your sister committed suicide—"

"No! No! I have always prayed that I might have misjudged her."

Arthurs at the bath-chair spoke up: "Oh, Miss Mary! you *would* 'ave it from the first that poor Miss Aggie 'ad made away with herself; an', of course, Miss Bessie took the notion from you. Only Master—Mister John stood out, and—and I'd 'ave taken my Bible oath *you* was making away with yourself last night."

Miss Mary leaned towards me, one finger on my sleeve.

"If going to Holmescroft kills me," she said, "you will have the murder of a fellow-creature on your conscience for all eternity."

"I'll risk it," I answered. Remembering what torment the mere reflection of her torments had cast on Holmescroft, and remembering, above all, the dumb Thing that filled the house with its desire to speak, I felt that there might be worse things.

Baxter was amazed at the proposed visit, but at a nod from that terrible woman went off to make arrangements. Then I sent a telegram to McLeod bidding him and his vacate Holmescroft for that afternoon. Miss Mary should be alone with her dead, as I had been alone.

I expected untold trouble in transporting her, but to do her justice, the promise given for the journey, she underwent it without murmur, spasm, or unnecessary word. Miss Bessie, pressed in a corner by the window, wept behind her veil, and from time to time tried to take hold of her sister's hand. Baxter wrapped himself in his newly-found happiness as selfishly as a bridegroom, for he sat still and smiled.

"So long as I know that Aggie didn't make away with herself," he explained, "I tell you frankly I don't care what happened. She's as hard as a rock—Mary. Always was. *She* won't die."

We led her out on to the platform like a blind woman, and so got her into the fly. The half-hour crawl to Holmescroft was the most racking experience of the day. McLeod had obeyed my instructions. There was no one visible in the house or the gardens; and the front door stood open.

Miss Mary rose from beside her sister, stepped forth first, and entered the hall.

"Come, Bessie," she cried.

"I daren't. Oh, I daren't."

"Come!" Her voice had altered. I felt Baxter start. "There's nothing to be afraid of."

"Good heavens!" said Baxter. "She's running up the stairs. We'd better follow."

"Let's wait below. She's going to the room."

We heard the door of the bedroom I knew open and shut, and we waited in the lemon-colored hall, heavy with the scent of flowers.

"I've never been into it since it was sold," Baxter sighed. "What a lovely restful place it is! Poor Aggie used to arrange the flowers."

"Restful?" I began, but stopped of a sudden, for I felt all over my bruised soul that Baxter was speaking truth. It was a light, spacious, airy house, full of the sense of well-being and peace—above all things, of peace. I ventured into the dining-room where the thoughtful McLeods had left a small fire. There was no terror there, present or lurking; and in the drawing-room, which for good reasons we had never cared to enter, the sun and the peace and the scent of the flowers worked together as is fit in an inhabited house. When I returned to the hall, Baxter was sweetly asleep on a couch, looking most unlike a middle-aged solicitor who had spent a broken night with an exacting cousin.

There was ample time for me to review it all—to felicitate myself upon my magnificent acumen (barring some errors about Baxter as a thief and possibly a murderer), before the door above opened, and Baxter, evidently a light sleeper, sprang awake.

"I've had a heavenly little nap," he said, rubbing his eyes with the backs of his hands like a child. "Good Lord! That's not *their* step!"

But it was. I had never before been privileged to see the Shadow turned backward on the dial—the years ripped bodily off poor human shoulders—old sunken eyes filled and alight—harsh lips moistened and human.

"John," Miss Mary called, "I know now. Aggie didn't do it!" and "She didn't do it!" echoed Miss Bessie, and giggled.

"I did not think it wrong to say a prayer," Miss Mary continued. "Not for her soul, but for our peace. Then I was convinced."

"Then we got conviction," the younger sister piped.

"We've misjudged poor Aggie, John. But I feel she knows now. Wherever she is, she knows that we know she is guiltless."

"Yes, she knows. I felt it too," said Miss Elizabeth.

"I never doubted," said John Baxter, whose face was beautiful at that hour. "Not from the first. Never have!"

"You never offered me proof, John. Now, thank God, it will not be the same any more. I can think henceforward of Aggie without sorrow." She tripped, absolutely tripped, across the hall. "What ideas these Jews have of arranging furniture!" She spied me behind a big cloisonné vase.

"I've seen the window," she said remotely. "You took a great risk in advising me to undertake such a journey. However, as it turns out . . . I forgive you, and I pray you may never know what mental anguish means! Bessie! Look at this peculiar piano! Do you suppose, Doctor, these people would offer one tea? I miss mine."

"I will go and see," I said, and explored McLeod's new-built servants' wing. It was in the servants' hall that I unearthed the McLeod family, bursting with anxiety.

"Tea for three, quick," I said. "If you ask me any questions now, I shall have a fit!" So Mrs. McLeod got it, and I was butler, amid murmured apologies from Baxter, still smiling and self-absorbed, and the cold disapproval of Miss Mary, who thought the pattern of the china vulgar. However, she ate well, and even asked me whether I would not like a cup of tea for myself.

They went away in the twilight—the twilight that I had once feared. They were going to an hotel in London to rest after the fatigues of the day, and as their fly turned down the drive, I capered on the doorstep, with the all-darkened house behind me.

Then I heard the uncertain feet of the McLeods, and bade them not to turn on the lights, but to feel—to feel what I had done; for the Shadow was gone, with the dumb desire in the air. They drew short, but afterwards deeper, breaths, like bathers entering chill water, separated one from the other, moved about the hall, tiptoed upstairs, raced down, and then Miss McLeod, and I believe her mother, though she denies this, embraced me. I know McLeod did.

It was a disgraceful evening. To say we rioted through the house is to put it mildly. We played a sort of Blind Man's Buff along the darkest passages, in the unlighted drawing-room, and little dining-room, calling cheerily to each other after each exploration that here, and here, and here, the trouble had removed itself. We came up to *the* bedroom—mine for the night again—and sat, the women on the bed, and we men on chairs, drinking in blessed drafts of peace and comfort and cleanliness of soul, while I told them my tale in full, and received fresh praise, thanks, and blessings.

When the servants, returned from their day's outing, gave us a supper of cold fried fish, McLeod had sense enough to open no wine. We had been practically drunk since nightfall, and grew incoherent on water and milk.

"I like that Baxter," said McLeod. "He's a sharp man. The death wasn't in the house, but he ran it pretty close, ain't it?"

"And the joke of it is that he supposes I want to buy the place from you," I said. "Are you selling?"

"Not for twice what I paid for it—now," said McLeod. "I'll keep you in furs all your life, but not our Holmescroft."

"No—never our Holmescroft," said Miss McLeod. "We'll ask *him* here on Tuesday, mamma." They squeezed each other's hands.

"Now tell me," said Mrs. McLeod—"that tall one I saw out of the scullery window—did *she* tell you she was always here in the spirit? I hate her. She made all this trouble. It was not her house after she had sold it. What do you think?"

"I suppose," I answered, "she brooded over what she believed was her sister's suicide night and day—she confessed she did—and her thoughts being concentrated on this place, they felt like a—like a burning glass."

"Burning glass is good," said McLeod.

"I said it was like a light of blackness turned on us," cried the girl, twiddling her ring. "That must have been when the tall one thought worst about her sister and the house."

"Ah, the poor Aggie!" said Mrs. McLeod. "The poor Aggie, trying to tell every one it was not so! No wonder we felt Something wished to say Something. Thea, Max, do you remember that night—"

"We need not remember any more," McLeod interrupted. "It is not our trouble. They have told each other now."

"Do you think, then," said Miss McLeod, "that those two, the living ones, were actually told something—upstairs—in your—in the room?"

"I can't say. At any rate they were made happy, and they ate a big tea afterwards. As your father says, it is not our trouble any longer—thank God!"

"Amen!" said McLeod. "Now, Thea, let us have some music

after all these months. 'With mirth, thou pretty bird,' ain't it? You ought to hear that."

And in the half-lighted hall, Thea sang an old English song that I had never heard before.

> "With mirth, thou pretty bird, rejoice
>   Thy Maker's praise enhanced;
> Lift up thy shrill and pleasant voice,
>   Thy God is high advanced!
> Thy food before He did provide,
> And gives it in a fitting side,
>   Wherewith be thou sufficed!
> Why shouldst thou now unpleasant be,
>   Thy wrath against God venting,
> That He a little bird made thee,
>   Thy silly head tormenting,
> Because He made thee not a man?
> Oh, Peace! He hath well thought thereon,
>   Therewith be thou sufficed!"

The Knife and the Naked Chalk

FROM *REWARDS AND FAIRIES* (1910)

No selection of Kipling's fantasies would be complete without one of the stories in which Puck introduces Dan and Una (children modeled on RK's own) to characters from England's past. Having been much tempted by at least two of those in *Puck of Pook's Hill*, I finally settled on this, because I know of few other works of fiction which in so narrow a compass successfully depict what it was like to live in a world where the Old Gods—in this case what the Scandinavians called the Æsir—were still worshipped. Perhaps RK's experiences in India, where the supernatural seems so much more immanent than in our cold western civilization, gave him the key to open this particular door to . . . I was about to say history, but strictly this tale is set in prehistoric times.

One might perhaps quibble that the People of the Chalk were unlikely to have known Tyr under that name, for it probably came into England with the folk who also bestowed their own name on the land they occupied, the Angles; previously the whole island had been known as Britain. But as Brian Branston shows in his study *The Lost Gods of England*, Tyr is one variant among many of a word that originally meant "resplendent, shining" and eventually came to signify just a god, or even God. So at least they could have been acquainted with his legend. Note, too, that the priestess of the Children of the Night says bluntly, "The God needs a proof."

It must be a terrible thing to find that the people you were born and grew up among will no longer treat you as one of themselves . . .

The Weald was formerly dense forest (cf. German *Wald*). "Bivvering" must be a dialect word; it is not in *O.E.D.* A dew-pond is a hollow in the ground water-proofed by lining it with clay. "Baff" in this case = pat; in golf it means to undercut and lift the ball (cf. the old name for one of the woods, a baffy).

The Knife and the Naked Chalk

THE RUN OF THE DOWNS

The Weald is good, the Downs are best
I'll give you the run of 'em, East to West.
Beachy Head and Winddoor Hill,
They were once and they are still.
Firle, Mount Caburn and Mount Harry
Go back as far as sums'll carry.
Ditchling Beacon and Chanctonbury Ring,
They have looked on many a thing;
And what those two have missed between 'em
I reckon Truleigh Hill has seen 'em.
Highden, Bignor and Duncton Down
Knew Old England before the Crown.
Linch Down, Treyford and Sunwood
Knew Old England before the Flood.
And when you end on the Hampshire side—
Butser's old as Time and Tide.
The Downs are sheep, the Weald is corn,
You be glad you are Sussex born!

The children went to the seaside for a month, and lived in a flint village on the bare windy chalk Downs, quite thirty miles away from home. They made friends with an old shepherd, called Mr. Dudeney, who had known their Father when their Father was little. He did not talk like their own people in the Weald of Sussex, and he used different names for farm things, but he understood how they felt, and let them go with him. He had a tiny cottage about half a mile from the village, where his wife made mead from thyme honey, and nursed sick lambs in front of a coal fire, while Old Jim, who was Mr. Dudeney's sheep-dog's father, lay at the door. They brought up beef bones for Old Jim (you must never give a sheep-dog mutton bones), and if Mr. Dudeney happened to be far in the Downs, Mrs. Dudeney would tell the dog to take them to him, and he did.

One August afternoon when the village water-cart had made the street smell specially townified, they went to look for their shepherd as usual, and, as usual, Old Jim crawled over the door-step and took them in charge. The sun was hot, the dry grass was very slippery, and the distances were very distant.

"It's just like the sea," said Una, when Old Jim halted in the shade of a lonely flint barn on a bare rise. "You see where you're going, and—you go there, and there's nothing between."

Dan slipped off his shoes. "When we get home I shall sit in the woods all day," he said.

"Whuff!" said Old Jim, to show he was ready, and struck across a long rolling stretch of turf. Presently he asked for his beef bone.

"Not yet," said Dan. "Where's Mr. Dudeney? Where's Master?"

Old Jim looked as if he thought they were mad, and asked again.

"Don't you give it him," Una cried. "I'm not going to be left howling in a desert."

"Show, boy! Show!" said Dan, for the Downs seemed as bare as the palm of your hand.

Old Jim sighed, and trotted forward. Soon they spied the blob of Mr. Dudeney's hat against the sky a long way off.

"Right! All right!" said Dan. Old Jim wheeled round, took his bone carefully between his blunted teeth, and returned to the shadow of the old barn, looking just like a wolf. The children went on. Two kestrels hung bivvering and squealing above them. A gull flapped lazily along the white edge of the cliffs. The curves of the Downs shook a little in the heat, and so did Mr. Dudeney's distant head.

They walked toward it very slowly and found themselves staring into a horseshoe-shaped hollow a hundred feet deep, whose steep sides were laced with tangled sheep-tracks. The flock grazed on the flat at the bottom, under charge of Young Jim. Mr. Dudeney sat comfortably knitting on the edge of the slope, his crook between his knees. They told him what Old Jim had done.

"Ah, he thought you could see my head as soon as he did. The closeter you be to the turf the more you see things. You look warm-like," said Mr. Dudeney.

"We be," said Una, flopping down. "*And* tired."

"Set beside o' me here. The shadow'll begin to stretch out in a little while, and a heat-shake o' wind will come up with it that'll overlay your eyes like so much wool."

"We don't want to sleep," said Una indignantly; but she settled herself as she spoke, in the first strip of early afternoon shade.

"O' course not. You come to talk with me same as your father used. *He* didn't need no dog to guide him to Norton Pit."

"Well, he belonged here," said Dan, and laid himself down at length on the turf.

"He did. And what beats me is why he went off to live among them messy trees in the Weald, when he might ha' stayed here and looked all about him. There's no profit to trees. They draw the lightning, and sheep shelter under 'em, and *so,* like as not, you'll lose a half-score ewes struck dead in one storm. Tck! Your father knew that."

"Trees aren't messy." Una rose on her elbow. "And what about firewood? I don't like coal."

"Eh? You lie a piece more uphill and you'll lie more natural," said Mr. Dudeney, with his provoking deaf smile. "Now press your face down and smell to the turf. That's Southdown thyme which makes our Southdown mutton beyond compare, and, my mother told me, 'twill cure anything except broken necks, or hearts. I forget which."

They sniffed, and somehow forgot to lift their cheeks from the soft thymy cushions.

"You don't get nothing like that in the Weald. Watercress, maybe?" said Mr. Dudeney.

"But we've water—brooks full of it—where you paddle in hot weather," Una replied, watching a yellow-and-violet-banded snail-shell close to her eye.

"Brooks flood. Then you must shift your sheep—let alone foot-rot afterward. I put more dependence on a dew-pond any day."

"How's a dew-pond made?" said Dan, and tilted his hat over his eyes. Mr. Dudeney explained.

The air trembled a little as though it could not make up its mind whether to slide into the Pit or move across the open. But it seemed easiest to go downhill, and the children felt one soft puff after another slip and sidle down the slope in fragrant breaths that baffed on their eyelids. The little whisper of the sea by the cliffs joined with the whisper of the wind over the grass, the hum of insects in the thyme, the ruffle and rustle of the flock below, and a thickish mutter deep in the very chalk beneath them. Mr. Dudeney stopped explaining, and went on with his knitting.

They were roused by voices. The shadow had crept half-way down the steep side of Norton Pit, and on the edge of it, his back to them, Puck sat beside a half-naked man who seemed busy at some work. The wind had dropped, and in that funnel of ground every least noise and movement reached them like whispers up a water-pipe.

"That is clever," said Puck, leaning over. "How truly you shape it!"

"Yes, but what does The Beast care for a brittle flint tip? Bah!" The man flicked something contemptuously over his shoulder. It fell between Dan and Una—a beautiful dark-blue flint arrowhead still hot from the maker's hand.

The man reached for another stone, and worked away like a thrush with a snail-shell.

"Flint work is fool's work," he said at last. "One does it because one always did it; but when it comes to dealing with The Beast—no good!" He shook his shaggy head.

"The Beast was dealt with long ago. He has gone," said Puck.

"He'll be back at lambing-time. *I* know him." He chipped very carefully, and the flints squeaked.

"Not he. Children can lie out on the Chalk now all day through and go home safe."

"Can they? Well, call The Beast by his True Name, and I'll believe it," the man replied.

"Surely!" Puck leaped to his feet, curved his hands round his mouth and shouted: "Wolf! Wolf!"

Norton Pit threw back the echo from its dry sides—"Wuff! Wuff!" like Young Jim's bark.

"You see? You hear?" said Puck. "Nobody answers. Grey Shepherd is gone. Feet-in-the-Night has run off. There are no more wolves."

"Wonderful!" The man wiped his forehead as though he were hot. "Who drove him away? You?"

"Many men through many years, each working in his own country. Were you one of them?" Puck answered.

The man slid his sheepskin cloak to his waist, and without a word pointed to his side, which was all seamed and blotched with scars. His arms, too, were dimpled from shoulder to elbow with horrible white dimples.

"I see," said Puck. "It is The Beast's mark. What did you use against him?"

"Hand, hammer, and spear, as our fathers did before us."

"So? Then how"—Puck twitched aside the man's dark-brown cloak—"how did a Flintworker come by *that*? Show, man, show!" He held out his little hand.

The man slipped a long dark iron knife, almost a short sword, from his belt, and after breathing on it, handed it hilt-first to Puck, who took it with his head on one side, as you should when you look at the works of a watch, squinted down the dark blade, and very delicately rubbed his forefinger from the point to the hilt.

"Good!" said he, in a surprised tone.

"It should be. The Children of the Night made it," the man answered.

"So I see by the iron. What might it have cost you?"

"This!" The man raised his hand to his cheek. Puck whistled like a Weald starling.

"By the Great Rings of the Chalk!" he cried. "Was *that* your price? Turn sunward that I may see better, and shut your eye."

He slipped his hand beneath the man's chin and swung him till he faced the children up the slope. They saw that his right eye was gone, and the eyelid lay shrunk. Quickly Puck turned him round again, and the two sat down.

"It was for the sheep. The sheep are the people," said the man, in an ashamed voice. "What else could I have done? *You* know, Old One."

Puck sighed a little fluttering sigh. "Take the knife. I listen."

The man bowed his head, drove the knife into the turf, and while it still quivered said: "This is witness between us that I speak the thing that has been. Before my Knife and the Naked Chalk I speak. Touch!"

Puck laid a hand on the hilt. It stopped shaking. The children wriggled a little nearer.

"I am of the People of the Worked Flint. I am the one son of the Priestess who sells the Winds to the Men of the Sea. I am the Buyer of the Knife—the Keeper of the People," the man began, in a sort of singing shout. "These are my names in this country of the Naked Chalk, between the Trees and the Sea."

"Yours was a great country. Your names are great too," said Puck.

"One cannot feed some things on names and songs." The man hit himself on the chest. "It is better—always better—to count one's children safe round the fire, their Mother among them."

"Ahai!" said Puck. "I think this will be a very old tale."

"I warm myself and eat at any fire that I choose, but there is no *one* to light me a fire or cook my meat. I sold all that when I bought the Magic Knife for my people. It was not right that The Beast should master man. What else could I have done?"

"I hear. I know. I listen," said Puck.

"When I was old enough to take my place in the Sheepguard, The Beast gnawed all our country like a bone between his teeth. He came in behind the flocks at watering-time, and watched them round the Dew-ponds; he leaped into the folds between our knees at the shearing; he walked out alongside the grazing flocks, and chose his meat on the hoof while our boys threw flints at him; he crept by night into the huts, and licked the babe from between the mother's hands; he called his companions and pulled down men in broad daylight on the Naked Chalk. No—not always did he do so! *this* was his cunning! He would go away for a while to let us forget him. A year—two years perhaps—we neither smelt, nor heard, nor saw him. When our flocks had increased; when our men did not always look behind them; when children strayed from the fenced places; when our women walked alone to draw water—back, back, back came the Curse of the Chalk, Grey Shepherd, Feet-in-the-Night—The Beast, The Beast, The Beast!

"He laughed at our little brittle arrows and our poor blunt spears. He learned to run in under the stroke of the hammer. I think he knew when there was a flaw in the flint. Often it does not show till you bring it down on his snout. Then—*Pouf!*—the false flint falls all to flinders, and you are left with the hammer-handle in your fist, and his teeth in your flank! I have felt them. At evening, too, in the dew, or when it has misted and rained, your spear-head lashings slack off, though you have kept them beneath your cloak all day. You are alone—but so close to the home ponds that you stop to tighten the sinews with hands, teeth, and a piece of driftwood. You bend over and pull—so! That is the minute for which he has followed you since the stars went out. 'Aarh!' he says. 'Wurr-aarh!' he says." (Norton Pit gave back the growl like a pack of real wolves.) "Then he is on your right shoulder feeling for the vein in your neck, and—perhaps your sheep run on without you. To fight The Beast is nothing, but to be despised by The Beast when he fights you—that is like his teeth in the heart! Old One, why is it that men desire so greatly, and can do so little?"

"I do not know. Did you desire so much?" said Puck.

"I desired to master The Beast. It is not right that The Beast should master man. But my people were afraid. Even my Mother, the Priestess, was afraid when I told her what I desired. We were accustomed to be afraid of The Beast. When I was made a man, and a maiden—she was a Priestess—waited for me at the Dew-ponds, The Beast flitted from off the Chalk. Perhaps it was a sickness; perhaps he had gone to his Gods to learn how to do us new harm. But he went, and we breathed more freely. The women sang again; the children were not so much guarded; our flocks grazed far out. I took mine yonder"—he pointed inland to the hazy line of the Weald—"where the new grass was best. They grazed north. I followed till we were close to the Trees"—he lowered his voice—"close *there* where the Children of the Night live." He pointed north again.

"Ah, now I remember a thing," said Puck. "Tell me, why did your people fear the Trees so extremely?"

"Because the Gods hate the Trees and strike them with lightning. We can see them burning for days all along the Chalk's edge. Besides, all the Chalk knows that the Children of the Night, though they worship our Gods, are magicians. When a man goes into their country, they change his spirit; they put words into his mouth; they make him like talking water. But a voice in my heart told me to go toward the north. While I watched my sheep there I saw three Beasts chasing a man, who ran toward the Trees. By this I knew he was a Child of the Night. We Flint-workers fear the Trees more than we fear The Beast. He had no hammer. He carried a knife like this one. A Beast leaped at him. He stretched out his knife. The Beast fell dead. The other Beasts ran away howling, which they would never have done from a Flint-worker. The man went in among the Trees. I looked for the dead Beast. He had been killed in a new way—by a single deep, clean cut, without bruise or tear, which had split his bad heart. Wonderful! So I saw that the man's knife was magic, and I thought how to get it—thought strongly how to get it.

"When I brought the flocks to the shearing, my Mother the Priestess asked me, 'What is the new thing which you have seen and I see in your face?' I said, 'It is a sorrow to me;' and she answered, 'All new things are sorrow. Sit in my place, and eat sorrow.' I sat down in her place by the fire, where she talks to the ghosts in winter, and two voices spoke in my heart. One voice said, 'Ask the Children of the Night for the Magic Knife. It is not fit that The Beast should master man.' I listened to that voice.

"One voice said, 'If you go among the Trees, the Children of the Night will change your spirit. Eat and sleep here.' The other voice said, 'Ask for the Knife.' I listened to that voice.

"I said to my Mother in the morning, 'I go away to find a thing for the people, but I do not know whether I shall return in my own shape.' She answered, 'Whether you live or die, or are made different, I am your Mother.' "

"True," said Puck. "The Old Ones themselves cannot change men's mothers even if they would."

"Let us thank the Old Ones! I spoke to my Maiden, the Priestess who waited for me at the Dew-ponds. She promised fine things too." The man laughed. "I went away to that place where I had seen the magician with the knife. I lay out two days on the short grass before I ventured among the Trees. I felt my way before me with a stick. I was afraid of the terrible talking Trees. I was afraid of the ghosts in the branches; of the soft ground underfoot; of the red and black waters. I was afraid, above all, of the Change. It came!"

They saw him wipe his forehead once again, and his strong back-muscles quivered till he laid his hand on the knife-hilt.

"A fire without a flame burned in my head; an evil taste grew in my mouth; my eyelids shut hot over my eyes; my breath was hot between my teeth, and my hands were like the hands of a stranger. I was made to sing songs and to mock the Trees, though I was afraid of them. At the same time I saw myself laughing, and I was very sad for this fine young man, who was myself. Ah! The Children of the Night know magic."

"I think that is done by the Spirits of the Mist. They change a man if he sleeps among them," said Puck. "Had you slept in any mists?"

"Yes—but *I* know it was the Children of the Night. After three days I saw a red light behind the Trees, and I heard a heavy noise. I saw the Children of the Night dig red stones from a hole, and lay them in fires. The stones melted like tallow, and the men beat the soft stuff with hammers. I wished to speak to these men, but the words were changed in my mouth, and all I could say was, 'Do not make that noise. It hurts my head.' By this I knew that I was bewitched, and I clung to the Trees, and prayed the Children of the Night to take off their spells. They were cruel. They asked me many questions which they would never allow me to answer. They changed my words between my teeth till I wept. Then they led me into a hut and covered the floor with hot stones and dashed water on the stones, and sang charms till the sweat poured off me like water. I slept. When I waked, my own spirit—not the strange, shouting thing—was back in my body, and I was like a cool bright stone on the shingle between the sea and the sunshine. The magicians came to hear me—women and men—each wearing a Magic Knife. Their Priestess was their Ears and their Mouth.

"I spoke. I spoke many words that went smoothly along like sheep in order when their shepherd, standing on a mound, can count those coming, and those far off getting ready to come. I asked for Magic Knives for my people. I said that my people would bring meat, and milk, and wool, and lay them in the short grass outside the Trees, if the Children of the Night would leave Magic Knives for our people to take away. They were pleased. Their Priestess said, 'For whose sake have you come?' I answered, 'The sheep are the people. If The Beast kills our sheep, our people die. So I come for a Magic Knife to kill The Beast.'

"She said, 'We do not know if our God will let us trade with the people of the Naked Chalk. Wait till we have asked.'

"When they came back from the Question-place (their Gods are our Gods), their Priestess said, 'The God needs a proof that your words are true.' I said, 'What is the proof?' She said, 'The God says that if you have come for the sake of your people you will give him your right eye to be put out; but if you have come for any other reason you will not give it. This proof is between you and the God. We ourselves are sorry.'

"I said, 'This is a hard proof. Is there no other road?'

"She said, 'Yes. You can go back to your people with your two eyes in your head if you choose. But then you will not get any Magic Knives for your people.'

"I said, 'It would be easier if I knew that I were to be killed.'

"She said, 'Perhaps the God knew this too. See! I have made my knife hot.'

"I said, 'Be quick, then!' With her knife heated in the flame she put out my right eye. She herself did it. I am the son of a Priestess. She was a Priestess. It was not work for any common man."

"True! Most true," said Puck. "No common man's work, that. And, afterwards?"

"Afterwards I did not see out of that eye any more. I found also that one eye does not tell you truly where things are. Try it!"

At this Dan put his hand over one eye, and reached for the flint arrow-head on the grass. He missed it by inches. "It's true," he whispered to Una. "You can't judge distances a bit with only one eye."

Puck was evidently making the same experiment, for the man laughed at him.

"I know it is so," said he. "Even now I am not always sure of my blow. I stayed with the Children of the Night till my eye healed. They said I was the son of Tyr, the God who put his right hand in a Beast's mouth. They showed me how they melted their red stone and made the Magic Knives of it. They told me the charms they sang over the fires and at the beatings. I can sing many charms." Then he began to laugh like a boy.

"I was thinking of my journey home," he said, "and of the surprised Beast. He had come back to the Chalk. I saw him—I smelt his lairs as soon as ever I left the Trees. He did not know I had the Magic Knife—I hid it under my cloak—the Knife that the Priestess gave me. Ho! Ho! That happy day was too short! See! A Beast would wind me. 'Wow!' he would say. 'Here is my Flint-worker!' He would come leaping, tail in air; he would roll; he would lay his head between his paws out of merriness of heart at his warm, waiting meal. He would leap—and, oh, his eye in mid-leap when he saw—when he saw the knife held ready for him! It pierced his hide as a rush pierces curdled milk. Often he had no time to howl. I did not trouble to flay any beasts I killed. Sometimes I missed my blow. Then I took my little flint hammer and beat out his brains as he cowered. He made no fight. He knew the Knife! But The Beast is very cunning. Before evening all The Beasts had smelt the blood on my knife, and were running from me like hares. *They* knew! Then I walked as a man should—the Master of The Beast!

"So came I back to my Mother's house. There was a lamb to be killed. I cut it in two halves with my knife, and I told her all my tale. She said, 'This is the work of a God.' I kissed her and laughed. I went to my Maiden who waited for me at the Dew-ponds. There was a lamb to be killed. I cut it in two halves with my knife, and told her all my tale. She said, 'It is the work of a God.' I laughed, but she pushed me away, and being on my blind side, ran off before I could kiss her. I went to the Men of the Sheepguard at watering-time. There was a sheep to be killed for their meat. I cut it in two halves with my knife, and told them all my tale. They said, 'It is the work of a God.' I said, 'We talk too much about Gods. Let us eat and be happy, and tomorrow I will take you to the Children of the Night, and each man will find a Magic Knife.'

"I was glad to smell our sheep again; to see the broad sky from edge to edge, and to hear the sea. I slept beneath the stars in my cloak. The men talked among themselves.

"I led them, the next day, to the Trees, taking with me meat, wool, and curdled milk, as I had promised. We found the Magic Knives laid out on the grass, as the Children of the Night had promised. They watched us from among the Trees. Their Priestess called to me and said, 'How is it with your people?' I said, 'Their hearts are changed. I cannot see their hearts as I used to.' She said, 'That is because you have only one eye. Come to me and I will be both your eyes.' But I said, 'I must show my people how to use their knives against The Beast, as you showed me how to use my knife.' I said this because the Magic Knife does not balance like the flint. She said, 'What you have done, you have done for the sake of a woman, and not for the sake of your people.' I asked of her, 'Then why did the God accept my right eye, and why are you so angry?' She answered, 'Because any man can lie to a God, but no man can lie to a woman. And I am not angry with you. I am only very sorrowful for you. Wait a little, and you will see out of your one eye why I am sorry.' So she hid herself.

"I went back with my people, each one carrying his Knife, and making it sing in the air—*tssee-sssse*. The Flint never sings. It mutters—*ump-ump*. The Beast heard. The Beast saw. *He* knew! Everywhere he ran away from us. We all laughed. As we walked over the grass my Mother's brother—the Chief on the Men's Side—he took off his Chief's necklace of yellow sea-stones."

"How? Eh? Oh, I remember! Amber," said Puck.

"And would have put them on my neck. I said, 'No, I am content. What does my one eye matter if my other eye sees fat sheep and fat children running about safely?' My Mother's brother said to them, 'I told you he would never take such things.' Then they began to sing a song in the Old Tongue—'The Song of Tyr.' I sang with them, but my Mother's brother said, 'This is *your* song, O Buyer of the Knife. Let *us* sing it, Tyr.'

"Even then I did not understand, till I saw that—that no man stepped on my shadow; and I knew that they thought me to be a God, like the God Tyr, who gave his right hand to conquer a Great Beast."

"By the Fire in the Belly of the Flint, was that so?" Puck rapped out.

"By my Knife and the Naked Chalk, so it was! They made way for my shadow as though it had been a Priestess walking to the Barrows of the Dead. I was afraid. I said to myself, 'My Mother and my Maiden will know I am not Tyr.' But *still* I was afraid, with the fear of a man who falls into a steep flint-pit while he runs, and feels that it will be hard to climb out.

"When we came to the Dew-ponds all our people were there. The men showed their knives and told their tale. The sheep-guards also had seen The Beast flying from us. The Beast went west across the river in packs—howling! He knew the Knife had come to the Naked Chalk at last—at last! *He* knew! So my work was done. I looked for my Maiden among the Priestesses. She looked at me, but she did not smile. She made the sign to me that our Priestesses must make when they sacrifice to the Old Dead in the Barrows. I would have spoken, but my Mother's brother made himself my Mouth, as though I had been one of the Old Dead in the Barrows for whom our Priests speak to the people on Midsummer Mornings."

"I remember. Well I remember those Midsummer Mornings!" said Puck.

"Then I went away angrily to my Mother's house. She would have knelt before me. Then I was more angry, but she said, 'Only a God would have spoken to me thus, a Priestess. A man would have feared the punishment of the Gods.' I looked at her and I laughed. I could not stop my unhappy laughing. They called me from the door by the name of Tyr himself. A young man with whom I had watched my first flocks, and chipped my first arrow, and fought my first Beast, called me by that name in the Old Tongue. He asked my leave to take my Maiden. His eyes were lowered, his hands were on his forehead. He was full of the fear of a God, but of *me,* a man, he had no fear when he asked. I did not kill him. I said, 'Call the maiden.' She came also without fear—this very one that had waited for me, that had talked with me, by our dew-ponds. Being a Priestess, she lifted her eyes to me. As I look on a hill or a cloud, so she looked at me. She spoke in the Old Tongue which Priestesses use when they make prayers to the Old Dead in the Barrows. She asked leave that she might light the fire in my companion's house—and that I should bless their children. I did not kill her. I heard my own voice, little and cold, say, 'Let it be as you desire,' and they went away hand in hand. My heart grew little and cold; a wind shouted in my ears; my eye darkened. I said to my Mother, 'Can a God die?' I heard her say, 'What is it? What is it, my son?' and I fell into darkness full of hammer-noises. I was not."

"Oh, poor—poor God!" said Puck. "And your wise Mother?"

"*She* knew. As soon as I dropped she knew. When my spirit came back I heard her whisper in my ear, 'Whether you live or die, or are made different, I am your Mother.' That was good—better even than the water she gave me and the going away of the sickness. Though I was ashamed to have fallen down, yet I was very glad. She was glad too. Neither of us wished to lose the other. There is only the one Mother for the one son. I heaped the fire for her, and barred the doors, and sat at her feet as before I went away, and she combed my hair, and sang.

"I said at last, 'What is to be done to the people who say that I am Tyr?'

"She said, 'He who has done a God-like thing must bear himself like a God. I see no way out of it. The people are now your sheep till you die. You cannot drive them off.'

"I said, 'This is a heavier sheep than I can lift.' She said, 'In time it will grow easy. In time perhaps you will not lay it down for any maiden anywhere. Be wise—be very wise, my son, for nothing is left you except the words, and the songs, and the worship of a God.' "

"Oh, poor God!" said Puck. "But those are not altogether bad things."

"I know they are not; but I would sell them all—all—all for one small child of my own, smearing himself with the ashes of our own house-fire."

He wrenched his knife from the turf, thrust it into his belt and stood up.

"And yet, what else could I have done?" he said. "The sheep are the people."

"It is a very old tale," Puck answered. "I have heard the like of it not only on the Naked Chalk, but also among the Trees—under Oak, and Ash, and Thorn."

The afternoon shadows filled all the quiet emptiness of Norton Pit. The children heard the sheep-bells and Young Jim's busy bark above them, and they scrambled up the slope to the level.

"We let you have your sleep out," said Mr. Dudeney, as the flock scattered before them. "It's making for tea-time now."

"Look what I've found," said Dan, and held up a little blue flint arrow-head as fresh as though it had been chipped that very day.

"Oh," said Mr. Dudeney, "the closeter you be to the turf the more you're apt to see things. I've found 'em often. Some says the fairies made 'em, but I say they was made by folks like ourselves—only a goodish time back. They're lucky to keep. Now, you couldn't ever have slept—not to any profit—among your father's trees same as you've laid out on Naked Chalk—could you?"

"One doesn't want to sleep in the woods," said Una.

"Then what's the good of 'em?" said Mr. Dudeney. "Might as well set in the barn all day. Fetch 'em 'long, Jim boy!"

The Downs, that looked so bare and hot when they came, were full of delicious little shadow-dimples; the smell of the thyme and the salt mixed together on the south-west drift from the still sea; their eyes dazzled with the low sun, and the long grass under it looked golden. The sheep knew where their fold was, so Young Jim came back to his master, and they all four strolled home, the scabious-heads swishing about their ankles, and their shadows streaking behind them like the shadows of giants.

SONG OF THE MEN'S SIDE

Once we feared The Beast—when he followed us we ran,
Ran very fast though we knew
It was not right that The Beast should master Man;
But what could we Flint-workers do?
The Beast only grinned at our spears round his ears—
Grinned at the hammers that we made;
But now we will hunt him for the life with the Knife—
And this is the Buyer of the Blade!

Room for his shadow on the grass—let it pass!
To left and right—stand clear!
This is the Buyer of the Blade—be afraid!
This is the great God Tyr!

Tyr thought hard till he hammered out a plan,
For he knew it was not right
(And it *is* not right) that The Beast should master Man;
So he went to the Children of the Night.
He begged a Magic Knife of their make for our sake.
When he begged for the Knife they said:
"The price of the Knife you would buy is an eye!"
And that was the price he paid.

Tell it to the Barrows of the Dead—run ahead!
Shout it so the Women's Side can hear!
This is the Buyer of the Blade—be afraid!
This is the great God Tyr!

Our women and our little ones may walk on the Chalk,
As far as we can see them and beyond.

We shall not be anxious for our sheep when we keep
  Tally at the shearing-pond.
We can eat with both our elbows on our knees, if we please,
  We can sleep after meals in the sun;
For Shepherd-of-the-Twilight is dismayed at the Blade,
  Feet-in-the-Night have run!
Dog-without-a-Master goes away (Hai, Tyr aie!),
  Devil-in-the-Dusk has run!

Then:

Room for his shadow on the grass—let it pass!
  To left and right—stand clear!
This is the Buyer of the Blade—be afraid!
  This is the great God Tyr!

The Village That Voted the Earth Was Flat

FROM *A DIVERSITY OF CREATURES* (1917)

A certain gentleman in New York, who nearly stood godfather to this and its companion collection, insisted that I absolutely *must* include this story.

My automatic reaction was to say, "Hang on a moment! That one isn't a fantasy." Luckily I stopped myself in time. Turning the matter over, I started to chuckle (I always chuckle when I think about "The Village That Voted") because I'd realized that the guy was right: it is indeed a fantasy, one of perhaps the very oldest kind.

It's a wish-fulfilment fantasy . . . and, into the bargain, it's one of the funniest stories ever written.

As you may guess, it first appeared before the Great War broke out—in 1913, to be precise.

Some of the material on which the story is based is strictly factual. There were indeed rural magistrates who set up "speed traps" for motorists exceeding the official limit, which at the time was twenty miles an hour. They are well described in *This Motoring* (1931), a history of the Automobile Association. Quote:

" 'Here! What about that new Act with the speed limits, and fines, and things? Get the Police to set traps and make the beggars pay. There's money in this.'

"There was!

"A measured furlong on a nice, straight piece of road, safe and tempting to the motorist. Two policemen in plain clothes, one at each end, with stop-watches—hiding. A third in uniform, beyond the end of the measured distance. The scene was set."

M.P. of course = Member of Parliament. An *auto-da-fé* was the punishment inflicted on heretics by the Spanish Inquisition. Music halls were variety (vaudeville) theatres; in his early days in London, Kipling patronized them regularly, and was extremely proud when a song he had written was performed at one called Gatti's.

I have no confirmatory evidence, but I suspect that the restaurant here called the Chop Suey must have been the Cathay in Glasshouse Street, just off Piccadilly Circus, where I ate my first Chinese meal. It had opened in 1908 and was the first Chinese restaurant in London's West End. Incidentally, it's still there.

Brasenose is an Oxford college. *Eheu ab angulo* means "Alas, from the corner," in the sense of a nook or chimney-corner, a place of retirement. *Non nobis gloria* = "not to us the glory" (Psalm 115). A panel doctor belonged to a group (a panel) that treated patients subscribing to a health insurance scheme, prior to the National Health Service. The forty oil "combinations" would have been patent stoves (cookers). "Nuts in May" is a children's singing game.

There are several references to Ireland in the story; it should be borne in mind that at this time there was much agitation for Home Rule (i.e., independence from the British government at Westminster) and tempers, even in Parliament, ran high when the matter was under discussion.

A *char-à-banc* was an open bus, originally horse-drawn. Helio = heliograph, a signaling device using reflected sunlight. *Margaritas ante Porcos* = pearls before swine. A motor-brake is what would now be called an estate car (U.S. station wagon); for Cook's, see notes to "The Gardener." A Radical was a member of the reformist wing of the Liberals, then one of the two major British political parties. Pallant, presumably, is a Conservative, opposing them. (RK's sympathies lay to that direction.) The Question that "there must be" is a formal question in the House of Commons. A cross-bencher is an independent M.P., not belonging to a party. And Antaeus was the giant in Greek mythology whose strength was renewed by touching his mother the Earth.

The Village That Voted the Earth Was Flat

Our drive till then had been quite a success. The other men in the car were my friend Woodhouse, young Ollyett, a distant connection of his, and Pallant, the M.P. Woodhouse's business was the treatment and cure of sick journals. He knew by instinct the precise moment in a newspaper's life when the impetus of past good management is exhausted and it fetches up on the dead-center between slow and expensive collapse and the new start which can be given by gold injections—and genius. He was wisely ignorant of journalism; but when he stooped on a carcass there was sure to be meat. He had that week added a half-dead, half-penny evening paper to his collection, which consisted of a prosperous London daily, one provincial ditto, and a limp-bodied weekly of commercial leanings. He had also, that very hour, planted me with a large block of the evening paper's common shares, and was explaining the whole art of editorship to Ollyett, a young man three years from Oxford, with coir-matting-colored hair and a face harshly modeled by harsh experiences, who, I understood, was assisting in the new venture. Pallant, the long, wrinkled M.P., whose voice is more like a crane's than a peacock's, took no shares, but gave us all advice.

"You'll find it rather a knacker's yard," Woodhouse was saying. "Yes, I know they call me The Knacker; but it will pay inside a year. All my papers do. I've only one motto: Back your luck and back your staff. It'll come out all right."

Then the car stopped, and a policeman asked our names and addresses for exceeding the speed-limit. We pointed out that the road ran absolutely straight for half a mile ahead without even a side-lane. "That's just what we depend on," said the policeman unpleasantly.

"The usual swindle," said Woodhouse under his breath. "What's the name of this place?"

"Huckley," said the policeman. "H-u-c-k-l-e-y," and wrote something in his note-book at which young Ollyett protested. A large red man on a grey horse who had been watching us from the other side of the hedge shouted an order we could not catch. The policeman laid his hand on the rim of the right driving-door (Woodhouse carries his spare tires aft), and it closed on the button of the electric horn. The grey horse at once bolted, and we could hear the rider swearing all across the landscape.

"Damn it, man, you've got your silly fist on it! Take it off!" Woodhouse shouted.

"Ho!" said the constable, looking carefully at his fingers as though we had trapped them. "That won't do you any good either," and he wrote once more in his note-book before he allowed us to go.

This was Woodhouse's first brush with motor law, and since I expected no ill consequences to myself, I pointed out that it was very serious. I took the same view myself when in due time I found that I, too, was summonsed on charges ranging from the use of obscene language to endangering traffic.

Judgment was done in a little pale-yellow market-town with a small Jubilee clock-tower and a large corn-exchange. Woodhouse drove us there in his car. Pallant, who had not been included in the summons, came with us as moral support. While we waited outside, the fat man on the grey horse rode up and entered into loud talk with his brother magistrates. He said to one of them—for I took the trouble to note it down—"It falls away from my lodge-gates, dead straight, three-quarters of a mile. I'd defy any one to resist it. We rooked seventy pounds out of 'em last month. No car can resist the temptation. You ought to have one your side the county, Mike. They simply can't resist it."

"Whew!" said Woodhouse. "We're in for trouble. Don't you say a word—or Ollyett either! I'll pay the fines and we'll get it over as soon as possible. Where's Pallant?"

"At the back of the court somewhere," said Ollyett. "I saw him slip in just now."

The fat man then took his seat on the Bench, of which he was chairman, and I gathered from a bystander that his name was Sir

Thomas Ingell, Bart., M.P., of Ingell Park, Huckley. He began with an allocution pitched in a tone that would have justified revolt throughout empires. Evidence, when the crowded little court did not drown it with applause, was given in the pauses of the address. They were all very proud of their Sir Thomas, and looked from him to us, wondering why we did not applaud too.

Taking its time from the chairman, the Bench rollicked with us for seventeen minutes. Sir Thomas explained that he was sick and tired of processions of cads of our type, who would be better employed breaking stones on the road than in frightening horses worth more than themselves or their ancestors. This was after it had been proved that Woodhouse's man had turned on the horn purposely to annoy Sir Thomas, who "happened to be riding by"! There were other remarks too—primitive enough,—but it was the unspeakable brutality of the tone, even more than the quality of the justice, or the laughter of the audience that stung our souls out of all reason. When we were dismissed—to the tune of twenty-three pounds, twelve shillings and sixpence—we waited for Pallant to join us, while we listened to the next case—one of driving without a license. Ollyett with an eye to his evening paper, had already taken very full notes of our own, but we did not wish to seem prejudiced.

"It's all right," said the reporter of the local paper soothingly. "We never report Sir Thomas *in extenso*. Only the fines and charges."

"Oh, thank you," Ollyett replied, and I heard him ask who every one in court might be. The local reporter was very communicative.

The new victim, a large, flaxen-haired man in somewhat striking clothes, to which Sir Thomas, now thoroughly warmed, drew public attention, said that he had left his license at home. Sir Thomas asked him if he expected the police to go to his home address at Jerusalem to find it for him; and the court roared. Nor did Sir Thomas approve of the man's name, but insisted on calling him "Mr. Masquerader," and every time he did so, all his people shouted. Evidently this was their established *auto-da-fé*.

"He didn't summons me—because I'm in the House, I suppose. I think I shall have to ask a Question," said Pallant, reappearing at the close of the case.

"I think *I* shall have to give it a little publicity too," said Woodhouse. "We can't have this kind of thing going on, you know." His face was set and quite white. Pallant's, on the other hand, was black, and I know that my very stomach had turned with rage. Ollyett was dumb.

"Well, let's have lunch," Woodhouse said at last. "Then we can get away before the show breaks up."

We drew Ollyett from the arms of the local reporter, crossed the Market Square to the Red Lion and found Sir Thomas's "Mr. Masquerader" just sitting down to beer, beef and pickles.

"Ah!" said he, in a large voice. "Companions in misfortune. Won't you gentlemen join me?"

"Delighted," said Woodhouse. "What did you get?"

"I haven't decided. It might make a good turn, but—the public aren't educated up to it yet. It's beyond 'em. If it wasn't, that red dub on the Bench would be worth fifty a week."

"Where?" said Woodhouse. The man looked at him with unaffected surprise.

"At any one of My places," he replied. "But perhaps you live here?"

"Good heavens!" cried young Ollyett suddenly. "You *are* Masquerier, then? I thought you were!"

"Bat Masquerier." He let the words fall with the weight of an international ultimatum. "Yes, that's all I am. But you have the advantage of me, gentlemen."

For the moment, while we were introducing ourselves, I was puzzled. Then I recalled prismatic music-hall posters—of enormous acreage—that had been the unnoticed background of my visits to London for years past. Posters of men and women, singers, jongleurs, impersonators, and audacities of every draped and undraped brand, all moved on and off in London and the Provinces by Bat Masquerier—with the long wedge-tailed flourish following the final "r."

"*I* knew you at once," said Pallant, the trained M.P., and I promptly backed the lie. Woodhouse mumbled excuses. Bat Masquerier was not moved for or against us any more than the frontage of one of his own palaces.

"I always tell My people there's a limit to the size of the lettering," he said. "Overdo that and the ret'na doesn't take it in. Advertisin' is the most delicate of all the sciences."

"There's one man in the world who is going to get a little of it if I live for the next twenty-four hours," said Woodhouse, and explained how this would come about.

Masquerier stared at him lengthily with gun-metal-blue eyes.

"You mean it?" he drawled; the voice was as magnetic as the look.

"*I* do," said Ollyett. "That business of the horn alone ought to have him off the Bench in three months." Masquerier looked at him even longer than he had looked at Woodhouse.

"He told *me,*" he said suddenly, "that my home-address was Jerusalem. You heard that?"

"But it was the tone—the tone," Ollyett cried.

"You noticed that, too, did you?" said Masquerier. "That's the artistic temperament. You can do a lot with it. And I'm Bat Masquerier," he went on. He dropped his chin in his fists and scowled straight in front of him. . . . "I made the Silhouettes—I made the Trefoil and the Jocunda. I made 'Dal Benzaguen." Here Ollyett sat straight up, for in common with the youth of that year he worshiped Miss Vidal Benzaguen of the Trefoil immensely and unreservedly. " '*Is* that a dressing-gown or an ulster you're supposed to be wearing?' You heard *that?* . . . 'And I suppose you hadn't time to brush your hair either?' You heard *that?* . . . Now, you hear *me!*" His voice filled the coffee-room, then dropped to a whisper as dreadful as a surgeon's before an operation. He spoke for several minutes. Pallant muttered "Hear! hear!" I saw Ollyett's eye flash—it was to Ollyett that Masquerier addressed himself chiefly,—and Woodhouse leaned forward with joined hands.

"Are you *with* me?" he went on, gathering us all up in one sweep of the arm. "When I begin a thing I see it through, gentlemen. What Bat can't break, breaks him! But I haven't struck that thing yet. This is no one-turn turn-it-down show. This is business to the dead finish. Are you with me, gentlemen? Good! Now, we'll pool our assets. One London morning, and one provincial daily, didn't you say? One weekly commercial ditto and one M.P."

"Not much use, I'm afraid," Pallant smirked.

"But privileged. *But* privileged," he returned. "And we have also my little team—London, Blackburn, Liverpool, Leeds—I'll tell you about Manchester later—and Me! Bat Masquerier." He breathed the name reverently into his tankard. "Gentlemen, when our combination has finished with Sir Thomas Ingell, Bart., M.P., and everything else that is his, Sodom and Gomorrah will be a winsome bit of Merrie England beside 'em. I must go back to town now, but I trust you gentlemen will give me the pleasure of your company at dinner tonight at the Chop Suey—the Red Amber Room—and we'll block out the scenario." He laid his hand on young Ollyett's shoulder and added: "It's your brains I want." Then he left, in a good deal of astrakhan collar and nickel-plated limousine, and the place felt less crowded.

We ordered our car a few minutes later. As Woodhouse, Ollyett and I were getting in, Sir Thomas Ingell, Bart., M.P., came out of the Hall of Justice across the square and mounted his horse. I have sometimes thought that if he had gone in silence he might even then have been saved, but as he settled himself in the saddle he caught sight of us and must needs shout: "Not off yet? You'd better get away and you'd better be careful." At that moment Pallant, who had been buying picture-postcards, came out of the inn, took Sir Thomas's eye and very leisurely entered the car. It seemed to me that for one instant there was a shade of uneasiness on the baronet's grey-whiskered face.

"I hope," said Woodhouse after several miles, "I hope he's a widower."

"Yes," said Pallant. "For his poor, dear wife's sake I hope that, very much indeed. I suppose he didn't see me in Court. Oh, here's the parish history of Huckley written by the Rector and here's your share of the picture-postcards. Are we all dining with this Mr. Masquerier tonight?"

"Yes!" said we all.

If Woodhouse knew nothing of journalism, young Ollyett, who had graduated in a hard school, knew a good deal. Our halfpenny evening paper, which we will call *The Bun* to distinguish her from her prosperous morning sister, *The Cake,* was not only diseased but corrupt. We found this out when a man brought us the prospectus of a new oil-field and demanded sub-leaders on its prosperity. Ollyett talked pure Brasenose to him for three minutes. Otherwise he spoke and wrote trade-English—a toothsome amalgam of Americanisms and epigrams. But though the slang changes the game never alters, and Ollyett and I and, in the end, some others enjoyed it immensely. It was weeks ere we could see the wood for the trees, but so soon as the staff realized that they had proprietors who backed them right or wrong, and specially when they were wrong (which is the sole secret of journalism), and that their fate did not hang on any passing owner's passing mood, they did miracles.

But we did not neglect Huckley. As Ollyett said our first care was to create an "arresting atmosphere" round it. He used to visit the village of week-ends, on a motor-bicycle with a side-car; for which reason I left the actual place alone and dealt with it in the abstract. Yet it was I who drew first blood. Two inhabitants of Huckley wrote to contradict a small, quite solid paragraph in *The Bun* that a hoopoe had been seen at Huckley and had, "of course, been shot by the local sportsmen." There was some heat in their letters, both of which we published. Our version of how the hoopoe got his crest from King Solomon was, I grieve to say, so inaccurate that the Rector himself—no sportsman as he pointed out, but a lover of accuracy—wrote to us to correct it. We gave his letter good space and thanked him.

"This priest is going to be useful," said Ollyett. "He has the impartial mind. I shall vitalize him."

Forthwith he created M. L. Sigden, a recluse of refined tastes who in *The Bun* demanded to know whether this Huckley-of-the-Hoopoe was the Hugly of his boyhood and whether, by any chance, the fell change of name had been wrought by collusion between a local magnate and the railway, in the mistaken interests of spurious refinement. "For I knew it and loved it with the maidens of my day—*eheu ab angulo!*—as Hugly," wrote M. L. Sigden from Oxford.

Though other papers scoffed, *The Bun* was gravely sympathetic. Several people wrote to deny that Huckley had been changed at birth. Only the Rector—no philosopher as he pointed out, but a lover of accuracy—had his doubts, which he laid publicly before Mr. M. L. Sigden, who suggested, through *The Bun,* that the little place might have begun life in Anglo-Saxon days as "Hogslea" or among the Normans as "Argilé," on account of its much clay. The Rector had his own ideas too (he said it was mostly gravel), and M. L. Sigden had a fund of reminiscences. Oddly enough—which is seldom the case with free reading-matter—our subscribers rather relished the correspondence, and contemporaries quoted freely.

"The secret of power," said Ollyett, "is not the big stick. It's the liftable stick." (This means the "arresting" quotation of six or seven lines.) "Did you see the *Spec.* had a middle on 'Rural Tenacities' last week? That was all Huckley. I'm doing a 'Mobiquity' on Huckley next week."

Our "Mobiquities" were Friday evening accounts of easy

motor-bike-*cum*-side-car trips round London, illustrated (we could never get that machine to work properly) by smudgy maps. Ollyett wrote the stuff with a fervor and a delicacy which I always ascribed to the side-car. His account of Epping Forest, for instance, was simply young love with its soul at its lips. But his Huckley "Mobiquity" would have sickened a soap-boiler. It chemically combined loathsome familiarity, leering suggestion, slimy piety and rancid "social service" in one fuming compost that fairly lifted me off my feet.

"Yes," said he, after compliments. "It's the most vital, arresting and dynamic bit of tump I've done up to date. *Non nobis gloria!* I met Sir Thomas Ingell in his own park. He talked to me again. He inspired most of it."

"Which? The 'glutinous native drawl,' or 'the neglected adenoids of the village children'?" I demanded.

"Oh, no! That's only to bring in the panel doctor. It's the last flight we—I'm proudest of."

This dealt with "the crepuscular penumbra spreading her dim limbs over the boskage"; with "jolly rabbits"; with a herd of "gravid polled Angus"; and with the "arresting, gipsy-like face of their swart, scholarly owner—as well known at the Royal Agricultural Shows as that of our late King-Emperor."

" 'Swart' is good and so's 'gravid,' " said I, "but the panel doctor will be annoyed about the adenoids."

"Not half as much as Sir Thomas will about his face," said Ollyett. "And if you only knew what I've left out!"

He was right. The panel doctor spent his weekend (this is the advantage of Friday articles) in overwhelming us with a professional counterblast of no interest whatever to our subscribers. We told him so, and he, then and there, battered his way with it into the *Lancet* where they are keen on glands, and forgot us altogether. But Sir Thomas Ingell was of sterner stuff. He must have spent a happy weekend too. The letter which we received from him on Monday proved him to be a kinless loon of upright life, for no woman, however remotely interested in a man, would have let it pass the home wastepaper-basket. He objected to our references to his own herd, to his own labors in his own village, which he said was a Model Village, and to our infernal insolence; but he objected most to our invoice of his features. We wrote him courteously to ask whether the letter was meant for publication.

He, remembering, I presume, the Duke of Wellington, wrote back, "publish and be damned."

"Oh! This is too easy," Ollyett said as he began heading the letter.

"Stop a minute," I said. "The game is getting a little beyond us. Tonight's the Bat dinner." (I may have forgotten to tell you that our dinner with Bat Masquerier in the Red Amber Room of the Chop Suey had come to be a weekly affair.) "Hold it over till they've all seen it."

"Perhaps you're right," he said. "You might waste it."

At dinner, then, Sir Thomas's letter was handed round. Bat seemed to be thinking of other matters, but Pallant was very interested.

"I've got an idea," he said presently. "Could you put something into *The Bun* tomorrow about foot-and-mouth disease in that fellow's herd?"

"Oh, plague if you like," Ollyett replied. "They're only five measly Shorthorns. I saw one lying down in the park. She'll serve as a sub-stratum of fact."

"Then, do that; and hold the letter over meanwhile. I think *I* come in here," said Pallant.

"Why?" said I.

"Because there's something coming up in the House about foot-and-mouth, and because he wrote me a letter after that little affair when he fined you. Took ten days to think it over. Here you are," said Pallant. "House of Commons paper, you see."

We read:

> DEAR PALLANT—Although in the past our paths have not lain much together, I am sure you will agree with me that on the floor of the House all members are on a footing of equality. I make bold, therefore, to approach you in a matter which I think capable of a very different interpretation from that which perhaps was put upon it by your friends. Will you let them know that that was the case and that I was in no way swayed by animus in the exercise of my magisterial duties, which as you, as a brother magistrate, can imagine are frequently very distasteful to—Yours very sincerely,
>
> T. INGELL

P.S.—I have seen to it that the motor vigilance to which your friends took exception has been considerably relaxed in my district.

"What did you answer?" said Ollyett, when all our opinions had been expressed.

"I told him I couldn't do anything in the matter. And I couldn't—then. But you'll remember to put in that foot-and-mouth paragraph. I want something to work upon."

"It seems to me *The Bun* has done all the work up to date," I suggested. "When does *The Cake* come in?"

"*The Cake,*" said Woodhouse, and I remembered afterwards that he spoke like a Cabinet Minister on the eve of a Budget, "reserves to itself the fullest right to deal with situations as they arise."

"Ye-eh!" Bat Masquerier shook himself out of his thoughts. " 'Situations as they arise.' I ain't idle either. But there's no use fishing till the swim's baited. You"—he turned to Ollyett—"manufacture very good ground-bait. . . . I always tell My people—— What the deuce is that?"

There was a burst of song from another private dining-room across the landing. "It ees some ladies from the Trefoil," the waiter began.

"Oh, I know that. What are they singing, though?"

He rose and went out, to be greeted by shouts of applause from that merry company. Then there was silence, such as one hears in the form-room after a master's entry. Then a voice that we loved began again: "Here we go gathering nuts in May—nuts in May—nuts in May!"

"It's only 'Dal—and some nuts," he explained when he returned. "She says she's coming in to dessert." He sat down, humming the old tune to himself, and till Miss Vidal Benzaguen entered, he held us speechless with tales of the artistic temperament.

We obeyed Pallant to the extent of slipping into *The Bun* a wary paragraph about cows lying down and dripping at the mouth, which might be read either as an unkind libel or, in the hands of a capable lawyer, as a piece of faithful nature-study.

"And besides," said Ollyett, "we allude to 'gravid polled Angus.' I am advised that no action can lie in respect of virgin

Shorthorns. Pallant wants us to come to the House tonight. He's got us places for the Strangers' Gallery. I'm beginning to like Pallant."

"Masquerier seems to like you," I said.

"Yes, but I'm afraid of him," Ollyett answered with perfect sincerity. "I am. He's the Absolutely Amoral Soul. I've never met one yet."

We went to the House together. It happened to be an Irish afternoon, and as soon as I had got the cries and the faces a little sorted out, I gathered there were grievances in the air, but how many of them was beyond me.

"It's all right," said Ollyett of the trained ear. "They've shut their ports against—oh yes—export of Irish cattle! Foot-and-mouth disease at Ballyhellion. *I* see Pallant's idea!"

The House was certainly all mouth for the moment, but, as I could feel, quite in earnest. A Minister with a piece of typewritten paper seemed to be fending off volleys of insults. He reminded me somehow of a nervous huntsman breaking up a fox in the face of rabid hounds.

"It's question-time. They're asking questions," said Ollyett. "Look! Pallant's up."

There was no mistaking it. His voice, which his enemies said was his one parliamentary asset, silenced the hubbub as tooth-ache silences mere singing in the ears. He said:

"Arising out of that, may I ask if any special consideration has recently been shown in regard to any suspected outbreak of this disease on *this* side of the Channel?"

He raised his hand; it held a noon edition of *The Bun*. We had thought it best to drop the paragraph out of the later ones. He would have continued, but something in a grey frock-coat roared and bounded on a bench opposite, and waved another *Bun*. It was Sir Thomas Ingell.

"As the owner of the herd so dastardly implicated—" His voice was drowned in shouts of 'Order!' "—the Irish leading.

"What's wrong?" I asked Ollyett. "He's got his hat on his head, hasn't he?"

"Yes, but his wrath should have been put as a question."

"Arising out of that, Mr. Speaker, Sirrr!" Sir Thomas bellowed through a lull, "are you aware that—that all this is a conspiracy—part of a dastardly conspiracy to make Huckley ridiculous—to make *us* ridiculous? Part of a deep-laid plot to make *me* ridiculous, Mr. Speaker, Sir!"

The man's face showed almost black against his white whiskers, and he struck out swimmingly with his arms. His vehemence puzzled and held the House for an instant, and the Speaker took advantage of it to lift his pack from Ireland to a new scent. He addressed Sir Thomas Ingell in tones of measured rebuke, meant also, I imagine, for the whole House, which lowered its hackles at the word. Then Pallant, shocked and pained: "I can only express my profound surprise that in response to my simple question the honorable member should have thought fit to indulge in a personal attack. If I have in any way offended—"

Again the Speaker intervened, for it appeared that he regulated these matters.

He, too, expressed surprise, and Sir Thomas sat back in a hush of reprobation that seemed to have the chill of the centuries behind it. The Empire's work was resumed.

"Beautiful!" said I, and I felt hot and cold up my back.

"And now we'll publish his letter," said Ollyett.

We did—on the heels of his carefully reported outburst. We made no comment. With that rare instinct for grasping the heart of a situation which is the mark of the Anglo-Saxon, all our contemporaries and, I should say, two-thirds of our correspondents demanded how such a person could be made more ridiculous than he had already proved himself to be. But beyond spelling his name "Injle," we alone refused to hit a man when he was down.

"There's no need," said Ollyett. "The whole press is on the huckle from end to end."

Even Woodhouse was a little astonished at the ease with which it had come about, and said as much.

"Rot!" said Ollyett. "We haven't really begun. Huckley isn't news yet."

"What do you mean?" said Woodhouse, who had grown to have great respect for his young but by no means distant connection.

"Mean? By the grace of God, Master Ridley, I mean to have it so that when Huckley turns over in its sleep, Reuters and the Press Association jump out of bed to cable." Then he went off at score about certain restorations in Huckley Church which, he said—and he seemed to spend his every weekend there—had been perpetrated by the Rector's predecessor, who had abolished a "leper-window" or a "squinch-hole" (whatever these may be) to institute a lavatory in the vestry. It did not strike me as stuff for which Reuters or the Press Association would lose much sleep, and I left him declaiming to Woodhouse about a fourteenth-century font which, he said, he had unearthed in the sexton's tool-shed.

My methods were more on the lines of peaceful penetration. An odd copy, in *The Bun*'s rag-and-bone library, of Hone's *Every-Day Book* had revealed to me the existence of a village dance founded, like all village dances, on Druidical mysteries connected with the Solar Solstice (which is always unchallengeable) and Midsummer Morning, which is dewy and refreshing to the London eye. For this I take no credit—Hone being a mine any one can work—but that I rechristened that dance, after I had revised it, "The Gubby" is my title to immortal fame. It was still to be witnessed, I wrote, "in all its poignant purity at Huckley, that last home of significant mediæval survivals"; and I fell so in love with my creation that I kept it back for days, enameling and burnishing.

"You'd better put it in," said Ollyett at last. "It's time we asserted ourselves again. The other fellows are beginning to poach. You saw that thing in the *Pinnacle* about Sir Thomas's Model Village? He must have got one of their chaps down to do it."

"Nothing like the wounds of a friend," I said. "That account of the non-alcoholic pub alone was—"

"I liked the bit best about the white-tiled laundry and the Fallen Virgins who wash Sir Thomas's dress shirts. Our side couldn't come within a mile of that, you know. We haven't the proper flair for sexual slobber."

"That's what I'm always saying," I retorted. "Leave 'em alone. The other fellows are doing our work for us now. Besides I want to touch up my 'Gubby Dance' a little more."

"No. You'll spoil it. Let's shove it in today. For one thing it's Literature. I don't go in for compliments as you know, but, etc. etc."

I had a healthy suspicion of young Ollyett in every aspect, but though I knew that I should have to pay for it, I fell to his flattery, and my priceless article on the "Gubby Dance" appeared. Next Saturday he asked me to bring out *The Bun* in his absence, which

I naturally assumed would be connected with the little maroon side-car. I was wrong.

On the following Monday I glanced at *The Cake* at breakfast-time to make sure, as usual, of her inferiority to my beloved but unremunerative *Bun*. I opened on a heading: "The Village that Voted the Earth was Flat." I read . . . I read that the Geoplanarian Society—a society devoted to the proposition that the earth is flat—had held its Annual Banquet and Exercises at Huckley on Saturday, when after convincing addresses, amid scenes of the greatest enthusiasm, Huckley village had decided by an unanimous vote of 438 that the earth was flat. I do not remember that I breathed again till I had finished the two columns of description that followed. Only one man could have written them. They were flawless—crisp, nervous, austere yet human, poignant, vital, arresting—most distinctly arresting—dynamic enough to shift a city—and quotable by whole sticks at a time. And there was a leader, a grave and poised leader, which tore me in two with mirth, until I remembered that I had been left out—infamously and unjustifiably dropped. I went to Ollyett's rooms. He was breakfasting, and, to do him justice, looked conscience-stricken.

"It wasn't my fault," he began. "It was Bat Masquerier. I swear *I* would have asked you to come if—"

"Never mind that," I said. "It's the best bit of work you've ever done or will do. Did any of it happen?"

"Happen? Heavens! D'you think even *I* could have invented it?"

"Is it exclusive to *The Cake*?" I cried.

"It cost Bat Masquerier two thousand," Ollyett replied. "D'you think he'd let any one else in on that? But I give you my sacred word I knew nothing about it till he asked me to come down and cover it. He had Huckley posted in three colors, 'The Geoplanarians' Annual Banquet and Exercises.' Yes, he invented 'Geoplanarians.' He wanted Huckley to think it meant aeroplanes. Yes, I know that there is a real Society that thinks the world's flat—they ought to be grateful for the lift—but Bat made his own. He did! He created the whole show, I tell you. He swept out half his Halls for the job. Think of that—on a Saturday! They—we went down in motor char-à-bancs—three of 'em—one pink, one primrose, and one forget-me-not blue—twenty people in each one and 'The Earth *is* Flat' on each side and across the back. I went with Teddy Rickets and Lafone from the Trefoil, and both the Silhouette Sisters, and—wait a minute!—the Crossleigh Trio. You know the Every-Day Dramas Trio at the Jocunda—Ada Crossleigh, 'Bunt' Crossleigh, and little Victorine? Them. And there was Hoke Ramsden, the lightning-change chap in *Morgiana and Drexel*—and there was Billy Turpeen. Yes, you know him! The North London Star. 'I'm the Referee that got himself disliked at Blackheath.' *That* chap! And there was Mackaye—that one-eyed Scotch fellow that all Glasgow is crazy about. Talk of subordinating yourself for Art's sake! Mackaye was the earnest inquirer who got converted at the end of the meeting. And there was quite a lot of girls I didn't know, and—oh, yes—there was 'Dal! 'Dal Benzaguen herself! We sat together, going and coming. She's all the darling there ever was. She sent you her love, and she told me to tell you that she won't forget about Nellie Farren. She says you've given her an ideal to work for. She? Oh, she was the Lady Secretary to the Geoplanarians, of course. I forget who were in the other brakes—provincial stars mostly—but they played up gorgeously. The art of the music-hall's changed since your day. They didn't overdo it a bit. You see, people who believe the earth is flat don't dress quite like other people. You may have noticed that I hinted at that in my account. It's a rather flat-fronted Ionic style—neo-Victorian, except for the bustles, 'Dal told me,—but 'Dal looked heavenly in it! So did little Victorine. And there was a girl in the blue brake—she's a provincial—but she's coming to town this winter and she'll knock 'em—Winnie Deans. Remember that! She told Huckley how she had suffered for the Cause as a governess in a rich family where they believed that the world is round, and how she threw up her job sooner than teach immoral geography. That was at the overflow meeting outside the Baptist chapel. She knocked 'em to sawdust! We must look out for Winnie. . . . But Lafone! Lafone was beyond everything. Impact, personality—conviction—the whole bag o' tricks! He sweated conviction. Gad, he convinced *me* while he was speaking! (Him? He was President of the Geoplanarians, of course. Haven't you read my account?) It *is* an infernally plausible theory. After all, no one has actually proved the earth is round, have they?"

"Never mind the earth. What about Huckley?"

"Oh, Huckley got tight. That's the worst of these model villages if you let 'em smell fire-water. There's one alcoholic pub in the place that Sir Thomas can't get rid of. Bat made it his base.

He sent down the banquet in two motor lorries—dinner for five hundred and drinks for ten thousand. Huckley voted all right. Don't you make any mistake about that. No vote, no dinner. A unanimous vote—exactly as I've said. At least, the Rector and the Doctor were the only dissentients. We didn't count them. Oh yes, Sir Thomas was there. He came and grinned at us through his park gates. He'll grin worse today. There's an aniline dye that you rub through a stencil-plate that eats about a foot into any stone and wears good to the last. Bat had both the lodge-gates stencilled 'The Earth *is* flat!' and all the barns and walls they could get at. . . . Oh Lord, but Huckley was drunk! We had to fill 'em up to make 'em forgive us for not being aeroplanes. Unthankful yokels! D'you realize that Emperors couldn't have commanded the talent Bat decanted on 'em? Why, 'Dal alone was . . . And by eight o'clock not even a bit of paper left! The whole show packed up and gone, and Huckley hoo-raying for the earth being flat."

"Very good," I began. "I am, as you know, a one-third proprietor of *The Bun.*"

"I didn't forget that," Ollyett interrupted. "That was uppermost in my mind all the time. I've got a special account for *The Bun* today—it's an idyll—and just to show how I thought of you, I told 'Dal, coming home, about your Gubby Dance, and she told Winnie. Winnie came back in our char-à-banc. After a bit we had to get out and dance it in a field. It's quite a dance the way we did it—and Lafone invented a sort of gorilla lockstep procession at the end. Bat had sent down a film-chap on the chance of getting something. He was the son of a clergyman—a most dynamic personality. He said there isn't anything for the cinema in meetings *qua* meetings—they lack action. Films are a branch of art by themselves. But he went wild over the Gubby. He said it was like Peter's vision at Joppa. He took about a million feet of it. Then I photoed it exclusive for *The Bun*. I've sent 'em in already, only remember we must eliminate Winnie's left leg in the first figure. It's too arresting. . . . And there you are! But I tell you I'm afraid of Bat. That man's the Personal Devil. He did it all. He didn't even come down himself. He said he'd distract his people."

"Why didn't he ask me to come?" I persisted.

"Because he said you'd distract me. He said he wanted my brains on ice. He got 'em. I believe it's the best thing I've ever done." He reached for *The Cake* and re-read it luxuriously. "Yes, out and away the best—supremely quotable," he concluded, and—after another survey—"By God, what a genius I was yesterday!"

I would have been angry, but I had not the time. That morning, Press agencies groveled to me in *The Bun* office for leave to use certain photos, which, they understood, I controlled, of a certain village dance. When I had sent the fifth man away on the edge of tears, my self-respect came back a little. Then there was *The Bun's* poster to get out. Art being elimination, I fined it down to two words (one too many, as it proved)—"The Gubby!" in red, at which our manager protested; but by five o'clock he told me that I was *the* Napoleon of Fleet Street. Ollyett's account in *The Bun* of the Geoplanarians' Exercises and Love Feast lacked the supreme shock of his version in *The Cake,* but it bruised more; while the photos of "The Gubby" (which, with Winnie's left leg, was why I had set the doubtful press to work so early) were beyond praise and, next day, beyond price. But even then I did not understand.

A week later, I think it was, Bat Masquerier telephoned to me to come to the Trefoil.

"It's your turn now," he said. "I'm not asking Ollyett. Come to the stage-box."

I went, and, as Bat's guest, was received as Royalty is not. We sat well back and looked out on the packed thousands. It was *Morgiana and Drexel,* that fluid and electric review which Bat—though he gave Lafone the credit—really created.

"Ye-es," said Bat dreamily, after Morgiana had given "the nasty jar" to the Forty Thieves in their forty oil "combinations." "As you say, I've got 'em and I can hold 'em. What a man does doesn't matter much; and how he does it don't matter either. It's the *when*—the psychological moment. Press can't make up for it; money can't; brains can't. A lot's luck, but all the rest is genius. I'm not speaking about My people now. I'm talking of Myself."

Then 'Dal—she was the only one who dared—knocked at the door and stood behind us all alive and panting as Morgiana. Lafone was carrying the police-court scene, and the house was ripped up crossways with laughter.

"Ah! Tell a fellow now," she asked me for the twentieth time, "did you love Nellie Farren when you were young?"

"Did we love her?" I answered. " 'If the earth and the sky and the sea'—There were three million of us, 'Dal, and we worshiped her."

"How did she get it across?" 'Dal went on.

"She was Nellie. The houses used to coo over her when she came on."

"I've had a good deal, but I've never been cooed over yet," said 'Dal wistfully.

"It isn't the how, it's the when," Bat repeated. "Ah!"

He leaned forward as the house began to rock and peal full-throatedly. 'Dal fled. A sinuous and silent procession was filing into the police-court to a scarcely audible accompaniment. It was dressed—but the world and all its picture-palaces know how it was dressed. It danced and it danced, and it danced the dance which bit all humanity in the leg for half a year, and it wound up with the lockstep finale that mowed the house down in swathes, sobbing and aching. Somebody in the gallery moaned, "Oh Gord, the Gubby!" and we heard the word run like a shudder, for they had not a full breath left among them. Then 'Dal came on, an electric star in her dark hair, the diamonds flashing in her three-inch heels—a vision that made no sign for thirty counted seconds while the police-court scene dissolved behind her into Morgiana's Manicure Palace, and they recovered themselves. The star on her forehead went out, and a soft light bathed her as she took—slowly, slowly to the croon of adoring strings—the eighteen paces forward. We saw her first as a queen alone; next as a queen for the first time conscious of her subjects, and at the end, when her hands fluttered, as a woman delighted, awed not a little, but transfigured and illuminated with sheer, compelling affection and goodwill. I caught the broken mutter of welcome—the coo which is more than tornadoes of applause. It died and rose and died again lovingly.

"She's got it across," Bat whispered. "I've never seen her like this. I told her to light up the star, but I was wrong, and she knew it. She's an artist."

" 'Dal, you darling!" some one spoke, not loudly but it carried through the house.

"Thank *you!*" 'Dal answered, and in that broken tone one heard the last fetter riveted. "Good evening, boys! I've just come from—now—where the dooce was it I have come from?" She turned to the impassive files of the Gubby dancers, and went on: "Ah, so good of you to remind me, you dear, bun-faced things.

I've just come from the village—The Village that Voted the Earth was Flat."

She swept into that song with the full orchestra. It devastated the habitable earth for the next six months. Imagine, then, what its rage and pulse must have been at the incandescent hour of its birth! She only gave the chorus once. At the end of the second verse, "Are you *with* me, boys?" she cried, and the house tore it clean away from her—"*Earth* was flat—*Earth* was flat. Flat as my hat—Flatter than that"—drowning all but the bassoons and double-basses that marked the word.

"Wonderful," I said to Bat. "And it's only 'Nuts in May' with variations."

"Yes—but *I* did the variations," he replied.

At the last verse she gestured to Carlini the conductor, who threw her up his baton. She caught it with a boy's ease. "Are you *with* me?" she cried once more, and—the maddened house behind her—abolished all the instruments except the guttural belch of the double-basses on "*Earth*"—"The Village that voted the *Earth* was flat—*Earth* was flat!" It was delirium. Then she picked up the Gubby dancers and led them in a clattering improvised lockstep thrice round the stage till her last kick sent her diamond-hilted shoe catherine-wheeling to the electrolier.

I saw the forest of hands raised to catch it, heard the roaring and stamping pass through hurricanes to full typhoon; heard the song, pinned down by the faithful double-basses as the bull-dog pins down the bellowing bull, overbear even those; till at last the curtain fell and Bat took me round to her dressing-room, where she lay spent after her seventh call. Still the song, through all those white-washed walls, shook the reinforced concrete of the Trefoil as steam pile-drivers shake the flanks of a dock.

"I'm all out—first time in my life. Ah! Tell a fellow now, did I get it across?" she whispered huskily.

"You know you did," I replied as she dipped her nose deep in a beaker of barley-water. "They cooed over you."

Bat nodded. "And poor Nellie's dead—in Africa, ain't it?"

"I hope I'll die before they stop cooing," said 'Dal.

" '*Earth* was flat—*Earth* was flat!' " Now it was more like mine-pumps in flood.

"They'll have the house down if you don't take another," someone called.

"Bless 'em!" said 'Dal, and went out for her eighth, when in the face of that cataract she said yawning, "I don't know how *you* feel, children, but *I*'m dead. You be quiet."

"Hold a minute," said Bat to me. "I've got to hear how it went in the provinces. Winnie Deans had it in Manchester, and Ramsden at Glasgow—and there are all the films too. I had rather a heavy week-end."

The telephones presently reassured him.

"It'll do," said he. "And *he* said my home address was Jerusalem." He left me humming the refrain of "The Holy City." Like Ollyett I found myself afraid of that man.

When I got out into the street and met the disgorging picture-palaces capering on the pavements and humming it (for he had put the gramophones on with the films), and when I saw far to the south the red electrics flash "Gubby" across the Thames, I feared more than ever.

A few days passed which were like nothing except, perhaps, a suspense of fever in which the sick man perceives the searchlights of the world's assembled navies in act to converge on one minute fragment of wreckage—one only in all the black and agony-strewn sea. Then those beams focused themselves. Earth as we knew it—the full circuit of our orb—laid the weight of its impersonal and searing curiosity on this Huckley which had voted that it was flat. It asked for news about Huckley—where and what it might be, and how it talked—it knew how it danced—and how it thought in its wonderful soul. And then, in all the zealous, merciless press, Huckley was laid out for it to look at, as a drop of pond water is exposed on the sheet of a magic-lantern show. But Huckley's sheet was only coterminous with the use of type among mankind. For the precise moment that was necessary, Fate ruled it that there should be nothing of first importance in the world's idle eye. One atrocious murder, a political crisis, an incautious or heady continental statesman, the mere catarrh of a king, would have wiped out the significance of our message, as a passing cloud annuls the urgent helio. But it was halcyon weather in every respect. Ollyett and I did not need to lift our little fingers any more than the Alpine climber whose last sentence has unkeyed the arch of the avalanche. The thing roared and pulverized and swept beyond eyesight all by itself—all by itself. And once well away, the fall of kingdoms could not have diverted it.

Ours is, after all, a kindly earth. While The Song ran and raped it with the cataleptic kick of "Ta-ra-ra-boom-de-ay," multiplied by the West African significance of "Everybody's doing it," plus twice the infernal elementality of a certain tune in *Dona et Gamma;* when for all practical purposes, literary, dramatic, artistic, social, municipal, political, commercial, and administrative, the Earth *was* flat, the Rector of Huckley wrote to us—again as a lover of accuracy—to point out that the Huckley vote on "the alleged flatness of this scene of our labors here below" was *not* unanimous; he and the doctor having voted against it. And the great Baron Reuter himself (I am sure it could have been none other) flashed that letter in full to the front, back, and both wings of this scene of our labours. For Huckley was News. *The Bun* also contributed a photograph which cost me some trouble to fake.

"We are a vital nation," said Ollyett while we were discussing affairs at a Bat dinner. "Only an Englishman could have written that letter at this present juncture."

"It reminded me of a tourist in the Cave of the Winds under Niagara. Just one figure in a mackintosh. But perhaps you saw our photo?" I said proudly.

"Yes," Bat replied. "I've been to Niagara, too. And how's Huckley taking it?"

"They don't quite understand, of course," said Ollyett. "But it's bringing pots of money into the place. Ever since the motor-bus excursions were started—"

"I didn't know they had been," said Pallant.

"Oh yes. Motor char-à-bancs—uniformed guides and key-bugles included. They're getting a bit fed up with the tune there nowadays," Ollyett added.

"They play it under his windows, don't they?" Bat asked. "He can't stop the right of way across his park."

"He cannot," Ollyett answered. "By the way, Woodhouse, I've bought that font for you from the sexton. I paid fifteen pounds for it."

"What am I supposed to do with it?" asked Woodhouse.

"You give it to the Victoria and Albert Museum. It is fourteenth-century work all right. You can trust me."

"Is it worth it—now?" said Pallant. "Not that I'm weakening, but merely as a matter of tactics?"

"But this is true," said Ollyett. "Besides, it is my hobby, I always wanted to be an architect. I'll attend to it myself. It's too serious for *The Bun* and miles too good for *The Cake.*"

He broke ground in a ponderous architectural weekly, which had never heard of Huckley. There was no passion in his statement, but mere fact backed by a wide range of authorities. He established beyond doubt that the old font at Huckley had been thrown out, on Sir Thomas's instigation, twenty years ago, to make room for a new one of Bath stone adorned with Limoges enamels; and that it had lain ever since in a corner of the sexton's shed. He proved, with learned men to support him, that there was only one other font in all England to compare with it. So Woodhouse bought it and presented it to a grateful South Kensington which said it would see the earth still flatter before it returned the treasure to purblind Huckley. Bishops by the benchful and most of the Royal Academy, not to mention *"Margaritas ante Porcos,"* wrote fervently to the papers. *Punch* based a political cartoon on it; the *Times* a third leader, "The Lust of Newness"; and the *Spectator* a scholarly and delightful middle, "Village Hausmania." The vast amused outside world said in all its tongues and types: "Of course! This is just what Huckley would do!" And neither Sir Thomas nor the Rector nor the sexton nor any one else wrote to deny it.

"You see," said Ollyett, "this is much more of a blow to Huckley than it looks—because every word of it's true. Your Gubby dance was inspiration, I admit, but it hadn't its roots in—"

"Two hemispheres and four continents so far," I pointed out.

"Its roots in the hearts of Huckley was what I was going to say. Why don't you ever come down and look at the place? You've never seen it since we were stopped there."

"I've only my weekends free," I said, "and you seem to spend yours there pretty regularly—with the side-car. I was afraid—"

"Oh, *that's* all right," he said cheerily. "We're quite an old engaged couple now. As a matter of fact, it happened after 'the gravid polled Angus' business. Come along this Saturday. Woodhouse says he'll run us down after lunch. He wants to see Huckley too."

Pallant could not accompany us, but Bat took his place.

"It's odd," said Bat, "that none of us except Ollyett has ever set eyes on Huckley since that time. That's what I always tell My people. Local color is all right after you've got your idea. Before that, it's a mere nuisance." He regaled us on the way down with panoramic views of the success—geographical and financial—of "The Gubby" and The Song.

"By the way," said he, "I've assigned 'Dal all the gramophone rights of 'The Earth.' She's a born artist. Hadn't sense enough to hit me for triple-dubs the morning after. She'd have taken it out in coos."

"Bless her! And what'll she make out of the gramophone rights?" I asked.

"Lord knows!" he replied. "I've made fifty-four thousand my little end of the business, and it's only just beginning. Hear *that!*"

A shell-pink motor-brake roared up behind us to the music on a key-bugle of "The Village that Voted the Earth was Flat." In a few minutes we overtook another, in natural wood, whose occupants were singing it through their noses.

"I don't know that agency. It must be Cook's," said Ollyett. "They *do* suffer." We were never out of ear-shot of the tune the rest of the way to Huckley.

Though I knew it would be so, I was disappointed with the actual aspect of the spot we had—it is not too much to say—created in the face of the nations. The alcoholic pub; the village green; the Baptist chapel; the church; the sexton's shed; the Rectory whence the so-wonderful letters had come; Sir Thomas's park gate-pillars still violently declaring "The Earth *is* flat," were as mean, as average, as ordinary as the photograph of a room where a murder has been committed. Ollyett, who, of course, knew the place specially well, made the most of it to us. Bat, who had employed it as a back-cloth to one of his own dramas, dismissed it as a thing used and emptied, but Woodhouse expressed my feelings when he said: "Is that all—after all we've done?"

"*I* know," said Ollyett soothingly. " 'Like that strange song I heard Apollo sing: When Ilion like a mist rose into towers.' I've felt the same sometimes, though it has been Paradise for me. But they *do* suffer."

The fourth brake in thirty minutes had just turned into Sir Thomas's park to tell the Hall that "The *Earth* was flat"; a knot of obviously American tourists were kodaking his lodge gates; while the tea-shop opposite the lych-gate was full of people buying postcards of the old font as it had lain twenty years in the sexton's shed. We went to the alcoholic pub and congratulated the proprietor.

"It's bringin' money to the place," said he. "But in a sense you can buy money too dear. It isn't doin' us any good. People are laughin' at us. That's what they're doin'. . . . Now, with regard to that Vote of ours you may have heard talk about. . . ."

"For Gorze sake, chuck that votin' business," cried an elderly man at the door. "Money-gettin' or no money-gettin', we're fed up with it."

"Well, I do think," said the publican, shifting his ground, "I do think Sir Thomas might ha' managed better in some things."

"He tole me,"—the elderly man shouldered his way to the bar—"he tole me twenty years ago to take an' lay that font in my tool-shed. He *tole* me so himself. An' now, after twenty years, me own wife makin' me out little better than the common 'angman!"

"That's the sexton," the publican explained. "His good lady sells the postcards—if you 'aven't got some. But we feel Sir Thomas might ha' done better."

"What's he got to do with it?" said Woodhouse.

"There's nothin' we can trace 'ome to 'im in so many words, but we think he might 'ave saved us the font business. Now, in regard to that votin' business—"

"Chuck it! Oh, chuck it!" the sexton roared, "or you'll 'ave me cuttin' my throat at cock-crow. 'Ere's another parcel of fun-makers!"

A motor-brake had pulled up at the door and a multitude of men and women immediately descended. We went out to look. They bore rolled banners, a reading-desk in three pieces, and, I specially noticed, a collapsible harmonium, such as is used on ships at sea.

"Salvation Army?" I said, though I saw no uniforms.

Two of them unfurled a banner between poles which bore the legend: "The Earth *is* flat." Woodhouse and I turned to Bat. He shook his head. "No, no! Not me. . . . If I had only seen their costumes in advance!"

"Good Lord!" said Ollyett. "It's the genuine Society!"

The company advanced on the green with the precision of people well broke to these movements. Scene-shifters could not have been quicker with the three-piece rostrum, nor stewards with the harmonium. Almost before its cross-legs had been kicked into their catches, certainly before the tourists by the lodge-gates had begun to move over, a woman sat down to it and struck up a hymn:

Hear ther truth our tongues are telling,
  Spread ther light from shore to shore,
God hath given man a dwelling
  Flat and flat for evermore.

When ther Primal Dark retreated,
  When ther deeps were undesigned,
He with rule and level meted
  Habitation for mankind!

I saw sick envy on Bat's face. "Curse Nature," he muttered. "She gets ahead of you every time. To think *I* forgot hymns and a harmonium!"

Then came the chorus:

Hear ther truth our tongues are telling,
  Spread ther light from shore to shore—
Oh, be faithful! Oh, be truthful!
  Earth is flat for evermore.

They sang several verses with the fervor of Christians awaiting their lions. Then there were growlings in the air. The sexton, embraced by the landlord, two-stepped out of the pub-door. Each was trying to outroar the other. "Apologizing in advance for what he says," the landlord shouted: "You'd better go away" (here the sexton began to speak words). "This isn't the time nor yet the place for—for any more o' this chat."

The crowd thickened. I saw the village police-sergeant come out of his cottage buckling his belt.

"But surely," said the woman at the harmonium, "there must be some mistake. We are not suffragettes."

"Damn it! They'd be a change," cried the sexton. "You get out of this! Don't talk! *I* can't stand it for one! Get right out, or we'll font you!"

The crowd which was being recruited from every house in sight echoed the invitation. The sergeant pushed forward. A man beside the reading-desk said: "But surely we are among dear friends and sympathizers. Listen to me for a moment."

It was the moment that a passing char-à-banc chose to strike into The Song. The effect was instantaneous. Bat, Ollyett, and I, who by divers roads have learned the psychology of crowds, retreated towards the tavern door. Woodhouse, the newspaper proprietor, anxious, I presume, to keep touch with the public, dived into the thick of it. Every one else told the Society to go away at once. When the lady at the harmonium (I began to understand why it is sometimes necessary to kill women) pointed at the stencilled park pillars and called them "the cromlechs of our common faith," there was a snarl and a rush. The police-sergeant checked it, but advised the Society to keep on going. The Society withdrew into the brake fighting, as it were, a rearguard action of oratory up each step. The collapsed harmonium was hauled in last, and with the perfect unreason of crowds, they cheered it loudly, till the chauffeur slipped in his clutch and sped away. Then the crowd broke up, congratulating all concerned except the sexton, who was held to have disgraced his office by having sworn at ladies. We strolled across the green towards Woodhouse, who was talking to the police-sergeant near the park-gates. We were not twenty yards from him when we saw Sir Thomas Ingell emerge from the lodge and rush furiously at Woodhouse with an uplifted stick, at the same time shrieking: "I'll teach you to laugh, you—" but Ollyett has the record of the language. By the time we reached them, Sir Thomas was on the ground; Woodhouse, very white, held the walking-stick and was saying to the sergeant:

"I give this person in charge for assault."

"But, good Lord!" said the sergeant, whiter than Woodhouse. "It's Sir Thomas."

"Whoever it is, it isn't fit to be at large," said Woodhouse. The crowd suspecting something wrong began to reassemble, and all the English horror of a row in public moved us, headed by the sergeant, inside the lodge. We shut both park-gates and lodge-door.

"You saw the assault, sergeant," Woodhouse went on. "You can testify I used no more force than was necessary to protect myself. You can testify that I have not even damaged this person's property. (Here! take your stick, you!) You heard the filthy language he used."

"I—I can't say I did," the sergeant stammered.

"Oh, but *we* did!" said Ollyett, and repeated it, to the apron-veiled horror of the lodge-keeper's wife.

Sir Thomas on a hard kitchen chair began to talk. He said he had "stood enough of being photographed like a wild beast," and expressed loud regret that he had not killed "that man," who was "conspiring with the sergeant to laugh at him."

" 'Ad you ever seen 'im before, Sir Thomas?" the sergeant asked.

"No! But it's time an example was made here. I've never seen the sweep in my life."

I think it was Bat Masquerier's magnetic eye that recalled the past to him, for his face changed and his jaw dropped. "But I have!" he groaned. "I remember now."

Here a writhing man entered by the back door. He was, he said, the village solicitor. I do not assert that he licked Woodhouse's boots, but we should have respected him more if he had and been done with it. His notion was that the matter could be accommodated, arranged and compromised for gold, and yet more gold. The sergeant thought so too. Woodhouse undeceived them both. To the sergeant he said, "Will you or will you not enter the charge?" To the village solicitor he gave the name of his lawyers, at which the man wrung his hands and cried, "Oh, Sir T., Sir T.!" in a miserable falsetto, for it was a Bat Masquerier of a firm. They conferred together in tragic whispers.

"I don't dive after Dickens," said Ollyett to Bat and me by the window, "but every time *I* get into a row I notice the police-court always fills up with his characters."

"I've noticed that too," said Bat. "But the odd thing is you mustn't give the public straight Dickens—not in My business. I wonder why that is."

Then Sir Thomas got his second wind and cursed the day that he, or it may have been we, were born. I feared that though he was a Radical he might apologize and, since he was an M.P., might lie his way out of the difficulty. But he was utterly and truthfully beside himself. He asked foolish questions—such as what we were doing in the village at all, and how much blackmail Woodhouse expected to make out of him. But neither Woodhouse nor the sergeant nor the writhing solicitor listened. The upshot of their talk, in the chimney-corner, was that Sir Thomas stood engaged to appear next Monday before his brother magistrates on charges of assault, disorderly conduct, and language calculated, etc. Ollyett was specially careful about the language.

Then we left. The village looked very pretty in the late light—pretty and tuneful as a nest of nightingales.

"You'll turn up on Monday, I hope," said Woodhouse, when we reached town. That was his only allusion to the affair.

So we turned up—through a world still singing that the Earth was flat—at the little clay-colored market-town with the large Corn Exchange and the small Jubilee memorial. We had some difficulty in getting seats in the court. Woodhouse's imported London lawyer was a man of commanding personality, with a voice trained to convey blasting imputations by tone. When the case was called, he rose and stated his client's intention not to proceed with the charge. His client, he went on to say, had not entertained, and, of course, in the circumstances could not have entertained, any suggestion of accepting on behalf of public charities any moneys that might have been offered to him on the part of Sir Thomas's estate. At the same time, no one acknowledged more sincerely than his client the spirit in which those offers had been made by those entitled to make them. But, as a matter of fact—here he became the man of the world colloguing with his equals—certain—er—details had come to his client's knowledge *since* the lamentable outburst, which . . . He shrugged his shoulders. Nothing was served by going into them, but he ventured to say that, had those painful circumstances only been known earlier, his client would—again "of course"—never have dreamed— A gesture concluded the sentence, and the ensnared Bench looked at Sir Thomas with new and withdrawing eyes. Frankly, as they could see, it would be nothing less than cruelty to proceed further with this—er—unfortunate affair. He asked leave, therefore, to withdraw the charge *in toto,* and at the same time to express his client's deepest sympathy with all who had been in any way distressed, as his client had been, by the fact and the publicity of proceedings which he could, of course, again assure them that his client would never have dreamed of instituting if, as he hoped he had made plain, certain facts had been before his client at the time when . . . But he had said enough. For his fee it seemed to me that he had.

Heaven inspired Sir Thomas's lawyer—all of a sweat lest his client's language should come out—to rise up and thank him. Then, Sir Thomas—not yet aware what leprosy had been laid upon him, but grateful to escape on any terms—followed suit. He was heard in interested silence, and people drew back a pace as Gehazi passed forth.

"You hit hard," said Bat to Woodhouse afterwards. "His own people think he's mad."

"You don't say so? I'll show you some of his letters tonight at dinner," he replied.

He brought them to the Red Amber Room of the Chop Suey. We forgot to be amazed, as till then we had been amazed, over The Song or "The Gubby," or the full tide of Fate that seemed to run only for our sakes. It did not even interest Ollyett that the verb "to huckle" had passed into the English leader-writers' language. We were studying the interior of a soul, flash-lighted to its grimiest corners by the dread of "losing its position."

"And then it thanked you, didn't it, for dropping the case?" said Pallant.

"Yes, and it sent me a telegram to confirm." Woodhouse turned to Bat. "Now d'you think I hit too hard?" he asked.

"No—o!" said Bat. "After all—I'm talking of everyone's business now—one can't ever do anything in Art that comes up to Nature in any game in life. Just think how this thing has—"

"Just let me run through that little case of yours again," said Pallant, and picked up *The Bun* which had it set out in full.

"Any chance of 'Dal looking in on us tonight?" Ollyett began.

"She's occupied with her Art too," Bat answered bitterly. "What's the use of Art? Tell me, some one!" A barrel-organ outside promptly pointed out that the *Earth* was flat. "The gramophone's killing street organs, but I let loose a hundred-and-seventy-four of those hurdygurdys twelve hours after The Song," said Bat. "Not counting the Provinces." His face brightened a little.

"Look here!" said Pallant over the paper. "I don't suppose you or those asinine J.P.s knew it—but your lawyer ought to have known that you've all put your foot in it most confoundedly over this assault case."

"What's the matter?" said Woodhouse.

"It's ludicrous. It's insane. There isn't two penn'orth of legality in the whole thing. Of course, you could have withdrawn the charge, but the way you went about it is childish—besides being illegal. What on earth was the Chief Constable thinking of?"

"Oh, he was a friend of Sir Thomas's. They all were for that matter," I replied.

"He ought to be hanged. So ought the Chairman of the Bench. I'm talking as a lawyer now."

"Why, what have we been guilty of? Misprision of treason or compounding a felony—or what?" said Ollyett.

"I'll tell you later." Pallant went back to the paper with knitted brows, smiling unpleasantly from time to time. At last he laughed.

"Thank you!" he said to Woodhouse. "It ought to be pretty useful—for us."

"What d'you mean?" said Ollyett.

"For our side. They are all Rads who are mixed up in this—from the Chief Constable down. There must be a Question. There must be a Question."

"Yes, but I wanted the charge withdrawn in my own way," Woodhouse insisted.

"That's nothing to do with the case. It's the legality of your silly methods. You wouldn't understand if I talked till morning." He began to pace the room, his hands behind him. "I wonder if I can get it through our Whip's thick head that it's a chance. . . . That comes of stuffing the Bench with radical tinkers," he muttered.

"Oh, sit down!" said Woodhouse.

"Where's your lawyer to be found now?" he jerked out.

"At the Trefoil," said Bat promptly. "I gave him the stage-box for tonight. He's an artist too."

"Then I'm going to see him," said Pallant. "Properly handled this ought to be a godsend for our side." He withdrew without apology.

"Certainly, this thing keeps on opening up, and up," I remarked inanely.

"It's beyond me!" said Bat. "I don't think if I'd known I'd have ever . . . Yes, I would, though. He said my home address was—"

"It was his tone—his tone!" Ollyett almost shouted. Woodhouse said nothing, but his face whitened as he brooded.

"Well, anyway," Bat went on, "I'm glad I always believed in God and Providence and all those things. Else I should lose my nerve. We've put it over the whole world—the full extent of the geographical globe. We couldn't stop it if we wanted to now. It's got to burn itself out. I'm not in charge any more. What d'you expect'll happen next. Angels?"

I expected nothing. Nothing that I expected approached what I got. Politics are not my concern, but, for the moment, since it seemed that they were going to "huckle" with the rest, I took an interest in them. They impressed me as a dog's life without a dog's decencies, and I was confirmed in this when an unshaven and unwashen Pallant called on me at ten o'clock one morning, begging for a bath and a couch.

"Bail too?" I asked. He was in evening dress and his eyes were sunk feet in his head.

"No," he said hoarsely. "All night sitting. Fifteen divisions. 'Nother tonight. Your place was nearer than mine, so—" He began to undress in the hall.

When he awoke at one o'clock he gave me lurid accounts of what he said was history, but which was obviously collective hysteria. There had been a political crisis. He and his fellow M.P.'s had "done things"—I never quite got at the things—for eighteen hours on end, and the pitiless Whips were even then at the telephones to herd 'em up to another dog-fight. So he snorted and grew hot all over again while he might have been resting.

"I'm going to pitch in my question about that miscarriage of justice at Huckley this afternoon, if you care to listen to it," he said. "It'll be absolutely thrown away—in our present state. I told 'em so; but it's my only chance for weeks. P'raps Woodhouse would like to come."

"I'm sure he would. Anything to do with Huckley interests us," I said.

"It'll misfire, I'm afraid. Both sides are absolutely cooked. The present situation has been working up for some time. You see the row was bound to come, etc. etc.," and he flew off the handle once more.

I telephoned to Woodhouse, and we went to the House together. It was a dull, sticky afternoon with thunder in the air. For some reason or other, each side was determined to prove its virtue and endurance to the utmost. I heard men snarling about it all round me. "If they won't spare us, we'll show 'em no mercy." "Break the brutes up from the start. They can't stand late hours." "Come on! No shirking! I know *you've* had a Turkish bath," were some of the sentences I caught on our way. The House was packed already, and one could feel the negative electricity of a jaded crowd wrenching at one's own nerves, and depressing the afternoon soul.

"This is bad!" Woodhouse whispered. "There'll be a row before they've finished. Look at the Front Benches!" And he pointed out little personal signs by which I was to know that each man was on edge. He might have spared himself. The House was ready to snap before a bone had been thrown. A sullen minister rose to reply to a staccato question. His supporters cheered defiantly. "None o' that! None o' that!" came from the Back Benches. I saw the Speaker's face stiffen like the face of a helmsman as he humors a hard-mouthed yacht after a sudden following sea. The trouble was barely met in time. There came a fresh, apparently causeless gust a few minutes later—savage, threatening, but futile. It died out—one could hear the sigh—in sudden wrathful realization of the dreary hours ahead, and the ship of state drifted on.

Then Pallant—and the raw House winced at the torture of his voice—rose. It was a twenty-line question, studded with legal technicalities. The gist of it was that he wished to know whether the appropriate Minister was aware that there had been a grave miscarriage of justice on such and such a date, at such and such a place, before such and such justices of the peace, in regard to a case which arose—

I heard one desperate, weary "damn!" float up from the pit of that torment. Pallant sawed on—"out of certain events which occurred at the village of Huckley."

The House came to attention with a parting of the lips like a hiccup, and it flashed through my mind . . . Pallant repeated, "Huckley. The village—"

"That voted the *Earth* was flat." A single voice from a back Bench sang it once like a lone frog in a far pool.

"*Earth* was flat," croaked another voice opposite.

"*Earth* was flat." There were several. Then several more.

It was, you understand, the collective, over-strained nerve of the House, snapping, strand by strand to various notes, as the hawser parts from its moorings.

"The Village that voted the *Earth* was flat." The tune was beginning to shape itself. More voices were raised and feet began to beat time. Even so it did not occur to me that the thing would—

"The Village that voted the *Earth* was flat!" It was easier now to see who were not singing. There were still a few. Of a sudden (and this proves the fundamental instability of the cross-bench mind) a cross-bencher leaped on his seat and there played an imaginary double-bass with tremendous maestro-like wagglings of the elbow.

The last strand parted. The ship of state drifted out helpless on the rocking tide of melody.

> "The Village that voted the *Earth* was flat!
> The Village that voted the *Earth* was flat!"

The Irish first conceived the idea of using their order-papers as funnels wherewith to reach the correct *"vroom—vroom"* on *"Earth."* Labor, always conservative and respectable at a crisis, stood out longer than any other section, but when it came in it was howling syndicalism. Then, without distinction of Party, fear of constituents, desire for office, or hope of emolument, the House sang at the tops and at the bottoms of their voices, swaying their stale bodies and epileptically beating with their swelled feet. They sang "The Village that voted the *Earth* was flat": first, because they wanted to, and secondly—which is the terror of that song—because they could not stop. For no consideration could they stop.

Pallant was still standing up. Some one pointed at him and they laughed. Others began to point, lunging, as it were, in time with the tune. At this moment two persons came in practically abreast from behind the Speaker's chair, and halted appalled. One happened to be the Prime Minister and the other a messenger. The House, with tears running down their cheeks, transferred their attention to the paralyzed couple. They pointed six hundred forefingers at them. They rocked, they waved, and they rolled while they pointed, but still they sang. When they weakened for an instant, Ireland would yell: "Are ye *with* me, bhoys?" and they all renewed their strength like Antaeus. No man could say afterwards what happened in the Press or the Strangers' Gallery. It was the House, the hysterical and abandoned House of Commons that held all eyes, as it deafened all ears. I saw both Front Benches bend forward, some with their foreheads on their despatch-boxes, the rest with their faces in their hands; and their moving shoulders jolted the House out of its last rag of decency. Only the Speaker remained unmoved. The entire press of Great Britain bore witness next day that he had not even bowed his head. The Angel of the Constitution, for vain was the help of man, foretold him the exact moment at which the House would have broken into "The Gubby." He is reported to have said: "I heard the Irish beginning to shuffle it. So I adjourned." Pallant's version is that he added: "And I was never so grateful to a private member in all my life as I was to Mr. Pallant."

He made no explanation. He did not refer to orders or disorders. He simply adjourned the House till six that evening. And the House adjourned—some of it nearly on all fours.

I was not correct when I said that the Speaker was the only man who did not laugh. Woodhouse was beside me all the time. His face was set and quite white—as white, they told me, as Sir Thomas Ingell's when he went, by request, to a private interview with his Chief Whip.

The Gardener

FROM *DEBITS AND CREDITS* (1926)

In a sense this is the most deeply felt story Kipling ever wrote.

His work with the War Graves Commission, that created cemeteries for the countless dead of World War I, and also his history of *The Irish Guards in the Great War*, were memorials to his dead son. So is "The Gardener."

In addition, it's an attack on the so-called "morality" that compelled so many decent women to live a lie rather than admit that they had loved "not wisely but too well"—an attack he made in other stories, particularly "On the Gate," from the same collection, where St. Peter admits to Heaven a prostitute turned battlefield nurse under the ruling "QMA," *quia multum amavit:* "for she has greatly loved."

And, once again, it demonstrates that sense of the immanence of the supernatural which characterized his work from his earliest days in India right up to the end. But this time it is the divine which enters the everyday world . . .

Kipling wrote very few stories with a "switch" or trick ending. Watch for this one. It is masterfully subtle. It consists in the alteration of a single word.

In Britain a prep (preparatory) school is a boarding school for children typically up to the age of thirteen, preparing for "public" school (private and expensive!)

afterward. O.T.C. = Officer Training Corps, which most public schools then had, and many still do under a different name. Enlistment (as a private soldier) is here contrasted with being commissioned (as an officer). "A wire" = U.S. cable.

It was during the Battle of Loos in September 1915 that RK's only son was killed. Along the River Somme there were constant battles from 1916 to 1918; it was one of the worst fronts of the entire war. "Hun" was a derogatory term applied to Germans, allegedly because the Kaiser ordered his troops to be as ruthless and as victorious as the Huns of history.

"Dickiebush" was army slang for a Flemish place-name meaning "thick wood." The A.S.C., if memory serves (my dictionaries fail me), would I think have been the Auxiliary Service Corps. Cook's—Thomas Cook's—was the first modern tourist agency, and it's still in business.

As to the Gardener Himself: see the Gospel of John, chapter 20, verse 15.

The Gardener

One grave to me was given,
  One watch till Judgement Day;
And God looked down from Heaven
  And rolled the stone away.

One day in all the years,
  One hour in that one day,
His Angel saw my tears,
  And rolled the stone away!

Everyone in the village knew that Helen Turrell did her duty by all her world, and by none more honorably than by her only brother's unfortunate child. The village knew, too, that George Turrell had tried his family severely since early youth, and were not surprised to be told that, after many fresh starts given and thrown away, he, an Inspector of Indian Police, had entangled himself with the daughter of a retired non-commissioned officer, and had died of a fall from a horse a few weeks before his child was born. Mercifully, George's father and mother were both dead, and though Helen, thirty-five and independent, might well have washed her hands of the whole disgraceful affair, she most nobly took charge, though she was, at the time, under threat of lung trouble which had driven her to the South of France. She arranged for the passage of the child and a nurse from Bombay, met them at Marseilles, nursed the baby through an attack of infantile dysentery due to the carelessness of the nurse, whom she had had to dismiss, and at last, thin and worn but triumphant, brought the boy late in the autumn, wholly restored, to her Hampshire home.

All these details were public property, for Helen was as open as the day, and held that scandals are only increased by hushing them up. She admitted that George had always been rather a black sheep, but things might have been much worse if the mother had insisted on her right to keep the boy. Luckily, it seemed that people of that class would do almost anything for money, and, as George had always turned to her in his scrapes, she felt herself justified—her friends agreed with her—in cutting the whole non-commissioned officer connection, and giving the child every advantage. A christening, by the Rector, under the name of Michael, was the first step. So far as she knew herself, she was not, she said, a child-lover, but, for all his faults, she had been very fond of George, and she pointed out that little Michael had his father's mouth to a line; which made something to build upon.

As a matter of fact, it was the Turrell forehead, broad, low, and well-shaped, with the widely spaced eyes beneath it, that Michael had most faithfully reproduced. His mouth was somewhat better cut than the family type. But Helen, who would concede nothing good to his mother's side, vowed he was a Turrell all over, and, there being no one to contradict, the likeness was established.

In a few years Michael took his place, as accepted as Helen had always been—fearless, philosophical, and fairly good-looking. At six, he wished to know why he could not call her "Mummy," as other boys called their mothers. She explained that she was only his auntie, and that aunties were not quite the same as mummies, but that, if it gave him pleasure, he might call her "Mummy" at bedtime, for a pet-name between themselves.

Michael kept his secret most loyally, but Helen, as usual, explained the fact to her friends; which when Michael heard, he raged.

"Why did you tell? *Why* did you tell?" came at the end of the storm.

"Because it's always best to tell the truth," Helen answered, her arm round him as he shook in his cot.

"All right, but when the troof's ugly I don't think it's nice."

"Don't you, dear?"

"No, I don't, and"—she felt the small body stiffen—"now you've told, I won't call you 'Mummy' any more—not even at bedtimes."

"But isn't that rather unkind?" said Helen softly.

"I don't care! I don't care! You've hurted me in my insides and I'll hurt you back. I'll hurt you as long as I live!"

"Don't, oh, don't talk like that, dear! You don't know what—"

"I will! And when I'm dead I'll hurt you worse!"

"Thank goodness, I shall be dead long before you, darling."

"Huh! Emma says, 'Never know your luck.' " (Michael had been talking to Helen's elderly, flat-faced maid.) "Lots of little boys die quite soon. So'll I. *Then* you'll see!"

Helen caught her breath and moved towards the door, but the wail of "Mummy! Mummy!" drew her back again, and the two wept together.

At ten years old, after two terms at a prep. school, something or somebody gave him the idea that his civil status was not quite regular. He attacked Helen on the subject, breaking down her stammered defences with the family directness.

"Don't believe a word of it," he said, cheerily, at the end. "People wouldn't have talked like they did if my people had been married. But don't you bother, Auntie. I've found out all about my sort in English Hist'ry and the Shakespeare bits. There was William the Conqueror to begin with, and—oh, heaps more, and they all got on first-rate. 'Twon't make any difference to you, my being *that*—will it?"

"As if anything could—" she began.

"All right. We won't talk about it any more if it makes you cry." He never mentioned the thing again of his own will, but when, two years later, he skilfully managed to have measles in the holidays, as his temperature went up to the appointed one hundred and four he muttered of nothing else, till Helen's voice, piercing at last his delirium, reached him with assurance that nothing on earth or beyond could make any difference between them.

The terms at his public school and the wonderful Christmas, Easter, and Summer holidays followed each other, variegated and glorious as jewels on a string; and as jewels Helen treasured them. In due time Michael developed his own interests, which ran their courses and gave way to others; but his interest in Helen was constant and increasing throughout. She repaid it with all that she had of affection or could command of counsel and money; and since Michael was no fool, the War took him just before what was like to have been a most promising career.

He was to have gone up to Oxford, with a scholarship, in October. At the end of August he was on the edge of joining the first holocaust of public-school boys who threw themselves into the Line; but the captain of his O.T.C., where he had been sergeant for nearly a year, headed him off and steered him directly to a commission in a battalion so new that half of it still wore the old Army red, and the other half was breeding meningitis through living overcrowdedly in damp tents. Helen had been shocked at the idea of direct enlistment.

"But it's in the family," Michael laughed.

"You don't mean to tell me that you believed that old story all this time?" said Helen. (Emma, her maid, had been dead now several years.) "I gave you my word of honor—and I give it again—that—that it's all right. It is indeed."

"Oh, *that* doesn't worry me. It never did," he replied valiantly. "What I meant was, I should have got into the show earlier if I'd enlisted—like my grandfather."

"Don't talk like that! Are you afraid of its ending so soon, then?"

"No such luck. You know what K. says."

"Yes. But my banker told me last Monday it couldn't *possibly* last beyond Christmas—for financial reasons."

"Hope he's right, but our Colonel—and he's a Regular—says it's going to be a long job."

Michael's battalion was fortunate in that, by some chance which meant several "leaves," it was used for coast-defense among shallow trenches on the Norfolk coast; thence sent north to watch the mouth of a Scotch estuary, and, lastly, held for weeks on a baseless rumour of distant service. But, the very day that Michael was to have met Helen for four whole hours at a railway-junction up the line, it was hurled out, to help make good the wastage of Loos, and he had only just time to send her a wire of farewell.

In France luck again helped the battalion. It was put down near the Salient, where it led a meritorious and unexacting life, while the Somme was being manufactured; and enjoyed the peace of the Armentières and Laventie sectors when the battle began. Finding that it had sound views on protecting its own flanks and could dig, a prudent Commander stole it out of its own Division, under pretence of helping to lay telegraphs, and used it round Ypres at large.

A month later, and just after Michael had written Helen that there was nothing special doing and therefore no need to worry, a shell-splinter dropping out of a wet dawn killed him at once. The next shell uprooted and laid down over the body what had been the foundation of a barn wall, so neatly that none but an expert would have guessed that anything unpleasant had happened.

By this time the village was old in experience of war, and, English fashion, had evolved a ritual to meet it. When the postmistress handed her seven-year-old daughter the official telegram to take to Miss Turrell, she observed to the Rector's gardener: "It's Miss Helen's turn now." He replied, thinking of his own son: "Well, he's lasted longer than some." The child herself came to the front-door weeping aloud, because Master Michael had often given her sweets. Helen, presently, found herself pulling down the house-blinds one after one with great care, and saying earnestly to each: "Missing *always* means dead." Then she took her place in the dreary procession that was impelled to go through an inevitable series of unprofitable emotions. The Rector, of course, preached hope and prophesied word, very soon, from a prison camp. Several friends, too, told her perfectly truthful tales, but always about other women, to whom, after months and months of silence, their missing had been miraculously restored. Other people urged her to communicate with infallible Secretaries of organizations who could communicate with benevolent neutrals, who could extract accurate information from the most secretive of Hun prison commandants. Helen did and wrote and signed everything that was suggested or put before her.

Once, on one of Michael's leaves, he had taken her over a munition factory, where she saw the progress of a shell from blank-iron to the all but finished article. It struck her at the time that the wretched thing was never left alone for a single second; and "I'm being manufactured into a bereaved next of kin," she told herself, as she prepared her documents.

In due course, when all the organizations had deeply or sincerely regretted their inability to trace, etc., something gave way within her and all sensation—save of thankfulness for the release—came to an end in blessed passivity. Michael had died and her world had stood still and she had been one with the full shock of that arrest. Now she was standing still and the world was going forward, but it did not concern her—in no way or relation did it touch her. She knew this by the ease with which she could slip Michael's name into talk and incline her head to the proper angle, at the proper murmur of sympathy.

In the blessed realization of that relief, the Armistice with all its bells broke over her and passed unheeded. At the end of another year she had overcome her physical loathing of the living and returned young, so that she could take them by the hand and almost sincerely wish them well. She had no interest in any aftermath, national or personal, of the war, but, moving at an immense distance, she sat on various relief committees and held strong views—she heard herself delivering them—about the site of the proposed village War Memorial.

Then there came to her, as next of kin, an official intimation, backed by a page of a letter to her in indelible pencil, a silver identity-disc, and a watch, to the effect that the body of Lieutenant Michael Turrell had been found, identified, and reinterred in Hagenzeele Third Military Cemetery—the letter of the row and the grave's number in that row duly given.

So Helen found herself moved on to another process of the manufacture—to a world full of exultant or broken relatives, now strong in the certainty that there was an altar upon earth where they might lay their love. These soon told her, and by means of time-tables made clear, how easy it was and how little it interfered with life's affairs to go and see one's grave.

"*So* different," as the Rector's wife said, "if he'd been killed in Mesopotamia, or even Gallipoli."

The agony of being waked up to some sort of second life drove Helen across the Channel, where, in a new world of abbreviated titles, she learnt that Hagenzeele Third could be comfortably reached by an afternoon train which fitted in with the morning boat, and that there was a comfortable little hotel not three kilometers from Hagenzeele itself, where one could spend quite a comfortable night and see one's grave next morning. All this she had from a Central Authority who lived in a board and tar-paper shed on the skirts of a razed city full of whirling lime-dust and blown papers.

"By the way," said he, "you know your grave, of course?"

"Yes, thank you," said Helen, and showed its row and number typed on Michael's own little typewriter. The officer would have checked it, out of one of his many books; but a large Lancashire woman thrust between them and bade him tell her where she might find her son, who had been corporal in the A.S.C. His proper name, she sobbed, was Anderson, but, coming of respectable folk, he had of course enlisted under the name of Smith; and had been killed at Dickiebush, in early 'Fifteen. She had not his number nor did she know which of his two Christian names he might have used with his alias; but her Cook's tourist ticket expired at the end of Easter week, and if by then she could not find her child she should go mad. Whereupon she fell forward on Helen's breast; but the officer's wife came out quickly from a little bedroom behind the office, and the three of them lifted the woman on to the cot.

"They are often like this," said the officer's wife, loosening the tight bonnet-strings. "Yesterday she said he'd been killed at Hooge. Are you sure you know your grave? It makes such a difference."

"Yes, thank you," said Helen, and hurried out before the woman on the bed should begin to lament again.

Tea in a crowded mauve and blue striped wooden structure, with a false front, carried her still further into the nightmare. She paid her bill beside a stolid, plain-featured Englishwoman, who, hearing her inquire about the train to Hagenzeele, volunteered to come with her.

"I'm going to Hagenzeele myself," she explained. "Not to Hagenzeele Third; mine is Sugar Factory, but they call it La Rosière now. It's just south of Hagenzeele Three. Have you got your room at the hotel there?"

"Oh yes, thank you. I've wired."

"That's better. Sometimes the place is quite full, and at others there's hardly a soul. But they've put bathrooms into the old Lion d'Or—that's the hotel on the west side of Sugar Factory—and it draws off a lot of people, luckily."

"It's all new to me. This is the first time I've been over."

"Indeed! This is my ninth time since the Armistice. Not on my own account. *I* haven't lost anyone, thank God—but, like everyone else, I've a lot of friends at home who have. Coming over as often as I do, I find it helps them to have someone just look at the—the place and tell them about it afterwards. And one can take photos for them, too. I get quite a list of commissions to execute." She laughed nervously and tapped her slung Kodak. "There are two or three to see at Sugar Factory this time, and plenty of others in the cemeteries all about. My system is to save them up, and arrange them, you know. And when I've got enough commissions for one area to make it worth while, I pop over and execute them. It *does* comfort people."

"I suppose so," Helen answered, shivering as they entered the little train.

"Of course it does. (Isn't it lucky we've got window-seats?) It must do or they wouldn't ask one to do it, would they? I've a list of quite twelve or fifteen commissions here"—she tapped the Kodak again—"I must sort them out tonight. Oh, I forgot to ask you. What's yours?"

"My nephew," said Helen. "But I was very fond of him."

"Ah, yes! I sometimes wonder whether *they* know after death? What do you think?"

"Oh, I don't—I haven't dared to think much about that sort of thing," said Helen, almost lifting her hands to keep her off.

"Perhaps that's better," the woman answered. "The sense of loss must be enough, I expect. Well, I won't worry you any more."

Helen was grateful, but when they reached the hotel Mrs. Scarsworth (they had exchanged names) insisted on dining at the same table with her, and after the meal, in the little, hideous salon full of low-voiced relatives, took Helen through her "commissions" with biographies of the dead, where she happened to know them, and sketches of their next of kin. Helen endured till nearly half-past nine, ere she fled to her room.

Almost at once there was a knock at her door and Mrs. Scarsworth entered; her hands, holding the dreadful list, clasped before her.

"Yes—yes—*I* know," she began. "You're sick of me, but I want to tell you something. You—you aren't married, are you? Then perhaps you won't . . . But it doesn't matter. I've *got* to tell someone. I can't go on any longer like this."

"But please—" Mrs. Scarsworth had backed against the shut door, and her mouth worked dryly.

"In a minute," she said. "You—you know about these graves of mine I was telling you about downstairs, just now? They really *are* commissions. At least several of them are." Her eye wandered round the room. "What extraordinary wall-papers they have in Belgium, don't you think? . . . Yes. I swear they are commissions. But there's *one,* d'you see, and—and he was more to me than anything else in the world. Do you understand?"

Helen nodded.

"More than anyone else. And, of course, he oughtn't to have been. He ought to have been nothing to me. But he *was*. He *is*. That's why I do the commissions, you see. That's all."

"But why do you tell me?" Helen asked desperately.

"Because I'm *so* tired of lying. Tired of lying—always lying—year in and year out. When I don't tell lies I've got to act 'em and I've got to think 'em, always. *You* don't know what that means. He was everything to me that he oughtn't to have been—the one real thing—the only thing that ever happened to me in all my life; and I've had to pretend he wasn't. I've had to watch every word I said, and think out what lie I'd tell next, for years and years!"

"How many years?" Helen asked.

"Six years and four months before, and two and three-quarters after. I've gone to him eight times, since. Tomorrow'll make the ninth, and—and I can't—I *can't* go to him again with nobody in the world knowing. I want to be honest with someone before I go. Do you understand? It doesn't matter about *me*. I was never truthful, even as a girl. But it isn't worthy of *him*. So—so I—I had to tell you. I can't keep it up any longer. Oh, I can't!"

She lifted her joined hands almost to the level of her mouth, and brought them down sharply, still joined, to full arms' length below her waist. Helen reached forward, caught them, bowed her head over them, and murmured: "Oh, my dear! My dear!" Mrs. Scarsworth stepped back, her face all mottled.

"My God!" said she. "Is *that* how you take it?"

Helen could not speak, and the woman went out; but it was a long while before Helen was able to sleep.

Next morning Mrs. Scarsworth left early on her round of commissions, and Helen walked alone to Hagenzeele Third. The place was still in the making, and stood some five or six feet above the metaled road, which it flanked for hundreds of yards. Culverts across a deep ditch served for entrances through the unfinished boundary wall. She climbed a few wooden-faced earthen steps and then met the entire crowded level of the thing in one held breath. She did not know that Hagenzeele Third counted twenty-one thousand dead already. All she saw was a merciless sea of black crosses, bearing little strips of stamped tin at all angles across their faces. She could distinguish no order or arrangement in their mass; nothing but a waist-high wilderness as of weeds stricken dead, rushing at her. She went forward, moved to the left and the right hopelessly, wondering by what guidance she should ever come to her own. A great distance away there was a line of whiteness. It proved to be a block of some two or three hundred graves whose headstones had already been set, whose flowers were planted out, and whose new-sown grass showed green. Here she could see clear-cut letters at the ends of the rows, and, referring to her slip, realized that it was not here she must look.

A man knelt behind a line of headstones—evidently a gardener, for he was firming a young plant in the soft earth. She went towards him, her paper in her hand. He rose at her approach and without prelude or salutation asked: "Who are you looking for?"

"Lieutenant Michael Turrell—my nephew," said Helen slowly and word for word, as she had many thousands of times in her life.

The man lifted his eyes and looked at her with infinite compassion before he turned from the fresh-sown grass toward the naked black crosses.

"Come with me," he said, "and I will show you where your son lies."

When Helen left the Cemetery she turned for a last look. In the distance she saw the man bending over his young plants; and she went away, supposing him to be the gardener.

When Earth's Last Picture Is Painted

FROM L'ENVOI TO "THE SEVEN SEAS" (1892)

So now to our envoi . . . at the special request of Tom Doherty, publisher of TOR Books, to whom I am greatly indebted because thanks to him this labor of love, which I have nurtured among my ambitions for lo! these many years, has finally attained publication. Tom—a Kipling buff since 'way back, like myself, like my many colleagues who have generously commended this and its companion collection to the public—has a particular affection for this splendid version of the ultimate fantasy: that which transcends even Judgment Day . . .

When Earth's Last Picture Is Painted

When Earth's last picture is painted and the tubes are twisted and dried,
When the oldest colors have faded, and the youngest critic has died,
We shall rest, and, faith, we shall need it—lie down for an aeon or two,
Till the Master of All Good Workmen shall put us to work anew.

And those that were good shall be happy: they shall sit in a golden chair;
They shall splash at a ten-league canvas with brushes of comets' hair.
They shall find real saints to draw from—Magdalene, Peter, and Paul;
They shall work for an age at a sitting and never be tired at all!

And only The Master shall praise us, and only The Master shall blame;
And no one shall work for money, and no one shall work for fame,
But each for the joy of the working, and each, in his separate star,
Shall draw the Thing as he sees It for the God of Things as They are!